SEVGI SOYSAL

DAWN

TRANSLATED FROM THE TURKISH BY
Maureen Freely

archipelago books

First Archipelago Books Edition, 2022

Library of Congress Cataloging-in-Publication Data available upon request.
ISBN 978-1-953861-38-2

Archipelago Books
232 3rd Street #A111
Brooklyn, NY 11215
www.archipelagobooks.org

Distributed by Penguin Random House
www.penguinrandomhouse.com

Cover art by Etel Adnan.
Copyright © The Estate of Etel Adnan
Courtesy Galerie Lelong & Co

This work is made possible by the New York State Council on the Arts
with the support of the Office of the Governor and the New York State
Legislature. Funding for the publication of this book was provided
by a grant from the Carl Lesnor Family Foundation.

This publication was made possible with support from Lannan Foundation,
the National Endowment for the Arts, the Nimick Forbesway Foundation, and the
New York City Department of Cultural Affairs.

Printed in the United Kingdom

Preface

WHEN MUSTAFA KEMAL ATATÜRK founded the Republic of Turkey in 1923, he put women at the epicenter of his modernizing vision. At home and in the workplace, they would be the ones to bring the nation up to Western standards. In 1926, he replaced sharia law with the Swiss civil code, thereby bringing an end to polygamy and a husband's right to unilaterally repudiate a wife at his discretion. He gave women the right to vote and run for office in 1934, well in advance of many countries in Europe, including France. But the very next year, he closed the Turkish Women's Union, which had been instrumental in effecting this change. His authoritarian single-party regime saw no need for women to organize on behalf of women, now that they had "full and equal status" with men.

This was the paradox into which Sevgi Soysal was born: a nation that had granted women equality, on condition they did not question its terms. And that's how it remained for the first thirty years of her life. All around her, women were rising in the ranks. Their many contributions to the national cause were much heralded. What they themselves thought about their lives, the world, and what it required of its women was politically irrelevant. But for those with the inclination, there was always the disobedient pen.

There was rarely a moment in her short life when Sevgi did not have that pen to hand. Even as a student, she was writing in arts journals, not so much to expound on what she knew but to explore what she did not. She grew up in Ankara, Turkey's new and fiercely patriotic capital. Her mother was German. Her architect father was a refugee from Greece. She had many doors open to her and she walked through them all. In sharp contrast to what might have been expected in 1950s Europe and America, an early marriage proved no impediment. She already had a young son when she took up jobs with Radio Ankara and the German Cultural Center. In the same years she began a distinguished side career as a translator, published her first book of short stories, and performed at the National Theater in two plays she herself had translated.

Her husband was away doing his military service when she took to the stage. She fell in love with a fellow performer, who became her second husband. Suddenly the main breadwinner, she took up a senior post at Turkish Radio and Television, where she proved herself a pioneer in progressive women's programming. Even during the fallow years before second-wave feminism came to Turkey as it did everywhere, she was bringing women's voices into questioning conversations about sex, marriage, children, and families. Her first novel, *Walking*, explored the same terrain with eloquence and daring. It won a national prize, only to be banned for obscenity. Undeterred, Sevgi went on to write *Tante Rosa*, about the women on the German side of her family. Now a classic, it was derided at the time for "sounding like a translation."

And here we come to the troubles for which she is unfortunately best known. While her second husband was away doing his military service, she met and fell in love with the distinguished professor of constitutional law Mümtaz Soysal. Their happy days were soon cut short by the infamous memorandum of March 12th, 1971, by which the military seized control of the country. For most of the next two years, much of Turkey was under martial law, as the generals now in charge did their utmost to crush the left. Sevgi was among the first to be removed from her job. Mümtaz was sent to Mamak Prison, charged with spreading communist propaganda, and it was here that the two married. Soon Sevgi was in prison herself, charged not just with spreading communist propaganda but also with obscenity.

All three of the books for which she is best known have their roots in the eight months she spent behind bars. The first is

Noontime in Yenişehir, the novel that she wrote in prison at the rate of eight pages a day between breakfast and gymnastics. The second is *Yıldırım District Women's Barracks*, her memoir of life inside. The third is the book in your hand.

I first read *Dawn* forty-five years ago. I translated it during lockdown, as democracy foundered everywhere, and it broke my heart once again. For though it is set in the early 1970s, it could just as easily have happened yesterday. Like Orhan Pamuk's *Snow*, it is the Turkish tragedy writ small. In contrast to *Snow*, it subjects that tragedy's scars and fissures to a female gaze. Oya, the protagonist, has just served a year in a political prison and a shorter spell in a civil prison. She is in the southeastern city of Adana to serve out the third part of her sentence – exile – as Sevgi herself did in real life. The novel covers just twelve hours. There is an evening meal in a shantytown, brought to an abrupt end by a police raid. There is a long night at police headquarters, followed by a dawn in name only.

The novel was published to great acclaim in 1975, during a lull in the Turkish state's long war against dissenters. Later that same year, Sevgi was diagnosed with breast cancer. She died in 1976, leaving behind one almost grown son and two very young daughters. It is thanks to her youngest, Funda Soysal, that all her books are back in print and enjoying a renaissance, especially among women who (like so many of us of all ages elsewhere) see their basic rights under threat. We read her to understand how it came to this, and how to keep going, guided by her beautiful words.

Maureen Freely
Bath
May 2022

DAWN

The Raid

THE SUN presses down on the city of Adana: it knows no other way. Autumn is here and evening has fallen, but still this suffocating humidity, this relentless heat. The Çukurova plains cannot bear much more. Let there be rain, and soon.

There is the blistering sun, and the rainy season. The rich in their grand villas and gardens of paradise share generously of the seasons with the city's poor, but what comes from this fertile earth belongs to the rich alone. No sign of nature's abundance in the outlying shantytowns. No orange trees or palms. No bright southern flowers, or fleshy, broad-leafed ornamental plants. Just these hot and humid fumes that pass for air, choking up the mean and narrow streets of the Independence District, seeping under every door. Soon the rain will come.

The only plenty to be found is in the crowded rooms where night has already fallen. Where the trays sit on the floor, and forks pile bright red radishes, green peppers, parsley, and spring onions over thick-sliced bread. Where the bed mats lie side by side, while outside the watchman blows his whistle, and fighting men spill out of the coffeehouses, to settle their scores in the street. Never a night in this district without a fight and a watchman's whistle. No one is surprised if a woman of low virtue has her face cut up by a razor. An evening begun with a few friendly drinks can drive a man of passion to violent excess. The district's liveliest nightspot is its police station. There are also the round-ups of hashish and cigarette smugglers. These, too, are routine.

No one is surprised to see a police car crawling down a street, blue light blinking, pausing before each house. The Arab workmen making their homes in these parts have long since wearied of such attentions. They close their doors. The police car crawls on. Creeps down the road, one house at a time. Each one identical to the last. A tricky business, locating an address in a neighborhood like this. To do so without attracting undue attention, the byword is stealth.

It took just one rough kick to break down the flimsy door. One rough kick, and at last Oya understood. Since the moment of her arrival, tensions had been building. And now it was as if Hüseyin had vanished, taking Mustafa with him, and their host, Ali of Maraş, and all those others. Even Gülşah, who'd only moments earlier carried in their supper on a tray. She was gone, too. It was just Oya in the room now, Oya the only unexpected guest, perched amongst the calico cushions at the end of the makeshift sofa. She'd never managed to draw these people out. One rough kick and they'd vanished inside themselves, locked themselves away. She was alone now, alone with the smashed door and the police flooding through it. The house and everyone in it: they were unraveling. They were spiraling out of reach, abandoning her to a self she'd too long taken for granted, a center that could no longer hold.

She'd seen a lot of the real world in recent years, but its ugly face still shocked her. This was not to say she thought reality could be given a face, and so be judged as beautiful or ugly. It was just that she was more attuned to beauty – having been raised to appreciate beauty to a degree that some might find odd. Though she knew full well that there was beauty and ugliness in all things under the sun, she was still in the habit of closing one eye, so as to separate out the beauty from the rest. In the name of beauty, she was willing to take any risk. She took courageous stands for no other reason than she found beauty in courage itself. Ask her to confront an ugly fact or deed, though, and she collapsed. Oya was shocked by her own cowardice. This, at least, was how she would come to understand her panic when that door was so suddenly kicked in, even after all she'd been through.

But this was not the time for idle soul searching. All over the city, police were kicking in doors. This was just one raid of many. Like it or not, Oya was going to have to accept that she was one of an angry, shocked, and terrified multitude. Think of all the others in this house alone. So many people, and she didn't know a single one. Ali of Maraş. Hüseyin, and Mustafa. Ekrem, Zekeriya, Gülşah, and Ziynet. They were strangers, or they had been, until the police kicked the door in. Now they were intimates, facing a single fate.

Ali of Maraş – their host – had been the last to work out what was happening. If he'd worked it out sooner, he would not have turned to his nephew to ask, "So where do you think we're headed, my boy?' He'd have left the question hanging. Instead, he'd acted as if he hadn't seen three policemen pushing their way into the room; while they stood there, glaring and glowering, he had finished his sentence. Hüseyin, meanwhile, had been so shocked as to pour his rakı back into the bottle. It was this bit of foolishness that had alerted Ali to the policemen. That same moment, he jumped to his feet.

They're all from Maraş, these people. Farmhands and factory workers who came to Adana to claim their share of the fertile Çukurova Plain. Hüseyin and Mustafa are Ali's nephews, and the only ones who've managed to break free. That's how Hüseyin sees it anyway. He's a lawyer. Mustafa, a teacher. Their family is still their family, though – if they feel somewhat distant from it, this is something they do their best to hide. That said. If Mustafa had not turned up without warning in Adana just today, Hüseyin would not be here at his uncle's. Because Ali – who worked for years at the Yüreğir plant, and for another long stretch at the

Mediterranean Textile Industries factory – has a long-standing dispute with Social Security that needs fixing. Ali is waiting for his nephew to fix it. Every last one of Hüseyin's relatives expects the same from him. Every time they have a problem that needs solving, or a question that needs answering, they come to him. It's beginning to try his patience. Do they really think he has a magic wand? It bothers him, though, that he's not managed to fix Ali's problem for him. He might be a lawyer – an educated man – but he is, first and foremost, a man from Maraş . . . and honor-bound, therefore, to fix his uncle's problem. It's not at all straightforward, this problem, and Hüseyin has only just finished his internship. He's still settling into the practice he's opened with two friends. What with the constant stream of relatives and acquaintances stopping by for tea and coffee, it's been a struggle to find time for anything that might bring in money. And it's Hüseyin's relatives who've come most often. They all have problems in need of a lawyer. Nothing that would bring in the sort of money that Hüseyin and his partners must bring in if they are to survive. These relatives are hoping Hüseyin will help them out of the goodness of his heart. The only abundance these people have seen since coming to the fertile Çukurova plain is in their ever-increasing numbers. And also, they keep ending up in court. Whenever that happens, they need a lawyer at their side. It doesn't stop there, either. They also need Hüseyin at their side whenever they get married or register the birth of a new child. They want him to write letters and petitions on their behalf. The drudgery has no end. And never do they come to him alone. They bring along friends. Involve neighbors. Any opportunity to show off this relative of theirs who got himself an education and is now a bona fide lawyer. None of this is new for Hüseyin, or surprising. It was one of the reasons his people made sure he got an education. Perhaps the main reason. To be clear: he has no wish to cut himself off from this family that has held him in its embrace since childhood. They might have loaded him down with responsibilities, but just as much, they've provided advantages. They were the ones who gave him the courage to set up a law practice in Adana. He has relatives working in all the cotton mills of Öte-Geçe. There's no end to the trouble they and their friends encounter with the state, the employers, the unions, social security, and life itself. If you're from Maraş, you'll take your business to Hüseyin. That's the sort of future he's dreaming of. But right now, Hüseyin and his partners can't even cover the rent. Every time a relation drops by for a coffee they can't afford, or tracks mud over the carpet they're still paying for, Hüseyin's heart sinks. In the meantime, he hasn't given his uncle's social security problem the attention it deserves. His relations might try his patience now and then, but the bond remains strong. He doesn't want to let them down, and it pains him to have disappointed his uncle, who has done so very much for him. On his way to his uncle's house this evening, he'd been fretting about how best to explain himself, but then Ali had welcomed him inside. Not a word about social security.

He's no fool, their Uncle Ali. He taught himself how to read. He reads the papers, listens to the news. He knows who's propping up the right these days and how the left is suffering. And he has questions. In fact, he'd just turned to Mustafa – the nephew he trusts more on these matters – at the very moment the door flew open. But Hüseyin, on seeing his uncle bite his lip, as was his habit before asking a serious question, had assumed he was about to ask about the social security business. As to why he then poured his raki back into the bottle – maybe it was shock, on seeing the door fly off its hinges. Maybe he just faltered, because he thought his uncle was about to ask him if he'd managed to fix his pension. This part is unclear.

But the rakı in the bottle – that did stay clear. Somehow, in the midst of all this commotion, when everything was happening so fast, Oya picked up on that small detail. Hüseyin drinks his rakı neat – no ice, no water. Which proves what they say: the best rakı drinkers are in the Southeast. Why would anyone drink ice with rakı? How long has the bottle been sitting outside the refrigerator? Tell me, did our grandfather ever put ice in his rakı? They didn't water down their drinks in those days, any more than they would water down their words. That's how Hüseyin likes to put it. But this evening he has a stomachache. An ulcer has turned his tongue black. In spite of which, he still declined the water. So when he poured his rakı back into the bottle – in shock, perhaps, at the sound of the door crashing down – the rakı in the bottle didn't cloud up.

When the police charged into the room, glaring and grimacing, Mustafa had wanted to take that bottle from his brother's hand and throw it at their heads. It was almost as if Hüseyin had guessed this and taken hold of the bottle to keep this from happening. The police have just raided our uncle's house, and there you are, pouring rakı from one vessel into another. Every day, a new outrage, and still you stay calm?

Mustafa is a mathematics teacher. He was still in his first year, in a school in Urfa, when he was arrested and sent to Istanbul. This was during martial law. After fourteen months in Selimiye Prison, he had resigned himself to being inside for years to come. But then, just two days ago, the prosecution had ordered his release. That was when he found out that he was still to be tried under Article 296 of the Turkish Penal Code, even though they were letting him go. They'd kept him locked up for more than a year, after all, and so they needed to charge him with something serious, conspiring to overturn the constitution, for instance. It was a lottery, in other words. And 296 turned out to be the winning number. Mustafa had no idea if he should be happy about this or upset. His release had been as sudden as his arrest. He had no money to get himself home, and no one in his family knew that. But his fellow prisoners, bless them all – they'd done what they always did. Without waiting to be asked, they'd organized a whip-round. Saved him from spending his first day in Istanbul in the gutter. He'd gone straight to the travel agency, to buy his bus ticket to Adana. To kill time while he was waiting for the bus to leave, he walked the streets of Istanbul. And soon he realized why he was humming the same songs he'd sung with his friends in prison. It was just like pacing the floor. They'd done a lot of that inside. To stop themselves thinking, to breathe new life into their cramped quarters, to escape the stranglehold of monotonous routine, to crack the damn shell, just in time to keep the joy inside from dying, they would hum as they marched. Singing out loud was forbidden. This humming was a defense, in other words. A way of keeping reality at bay. The same way a person might keep himself clean and powdered to avoid noticing how much he'd aged. And now? Mustafa was still pacing, but there were no walls. He could go where he liked, at whatever speed he chose. But how? What had he spent those fourteen months trying so hard to keep intact? What was it that had thrown him so, when suddenly they'd told him he was free?

Yes, that was it. He'd kept himself strong so that he could start again the moment he got out. Or that was what he'd told himself. Now he was out. One step at a time, he thought. His friends were who knew where. He had to find the strength inside himself. He had to pull himself together, but then what? He needed to think it through, but if he kept up this humming, wasn't he just numbing himself? *They grind iron into the dust, sprinkle ash on your blind eyes . . . They crush your heart, until it bleeds . . .* This was what he'd been humming when suddenly his wife came to mind. For the first time since he got out – but how could that be? He'd thought about Güler so much when he was inside. So very much! If she knew he was free . . . so what if she did? This question set off a chain of dark thoughts. He wasn't even sure if his wife was still in Urfa. There'd been no letters for a month. There'd been a revolt in his wing of the prison, after which they'd banned all letters and visits. Was this the sort of time you'd expect to be released? Just to think this made him angry. It was cowardice, this he knew. Now that he was out, he had to be ready for anything, more than that, even. Much more.

Stopping in Sebil, he'd bought himself a coffee and sat down to watch the passing ferries. He'd spend a night or two in Adana, he decided. As soon as he knew how things stood with Güler, he'd head back to Urfa. How things stood with Güler. It grieved him so, to feel his heart darkening with suspicion. Even under torture, he'd managed to keep her memory unsullied. In the last letter he'd received from her, she'd said she was thinking of leaving Urfa. With their daughter, born while he was inside. She'd never got along with his family. Before, when he was a free man, it hadn't really mattered. But now, things could so easily go wrong.

They'd met in Istanbul, while studying in the Faculty of Natural Sciences. She was in the movement, too. At least, she didn't come across as being outside it. She'd been so sure of herself in those days. As confident as any man. She'd commanded respect and given the same back. She'd had a warmth. All he can recall of those days now are her large black eyes, and her bony hands. What else? She came from a poor family. Not as poor as Mustafa's, but poor, nonetheless. Her mother was a bank clerk. No father – he'd died when she was tiny. So in a way she'd had it harder than Mustafa. His relations might be farm laborers and factory workers, but there were a lot of them. They helped each other out – put both Hüseyin and Mustafa through school. So even though Güler's mother was a bank clerk, her childhood had been lonelier and less secure. Her mother had struggled to get her an education. She'd expected to be rewarded for her trouble.

Güler had not finished university. She'd married Mustafa instead. Even with his degree in mathematics, he'd been lucky to land a job at a lycée in Urfa. Güler's mother had not wanted to move there with them. And you couldn't say Güler had liked Urfa much either. She'd already met members of Mustafa's huge family in Istanbul. She'd liked them well enough in those days, or at least that was how it had seemed. They're not like my mother, she'd say. They don't ask what's in it for them and turn away. They help each other out, not to get something in return, but to keep each other going. So many of them had dug deep into their pockets, just to keep Mustafa in school. But no one more than Ali. In those days, it would bring tears to Güler's eyes, to see such sacrifice. But not to Mustafa's eyes. He'd learned early what blood ties meant. You helped your relatives when they were studying, when they were in the army, and also when they were in jail. At the end of the day, a family had to be a single body. It had to use all its limbs to keep the blood flowing. There was no other way to survive.

After moving to Urfa, though, Güler had begun to lose patience with these relatives who came and went as they pleased. Couldn't they have waited until they'd managed to furnish the place? The relatives didn't mind at all, though. If there were no knives or forks, or pots or pans, then so be it. It didn't matter to them how their food was served. What mattered was how Güler served her husband. They'd like me to turn my hair into a broom, she'd say. They want me to be your slave. One day, when she was very angry, she said: they want you to use me the same way you used them. They want you to exploit me. Yes, she'd gone that far.

And now, on the day of his release, those long-ago words had flared up in him. How could Güler have ever said such a thing? He was the reason: she'd wanted him to support her the way he supported his relations. More to the point, she'd wanted him to stand up for her, forget what his relatives thought of her, and let her be herself – her old self. In this way, too, he had disappointed her. The truth was she didn't act the way his Maraş relations expected a wife to act, and she'd not been able to win them over. She counted for nothing in their eyes. Nothing.

The upshot of all this: she'd withdrawn into herself. A distance grew between them. She fell pregnant. Mustafa, meanwhile, was too busy to dwell on details. There was the movement: his heart and soul. Oh, to see it go from strength to strength! Nothing else mattered. He had no time in those days for the personal or the everyday. These were matters for later. And Güler? It was her job to keep him going. This she had done. But in silence. No sign now of the plain-speaking, backtalking girl he had married. Except for the day she'd said those ugly words, except for that last day. Unfair it might be, but he could no longer remember anything else. So what had been on her mind through all that? It had never occurred to him to ask, he now realizes. All he can remember is Güler cooking, Güler knitting in silence. He was happy with her then. She had his friends' approval. But did they have hers? He had absolutely no idea. But now here he was, drinking a coffee in Sebil, in a storm of doubt. Did she love me? Trust me? Believe in me? Was she happy? What sort of happiness could she have been expecting? She couldn't even make herself happy. But how could that be? She'd been so self-aware. At least she had been when they got married.

As he sipped the bitter dregs of his coffee, he thought, I only took from her, I never gave. And Güler – she'd asked for nothing. What if she had? It would have made no difference. Why not? He'd given everything he had to the movement, that was why. Which meant he'd never trusted her. As he drank his second coffee in Sebil, and then his third, he knew it was pointless, beating himself up like this, but he couldn't find a way to stop.

He couldn't help himself. She was one enormous question mark, looming over him. So very different from the Güler he'd conjured up in prison. Ever-smiling, ever-giving. No smiles, though, on the night before they took him away. That night, they'd argued. That night, she'd stood up to him. "Tomorrow I'm bringing some people back with me," he'd said. "Be ready." And Güler had asked, "Who are they?" In the same way she might have asked if he'd like another glass of tea. He could have just left the question unanswered, but something in Mustafa had snapped. "This is hardly the time to play the shrew!" he'd said. And Güler had sat up straight, and in the harsh voice he'd not heard since Istanbul, she'd said, "This is my house, too. So let me make this clear: no one can take shelter here unless I know who they are." And Mustafa had sprung from his chair and picked up her great pile of photo-novels – yes, she'd started reading photo-novels, she'd sunk that low. He'd torn them to shreds. Thrown those shreds into her face. And taunted her: was this where she'd picked up her vulgar notions? Güler had burst into tears. "What am I supposed to do? What choice do I have but foolishness? It's my only escape!" She'd lain in bed crying for hours. Mustafa had stroked her back until she fell asleep. As he finished his last coffee in Sebil, Mustafa wondered if he had stroked her back that night because he'd known somehow that he'd need her the next day.

As he sat there blankly watching the ferries pass, he remembered something else she had said that night: "I want to be involved. Why won't you let me be involved? I can't take this much longer. I've had it with these ideas of yours. With this movement, too. One day I'm going to pack my bags and run. Put as much distance between us as I can. As if you were the plague." And Mustafa had murmured, "If I'd known you were this upset . . ." At which point, Güler's sobs had given way to shrieks. "You're as backward as everyone else in your family! So backward you'll never succeed!" Yes, she had said that. Said he would never succeed. How could it be that he had not thought about this, not once, during his months in Selimiye Prison? So let's go back there now. What happened then? Maybe he'd cursed her. And hit her a few times, too. He can't bear thinking about it, and so he doesn't.

The next morning, though. He encounterd a very different Güler. He was in a rush to leave, gulping down his tea. And in the accommodating voice that marriage had bestowed on her, she asked, "Would you like me to make bumbar tonight?" Knowing that he liked this dish a lot. But she'd never made it for him. Intestines stuffed with meat, she'd say. Disgusting. Why had she suddenly offered to make it for me? Was it because she could see I was still upset? "Don't bother," he'd replied. "I don't care what you cook. What importance does food have, in times like these? Just make sure you have plenty of it."

It was at that exact moment that the bell had gone. The moment least expected. I must have turned pale. When my job was to stay calm – not react in any way to that bell – I just froze. I left my pregnant wife to open the door. To have four submachine guns press into her tummy. "Surrender!'"

I sent my pregnant wife to the door. I even did that. And now I'll have to live with it. These were the dark thoughts that came to plague him, on his first morning outside.

That night, he'd boarded the bus for Adana. From the station he'd gone straight to Hüseyin's office. Fighting sleep.

Mustafa stamped down hard on the floor. Or to be more precise, on his brother's foot. This really did throw him. So much so that he let the rakı bottle fall across the table. And that, for Mustafa, was the last straw. I sat with this man in his office all day, answering all his silly questions, but I couldn't bring myself to ask about Güler. Male pride, maybe. He'd told his brother he'd be heading to Urfa in the morning and left it at that. If Hüseyin were a man, he would have brought it up himself, given him some news of his wife and daughter. But Hüseyin never misses a chance to lord it over: you were wrong about such and such, you should have done such and such instead, and this fine dog should know!

The news had gone out fast – nothing faster than the family grapevine – and soon every last man from the Maraş tribe had heard he was back. Had rushed to his brother's office to greet him. Come back to the house, each one said. To accept all their invitations, he would have needed a month. Who cares about Güler? Who cares about a teaching job? They think I'll be fine, just because I'm a professional. While he was inside, the Teachers Association had given Güler assistance. The moment he was convicted, though, they'd ban him from teaching, if not before. It was good the Teachers Association had been there to help, because Güler hadn't wanted to ask his family. It was wrong of me to get angry at Hüseyin. He probably has no idea what Güler's up to.

Mustafa could never have turned down Ali's invitation. The man was like a father to him. He'd done so much for him. Brought him to Adana for middle school.

He'd never treated Mustafa differently from his own children. From his own sons, that is. Because he hadn't educated his daughters. Who could say how he'd scraped together the money to pay for all those pencils and erasers Mustafa had so carelessly lost at school? He'd often wondered about that afterward. Ali had never mentioned it, not even once. Someone in this house is studying already, he'd said. That was his reason for not sending his eldest daughter to middle school. At the time, Mustafa had found this natural. If anyone was to be educated, it was going to be a boy. If his father couldn't afford it on his own, then it fell to his uncles to find a way. It was the same when the time came for a boy to marry or do his military service. Everyone pitched in, most especially for the boys. They put their hope in their sons. Because their sons were their only hope.

When Mustafa was still in school in Adana, he'd promised that when he was older, he would be the one to send Ali's youngest son to school. In those days, Hasan was still a baby.

In the dark cells of Selimiye Prison, where night always fell so early, these words came to haunt him. For Ali's son was well into his school years by then. And it was Ali who was paying for his schooling, Ali who'd had to scrimp and save, and what of Mustafa's fine words now? This unpaid debt tormented him, kept him up all night smoking one cigarette after another. Before his arrest, it hadn't bothered him so much, probably. Back then, he'd managed not to think too much about his debts to Ali and his other Maraş relatives. If he'd thought about them at all during those heady, hopeful days. Back then, it wasn't his debt to Ali and those others that preoccupied him, but his debt to the people. What he owed the masses. Set against this great burden, his personal debt to Ali's son had seemed so very small. What could be achieved, by educating just one boy? Ali would just have one boulder less to carry. When there shouldn't be any boulders weighing him down. Or any man . . .

What tormented him in Selimiye Prison: the growing suspicion that this line of reasoning had been a pretext. What did I do, in all that time? What did I achieve? Was I truly dedicating my life to all the Alis of this world, or was I just fooling around? Was I letting myself off the hook, thinking myself a man of the struggle, when I couldn't meet even my own small obligations? What do I have to show for myself? What did I do for my own people? Why not even them? I didn't even manage to bring them to the cause. They didn't join in the cause, but still they were always there for me, even the ones who expected so much of me, even after I had spent all that time trying to bring them round. As for the masses – where were they? What did I do, beyond my own little circle of ten or fifteen friends – okay, let's say fifty? And what did we do, beyond staying out of trouble, and getting together to talk? Why, under interrogation, could we barely look at ourselves? These were the thoughts that had haunted him throughout his interrogation, as his beliefs were put to the test, and honor crushed. Later, in prison, he would brush them aside, and forget them.

In Urfa, on the day he was picked up, he remembered feeling relieved, to have been detained before he'd actually committed a crime. They'd found no fugitives in his home. But that wasn't why he was relieved. He was relieved because he'd not been caught in the act. Later, during those long nights in prison, it was this that had shaken his belief in himself as a man of the struggle, a man who could afford to overlook his personal debt to Ali. That morning, he had even believed that – having found no fugitives in his home – they would not be taking him in. The denunciation was unfounded. "Sir . . . May I go to work now, sir? My wife is pregnant, sir. . ." Yes, he'd even said that, and now he can hardly bear to remember that. What a look Güler had given him. But she'd kept silent. She hadn't said a thing to this major. She'd not even said, "Do come in." She'd said nothing. While he'd carried on babbling. Hiding his hatred, his disgust for these men who'd come barging into their home. He'd even shown them respect. Hoping this would keep them from taking him in. The major had not said anything either. He must have thought me small, to have sent my wife to answer the door. Whatever the major thought, though. These were dangerous times, and he'd let his wife answer the door, and that was unforgiveable. And then, to have told the major she was pregnant. These cheap, vile words would come back to him during those first nights in prison, to chase him like the plague.

And still they chase after him. There is the door crashing in, and Abdullah the policeman with his grimy face and filthy moustache. There is Ali asking, "So what are we going to do about this business, my boy?" and Hüseyin, stupidly pouring his rakı back into the bottle. And there is Güler's face, swinging at him like a string of prayer beads, hitting at his throat. Before they'd taken him off in their car, she'd smiled and said, "Don't worry." And: "Do you have any money?" Truth is, she was strong that morning. This was the Güler he'd treasured and exalted all these fourteen months. You had to have someone to look up to, those days. You had to have something.

Revulsion. The moment he felt Hüseyin's foot beneath his own, it claimed him yet again. Bringing with it thoughts that grated on his mind like fingernails scraping a wall. Who'd informed on whom? Everyone had informed on everyone. Now that was a humiliation worth sharing. And they'd shared it in record time. Between interrogations, they'd fallen even lower, and this shame, too, they had shared. That's how they faced up to it. "They know, somehow they know. They talked, for whatever reason, they talked. I talked. Somehow, for whatever reason, I talked." The aching soul. That was the hardest thing to bear. Worse than being stripped naked. Worse than the electric shocks. Worse than walking on ruptured soles. Worse even than the thoughts running rampant through the mind. The soiled and bloodied pajamas. The chains on his legs. The gnawing fear that he had nothing left to hide or confess. That there was nothing left to him. The fear. The yearning for deliverance. From the soiled pajamas. From the clanking chain. From the screaming and wailing that went on all night. From the rooms where they stripped him naked, and doused him with bucket after bucket of water, while the electric truncheon whirred. From his own hideous flesh. And his tears. If only his metabolism stopped working, he could escape all this. So he thought.

Deliverance was a garden full of apricot trees. There he slept, in the shadow of a tree newly blossomed. Far from Güler, and his friends, and their fine words. Their clenched fists, and himself. There he slept, like an empty sack.

In the end – when his tormentors were persuaded that he was indeed an empty sack – he was formally arrested and sent to Selimiye. What a relief it was, to be arrested. What sort of revolutionary did that make him, then? No, I was no longer a revolutionary by then. I was nothing. Absolutely nothing. Nothing but a sack they'd succeeded in emptying of its contents.

There'd been deaths. I didn't die, but some did. Death was something we'd been prepared for. But torture? In Mustafa's opinion, they'd not been ready for it. But they should have been. They should have been expecting to be turned into empty sacks. We talked death to death, but we didn't talk enough about torture, when it was the most important thing to understand. We turned away from it – and turned into empty sacks. Between interrogations, as he drifted in and out of sleep, this had been Mustafa's one and only thought. There was nothing left to him. Not even his past. Together they'd turned the old Mustafa in. His connection to his old life had snapped like a string of prayer beads. Hard to thread them back together. Mustafa was left with the beads and nothing more. Being arrested meant an end to torture, nothing more than that. But it freed the empty sack to look back and judge his performance. They ratted on me, of course they did. It was already known, what I'd done. I ratted on them, too. I said much too much. Where did betrayal begin and end? What could he have done differently? What was his fault, and his alone? Try as he might, he just couldn't work it out. His calculations kept going astray. He could not find his way to the clear and simple solution that he so desperately needed. That they all would need. Later on. If ever they managed to string together their thoughts. Fashion a new set of prayer beads, you might say. In the meantime. It had been left to Güler to make sense of things, and to Ali. The thought of Ali brought with it a flash of light. It was Ali he had ratted on. Ali and the whole Maraş tribe. He'd betrayed them first, and he'd gone on to betray all the rest. The masses. When I turned from Ali to the masses, and brushed aside my obligations, was I not committing myself to a greater cause? *They know all this already,* I told myself. But when I incriminated myself, I was really incriminating them all. So this was the crime. This was the offense. Forget about incriminating others. None of us had the right to incriminate ourselves. We couldn't have known that. Or rather, we didn't manage it. It wasn't just myself I betrayed. I brought the sky down on us all. Having reached this verdict, Mustafa had found new strength, as do so many, once they are able to measure the dimensions of defeat. How beautiful are new beginnings!

He'd begun with Güler. Güler as he'd last seen her, on the day they took him away. The other Güler – the bored and moody housewife who read photonovels and with every passing day looked more like the vegetables she served him – she didn't figure at all. He was never more at peace with himself than he was during those fourteen months in prison. He felt no fear. He was resolute. He believed himself to be moving on, making good progress. He didn't let himself be idle. He kept up his reading. Went on morning and evening strolls. Never forgot to exercise. Limited his food, but never his appetite for serious discussion. These were days for healing.

Why then, had he faltered once he was set free? Had he not given himself enough time to convalesce? He felt like a patient who'd discharged himself from hospital too soon. That first morning outside, it became clear to him: he hadn't healed yet, he still wasn't strong enough. And that was when his doubts about Güler had returned to him.

He didn't know if he'd find her in Urfa. If he even had a job there. With so much uncertainty looming, it was not the right time to be visiting Ali. He should have waited until he could present himself as a man who had put his life in order. Today he was a man in turmoil about what he might find tomorrow. Incapable even of ordering his thoughts. Ali's question had angered him. If you're in the wrong, your temper flares fast, after all.

"Let's put it like this: until you people start standing up for yourselves, there's no hope." That was how he had answered Ali, and there was some truth in that. But why had he left himself out of it? Why had he said "you people?" He didn't have time to ask himself that before they kicked in the door.

Ali's wife Gülşah and his sister-in-law, Ziynet had only just finished bringing out the food. Ziynet was brought up by her sister. She's married now, but still living here, in her brother-in-law's house. She has no interest in the food on the table. Hardly notices her older sister as she rushes back and forth. But her heart is beating as fast as a bird's. Zekeriya just got back from Iskenderun this morning, you see. He's found himself a job in a shipyard. They'll be moving to Iskenderun just as soon as they can. And Ziynet will at last be set free from her sister's house. Zekeriya, meanwhile. Seeing the house in such commotion, he did what any self-respecting man would do, and took off. But he's not what Ziynet is longing for right now. She's longing for these guests to be gone. She keeps glancing furtively at her husband, who is eating in silence as the other men speak. Now and then, she can feel herself blushing.

Gülşah took one last look at the food on the table. Okra, lettuce, and the biggest radishes. Parsley, bread, water, boiled eggs, bumbar – job done. She and Ziynet have remained on their feet. She's serving the köftes that Ziynet grilled on the brazier. One for each man, and another for little Hasan. But nothing for herself, or Ziynet. Let the men eat – that's what matters. When Gülşah sees men taking pleasure in the food that fills their cheeks, that's when she knows she's done her duty. And it is at just that moment that the door comes crashing down. What a shock! Gülşah stared at the door, as if it was accusing her of cooking the köftes badly, or not serving the men food in good time and leaving their stomachs empty.

Then the police charged in, and the supper was ruined. But she was so used to being ruined, and carrying all the blame for it, that she kept on running back and forth, as if she'd forgotten to bring the bread out to the table, or the salt, or the water. Until it dawned on her that she was not the one who had brought disorder to the house.

As for Oya, there on the edge of the sofa – the sudden disorder was something of a relief. She'd been feeling so ill at ease, and so out of place in this house, that even the sound of the door crashing down had come as a welcome change. It had shamed her, to be the only woman at the table, to be served by Gülşah and Ziynet and to see them left standing, her own privileges so starkly revealed.

But Gülşah and Ziynet didn't even question it. Oya is not like anyone they know. And that's fine with them. They hardly think about it.

In their eyes, Oya is neither a man nor a woman. She's simply an extension of the men they live to serve. And Oya – she's always made a point of acting like a man, she even enjoys it – but tonight it bothers her, that they think of her like this, and that may be why she turned down the rakı. Until that moment, she hadn't said a thing, either. How could she have let this happen, when her reason for coming here had been to welcome a few new people into her life? She loves meeting new people. People from all walks of life. But this evening, seeing Ziynet and Gülşah cut out of all conversation, she'd not felt able to join in either. How rude it would be, if she counted them for nothing, and turned her back on them, too. There at that cramped table, she feels like some sort of hybrid, half man, half woman. She'd wanted to get up and help them serve the food, and then invite them to sit down, but fearful they might find that laughable, she'd given up on the idea. She was still fretting about it though when they kicked in the door.

And she was the only one who noticed how shocked Gülşah looked, and also, how guilty. But this was no way to create a bond. On the contrary. Never mind that she had, however briefly, been so callous as to welcome this ugly intrusion. They're wondering if it's their fault this is happening. Each and every one of them. With every moment, they sink deeper into themselves.

Oya thinks it's her fault. She's the reason for the raid. She's the one who brought disorder to the house. It's her fault Gülşah's hard work has come to nothing, so how can she ever hope to make it up to her?

She'll be leaving Adana very soon. Her time of internal exile completed. She'd been careful from the outset. She'd needed to use her brains, and so she had. As much as possible, she'd kept herself from becoming an object of pity. Good could come of these things, as well as bad. Not to hold herself responsible for the distress she kept well hidden. Just to endure. Just to endure was to gain some sense of accomplishment. Like shielding yourself from a disease. As if her only responsibility was to her health. Keep herself safe from new microbes. All this could be calming, stabilizing even. The body could not fight too many microbes at one time. Which meant? She had to be alone.

There wasn't much she could do. Everywhere she went, she was followed. In the end she had decided to see this oppressive situation as the perfect opportunity to put herself and her health in order. Days would go by without a single person stopping by her hotel to ask her how she was. She knew no one in Adana. She had little opportunity to meet new people. Of the handful of contacts she'd been given, not a single one returned her calls. As if she were dying of a contagious disease, Oya thought. As if they'd decided she was best left to face death alone.

Though she had to admit that it wasn't altogether unpleasant to be seen as dangerous. There is a certain glamour in being shunned. And besides, as she well knew, not everyone in this city was like that. But she couldn't bring herself to seek those other people out. She may well have convinced herself that she was more dangerous than she really was, but she still hadn't wanted to put anyone in harm's way. She'd be leaving soon enough. These others would be staying, to weather the storm here. She might have enjoyed their company, but she would simply be providing new targets for the men who followed her everywhere she went. That's why she'd torn up the few addresses she'd been given.

Now, as she watches a befuddled Hüseyin pour his rakı back into the bottle, she asks herself what business she has sitting here right next to him. They'd only met by chance. She'd been ordered to make a statement for a trial going on in Ankara. She'd been making her gloomy way through the corridors of the Adana courthouse when she heard a voice asking, "Are you Oya Ertem?" He was young, this man. Dark-skinned. Hook-nosed. Swimming in his lawyer's robes. For months, she had spoken to no one. Why had she let this man befriend her? That Hüseyin had brought her here tonight – that the evening had ended in a raid – it was rotten luck. Nothing more.

Without preamble, Hüseyin had run through his history. Originally from Maraş. A degree in law from Istanbul University. His Adana internship recently completed. He'd heard that Oya was serving out her term of exile here, but he'd refrained from stopping by her hotel. He'd been a member of the old Workers' Party, you see. He hadn't wanted to taint her with the same brush! All this in one breath. And Oya had smiled to herself. We're all doing the same thing, she thought. Always worrying about putting other people at risk. He'd struck her as sincere, Hüseyin. Driven half mad by solitude, Oya was hungry for people she could believe in. Even though she'd promised herself she'd stay away from people like this, she'd not found it in herself to mistrust Hüseyin. She'd brushed aside her battle-hardened friends' warnings. *Never let your guard down,* they'd said. *They'll try to befriend you, but just to take words out of your mouth. Adana is crawling with police informers. Don't play into their hands.* Sitting here now, she cannot come up with a single reason why she should have trusted Hüseyin. Even if his sideburns and his fancy tie did give him the look of the sort of provincial playboy who'd belong to the Workers' Party. She'd certainly gained no sense of the man himself, though, in the time between that first meeting and this evening. What sort of man was he, this creature who'd just poured his rakı back into the bottle? It occurred to her now that she'd never asked herself this question.

"Are you Oya Ertem?" "Yes, I am." A short exchange. A brief escape from loneliness. A terrible lapse – there was no other word for it. From that day on, Hüseyin had checked in on her from time to time. Usually by phone. "How are you doing?" "Fine, thanks." "Is there anything you need?" "Not really, but thanks for asking." And that was it. They'd not exactly made friends. But Oya had felt grateful, that he'd made the effort to call. And Hüseyin had been courtesy itself.

Adana has three things in its favor: its sunny climate, its growing workforce, and its fertile soil. No hope, though, of seeing the sun set over the Çukurova Valley from Oya's hotel window. From here, the city was one enormous construction site, each new building uglier than the last. Day after day, she watched them slowly rising. Night after night, she kept herself safe behind tightly closed curtains. Trying not to feel sorry for herself. Trying to believe that her heart, though it ached so, was still strong. In the half-finished apartment building right across from her, there were always two plainclothes policemen on guard. Staring right at her, every time she opened her curtains. In the end it gave her strength, to watch them watching her. To wonder what they made of their pointless job, and where they found the patience.

To have to sit there, staring at her curtains, day after day, for months on end – this was a sentence not much different from Oya's. Their unfamiliar faces had unsettled her at first, but by the month's end, she'd grown used to them. She'd peek through the curtains now and again, to see if they were still on the job. It made her feel less lonely, to know that they were there. But it was such a farce, their being there at all. There was no need for them. If they wanted to make sure Oya was in her room, all they needed to do was check in with the receptionist. Every time she stepped outside, they wrote down the time. Every time she had a visitor or a phone call, they took down the caller's name. Over time she'd become convinced that a portion of her monthly hotel bill went to paying her own guards. She'd been tempted to lodge a complaint with the hotel manager. They were making her pay to be imprisoned. But what could she do? She would keep paying her hotel bills, and let the police do their business. She'd been sent to Adana with no advance notice. She'd not been able to find a house. They rented houses here by the year. And anyway, she was hardly in a position to furnish an apartment. She knew no one who might be in a position to put her up. And who would wish to put her up, when there was still martial law? Who would want to have everyone from the chestnut seller to the shoeshine man reporting on everyone they knew? She had no choice but to bow her head and pay to be marooned in this hotel. The hotel manager had heard plenty of grumbling about her being here at all. She'd have a hard time finding any other hotel to take her. The police were coming down hard on this hotel for taking her in. They could easily decide that enough was enough and show her the door.

It terrified her, to think that she might end up in the streets of this strange, angry, concrete city. And not to forget the police station where she went to sign in every evening. They'd take a dim view of her moving.

Her guards would call her late each night. Why? To make sure Oya Ertem had not escaped? Woken by the phone, Oya would never manage to get back to sleep before dawn. But over time, she grew fond of her nighttime companions – the footsteps, the creaking doors, the phones ringing in the distance. The boys bringing in tea and coffee, the postman with those infrequent letters – they warmed her heart. Oh, the mistakes you can make, when the longing for a friendly face grows too strong.

This was what she'd run away from. She never went out after dark. Every afternoon she went to the police station to sign in. Returning, she'd shut herself up in her room. She'd had no other choice. Her guards were waiting for her to make one wrong move. But she hadn't made a single one. All over the city, the police were raiding houses in the middle of the night and carting off any one they found. She didn't want to make their work easier for them. But it's painful, to be cautious all the time. A child who's never been allowed to perspire, who's never gone anywhere without a towel draped over her shoulders – the first time she goes out to play, she'll come back with pneumonia. Which is, more or less, what Oya has done this evening.

When the phone rang, Oya had been making tea on the electric range she hid in her closet. This was one of her great pleasures: waiting for the water to boil, and the tea to brew. Raising her glass to her lips for that first taste. How this ritual restored her. Like the morning paper and the setting sun. These were the things that kept her going, saved her from being swallowed up whole. She'd grown to love these little escapes from tedium. To hear the phone ring on a day like this: it counted as a major event.

"Oya Hanım, there's a gentleman waiting for you at reception?"

She'd hung up before so much as asking who this gentleman might be. That's how ready she'd been to throw caution to the wind. Ready to explode, that is. But before she could, there was the raid.

Hüseyin had been waiting for her outside the hotel entrance. To tell the truth, Oya had not been all that happy to see him. Had she been expecting someone else? Who knew? This was the first time she'd seen Mustafa. And she thought it surprising, that Hüseyin would think to bring along someone she'd never met. After that first meeting at the courthouse, Oya had dropped by Hüseyin's office on several occasions, there to drink tea as the Maraş brigade came and went. Their conversations had never strayed far from the superficial. Once or twice Hüseyin had checked in on her at the hotel and accompanied her to the police station. And yes, there had been that one time when they'd had tea together at that pastry shop on Atatürk Avenue. They'd talked about Adana and about martial law, but nothing more personal than that. So you couldn't really say they'd made friends. Had they been anywhere other than Adana, they might have, but under these conditions? They'd gone on a few walks together, shared a few glasses of tea. No more. What more could she have done? Fritter away whole afternoons at Hüseyin's office?

But that evening, when Hüseyin turned up after dark with a man she'd never met before, she thought nothing of it. No alarm bells whatsoever. Even knowing that Hüseyin knew she never ever went out at night.

But there he was, this man she'd come to know but never quite learned to trust. She couldn't quite make out the tall, dark, moustachioed man standing next to him.

"This is Mustafa. Another Maraş boy, you won't be surprised to hear. But this one's had it hard. He was released from Selimiye only yesterday."

Just what she needed. An outing with a man just released from prison. But even now, it didn't cross her mind to head back into the hotel.

"He's off to Urfa tomorrow. Before he went inside, he was teaching math at the lycée there. But we didn't let him go. Not much chance of a job waiting for him there. As any innkeeper could tell you."

Innkeeper. That's what prisoners called the ones who rented rooms to people like Oya. Hüseyin must have heard it from Mustafa. Heard it, and then sold it. Oya glanced over at Mustafa, to see if he had taken offense. But it was already too dark for her to see anything other than his inky black moustache.

"I'm Oya."

"She's serving out her exile sentence here. Adana's most famous case. Every shoeshine man in the city knows your name." Hüseyin gestured over at the shoeshine man stationed in front of the hotel entrance. Who had his shoes shined at this time of night? A wave of anger passed through her. And not just because of the shoeshine man. This Hüseyin had been too familiar.

"What's the word in Adana for people who can't help playing the clown?"

Silence. Even Oya was taken aback by what she'd just said. She should at least have made allowances for Hüseyin. She'd noticed then that he was wearing a full-length overcoat that looked new to her. This, too, struck her as laughable. But it was too late now, to dwell on the details of the evening. She'd come out because she was bored. just wanted to do something, anything at all. In spite of all she'd seen and suffered, she was still a card-carrying member of the bourgeoisie, content to let life unfurl as it may.

Hüseyin had resumed his patter, making as if he and Oya were old friends.

"Don't you read too much into what she just said," he'd told Mustafa. "She's not angry, she's having fun. She's one of those arty types – so hard on herself that she never lets anyone else criticize her."

Mustafa had said nothing. Leaving Oya to wonder what he must make of her.

From the first moment, then, she'd had that hanging over her.

Hüseyin, meanwhile. He wouldn't stop talking.

"So what do you say to some home cooking? Better than going hungry at this hotel, I'd say."

Oya had mentioned this to Hüseyin. They didn't serve food at her hotel, so she'd go to bed hungry. Sometimes she would make herself tea and treat herself to a sesame roll she'd brought back with her. Sometimes she'd have a yogurt. But she'd never found the nerve to go out to a restaurant. So tonight she was ready for whatever they suggested. A film would have been fine. Home cooking, even better. Anything for a change. But Hüseyin was still prattling on.

"We're off to see the proud proletarians of Kahramanmaraş," he said gormlessly. "Our uncle has invited us to supper. Even though we're branded anarchists. Even though we're just out of prison. He's still determined to welcome us with open arms . . ."

If he'd come to her hotel just one day earlier, and spoken to her like this, she would have bridled, and made her apologies, and gone back to her room. But this evening, none of this bothered her. She might as well have been the heroine of one of those soap operas housewives like so much. *Tomorrow Is Another Day. Fate Weaves Its Web.*

Hüseyin's impertinence had proved contagious. Wheeling around, she'd asked Mustafa: "Are you Alevi?"

Mustafa did not reply. At once, Oya regretted asking. Worse, she thought, than asking him which leftwing faction he belonged to. A thousand times worse. Now she really was angry with Hüseyin. It was not enough for him to boast about the people of Maraş. Now he had to boast about their being Alevi.

"When others look down on a man, the Alevis open their arms."

She'd asked a foolish question, and it was Hüseyin who answered it. The evening had begun with foolish talk, and so it would continue. Hüseyin prattled on. "They've made us Adana köfte. You're coming with us, aren't you? You don't get an opportunity to see a place like this any old day, you know."

What a clumsy invitation. But she hadn't stopped him from showing off his relatives like a herd of prize cows, and she didn't stop him now. "All right," she'd said. "I'll come." As a voyeur, in other words. Peeking through the keyhole to see how the other half lives.

Moments later, they were in a taxi. "Take us to the Independence District," Hüseyin said.

Mustafa sat in front, next to the driver. Out of habit, Oya looked over her shoulder, to watch the headlights following them. But she said nothing.

It would sound so foolish, after all. To being going anywhere at all, knowing they'd be followed. And then to whine about it. Hüseyin and Mustafa were busy talking.

"Don't ask Ali if he's left the CHP."

"So you're telling me you never got him to join the cause?"

"He's still an Ecevit man, I'm afraid."

"He'd be better off joining the Justice Party."

Oya was interested to know why Mustafa thought that, but she was not about to ask him in a taxi. Hüseyin had told her that his own sympathies went to Aybar.

"Sooner or later, it's going to cave in."

"If you'd joined the party, you could have been part of that."

"Who can dare to judge, in times like this? How do you justify your own position?"

"We're after what's possible!"

For a moment, Oya felt uneasy, to be hearing two men conversing like this in a city like Adana, and in a taxi, to boot. The further they go, the more nervous she becomes about the headlights just behind them. I'll just give my apologies the moment we get there, she tells herself, and then I'll head back to the hotel.

Suddenly Mustafa turned to Hüseyin and asked, "You joined the Unity Party, didn't you?"

"Of course. No party more socialist than that, after all."

"Knock it off. I know you too well. What in God's name are you after?"

"Clients. As you know, all of the party's Adana deputies are Alevi."

"So you've joined up so you can lead them down the wrong path?"

"If it's mistakes you want to talk about, Mustafa . . ."

With that, Mustafa falls silent. Which is fine with Oya. It doesn't matter, though. As soon as they get to where they're going, she's making her excuses and heading back to the hotel.

But when the moment comes, she doesn't do that. When they arrive to see children swarming around the car, she forgets her doubts. Her worries, too.

Ali had come to the door, too. He threw his arms around Mustafa. With tears in his eyes. How it warmed Oya's heart. She loved them all. Ali most of all. He was tall, with sunken cheeks and a concave chest. Half child, half old man. He spoke with a strong southeastern accent. He had the body and hands of a worker, and the face of an intellectual.

Opening the wooden door, he brought them all inside. And what a lovely, welcoming door it was, until the police kicked it in.

Gülsah and Ziynet. At first she didn't even notice them. The house was so crowded, that's why. A great crowd of children and men she'd never met. The photograph of Yilmaz Güney on the wall above the headboard – that was the first thing her eyes went to. And then to Ziynet. Her pink face bent over the brazier. Beads of perspiration on her forehead. Her wiry curls plastered over them. Like so many women in these parts, she had dark, very large, very beautiful eyes. She must be a very beautiful woman, all told, but she didn't know how to make it show. As if such a thing were possible for women in places like this. No one learned how to bring out their beauty unless they were taught.

The door keeps opening and shutting. This has never been the sort of door that sees the need for a key, after all. New children rush in. The ones inside rush out. No way of knowing which children live here and which belong to some other house nearby. After they'd taken their places around the low table, she tried striking up a conversation with a few of them. How she hated the way she sounded. So fake.

She fell silent then, to watch Gülşah and Ziynet race back and forth, bringing food to the table. She hardly looked at the others sitting around her. Maybe because she didn't want to be the sort of observer Hüseyin seemed to think she was. And anyway. She had no idea what to say here, or what to do. Instead she listened to the men of Maraş conversing.

"This is nothing other than reversing the course of history." This was Mustafa, talking about the CHP.

"Our union says otherwise." This was Ali. There followed a long account of the long years of support the union had enjoyed in exchange for supporting that party.

But from the moment Mustafa brought up the CHP, Oya's mind went into overdrive. What truly angered her – those were other matters entirely. But here was a subject on which she could speak.

"History... Industry... Capitalism... The wheels of unstoppable progress . . ." These words sent her mind buzzing. "The People's Party will lose people to those wheels," Mustafa said. With that, he fell silent. His face lit up. "So go ahead and vote for them, dear uncle. That's another matter entirely."

And for a moment Oya forgot her discomfort, to examine Mustafa more closely.

Dark, deep-set eyes. Feral, almost. Fierce, but not without a certain charm. His face, all angles. But his nose was flat. A man with a face like that, she thought, is either very bold or very fearful. One extreme or the other – that was for sure.

Mustafa could feel Oya's eyes on him. He felt himself judged. But the man Oya saw was prey to doubt and riddled with contradictions. What she saw most clearly: he was restless. Like an animal preparing to shed its skin. Seeing that, Oya wondered yet again what this Mustafa made of her. He found her interest in him troubling. And he was taking it out on his uncle Ali.

"So why are you even asking us?" he said. "Are we meant to ask for your permission? It's beyond us to help you. We don't need you. It's up to you to know where to stand up for your rights. If you want to claim them from the lion's mouth, that's your business. That's all."

Even Hüseyin was shocked, to hear these harsh words. He'd seen plenty of his brother's anger during their student years in Istanbul. But with Ali, he'd always been respectful. He'd made a point of it. Always saying that they had to show his family patience and respect. He'd always had a special place in his heart for Ali, after all. And Ali doted on Mustafa. He held him in higher regard than he did Hüseyin. Hüseyin had become a lawyer, Mustafa a teacher. The family had greater need of a lawyer than it did a teacher. But Ali had always preferred Mustafa, put more trust in him, too. Even in the '69 elections. Hüseyin had begged Ali to back the Worker's Party, but Mustafa had advised against it, so their uncle had not given them his vote. In those days, Mustafa had not been one to tell people to stew in their own juices. Whatever he said, he gave courage to Ali's tired heart. Things hadn't turned out as he'd predicted. But still, he shouldn't have rebuffed their uncle like that. That's what Hüseyin thought, anyway. He'd had no right. He'd been crowing long enough. Time for him to shut up! Truth be told, Mustafa's discourtesies had taken the edge off the guilt Hüseyin felt about the social security business. As hard as it was for him to share things with Mustafa, he was fine about sharing guilt with him. And that made for a change from the foul atmosphere in the office that afternoon. Mustafa had reminded him of their old arguments. Going so far as to say he'd been right. He shouldn't have said that. Should have let fury overtake him.

Or was Hüseyin the one who'd provoked Mustafa's outburst, by acting as he had that afternoon? That said. He'd always been quick to take offense. Or so it seemed to Hüseyin. In Istanbul, when Hüseyin was still studying law, they'd spent endless hours arguing in the meyhanes and coffeehouses of Kumkapı. Mustafa would punch the table with his fist and say: "That's the way it is, you fool. Understood?" Whatever Hüseyin said, he dismissed as idle chatter. In the end, Mustafa had stopped coming to those meyhanes and coffeehouses. If ever he ran into Hüseyin, he'd say, "What's happening, chatterbox?" Then came the year Hüseyin lost his scholarship. He'd gone around telling everyone it was because he was a member of the Socialist Youth Association, but really it was because he'd missed his exams. On account of all that drinking in meyhanes. All that chattering. That year, it had been Mustafa who'd supported him. Where he'd found the money, he didn't say. "I've dropped out," he'd said. "I'm working." But Hüseyin hadn't believed him. Later on, he'd decided that Mustafa must have rushed into his final exams. Then he'd found the job in Urfa. And married.

There were things between them, things he'd never managed to understand, let alone resolve.

That forum – when those people had tried to beat him up. It was Mustafa who'd saved him. But then again, hadn't it been Mustafa who'd dragged him into all that business? Who'd given Hüseyin the books that paved the way? He'd outrun his attackers, though. Yes, it was true. Mustafa had saved him. But not to forget that it had been Mustafa's team that had attacked him. He'd taken Hüseyin off to find a sink. Cleaned up his bloody nose. Told him it was time to stop his silly games. "You've gone way past your bus stop," he'd said. "Not everyone can expect to go all the way to the end of the line." These words now rumble inside Hüseyin like hot peppers. *You stayed on the bus. And look where you ended up!* Back then, Hüseyin had asked him. "Do you know where you're going?" And Mustafa had said, "Of course I do. I can see it just as clearly as I see Maraş and Siverek." And off he'd walked, leaving Hüseyin with the sink and its temperamental faucet.

This afternoon, he'd got his own back. "I thought you knew Maraş and Siverek like the back of your hand," he'd said. Mustafa hadn't liked that.

"What gives you the right to criticize me? The fact that they locked me up in prison? Say I made mistakes. I've paid for them in full! While you – you've burrowed your way back into this city like the mole you are. No one knows what you've done right, or wrong. Keep it up and you'll end up in the National Assembly. What does all this prove? You're a coward, pure and simple!"

To bring this ugly and untimely quarrel to a close, Hüseyin had launched into a long disquisition about Adana's growing importance. It was now the second largest industrial city in the country, he told Mustafa – as if his brother didn't already know that. He went on to describe workers' conditions, and the status of the unions, and the opportunities that the region might open up, until Mustafa gave him a look, as if to say, Hah! You haven't given up on idle chatter, I see! As if he could tell that Hüseyin had yet to get his practice up and running.

All this might explain his upset stomach. It felt like an alien beast, hurling itself against its walls. Echoing his brother's ugly words.

"Your union's worth nothing. They're just another bunch of chieftans. Chieftans in yellow turbans."

So Mustafa was upset, and he was taking it out on Ali. What was he thinking? Did they really have to start talking about the union? Next thing they knew, they'd be moving on to social security. And what then? But Ali didn't look to be in the mood for blaming anyone. All his attention was on his guests. Were their glasses full? Did they have cushions to lean on? Nothing else seemed to matter. He was the host, taking every opportunity to put them all at ease. He called out to his youngest son.

"Go fetch Uncle Ekremgil. Ask him to come join us."

Oya assumed that this Ekrem would be another member of the Maraş tribe.

But from the moment he walked in, she saw him to be another sort of fish entirely. Not from Maraş, and not Alevi. He had his sleek brown hair combed back. Sideburns and a thin, neat moustache. As far as Oya could see, this man had nothing in common with those already in the room. He was a neighbor, just back from Germany. Ali must have wanted to make him feel welcome. From what Oya could work out, he'd spent his first years in Germany working in a factory, eventually managing to set up a small business. Now he seemed to be traveling back and forth between Adana and Germany, buying and selling, with an eye on something bigger. It wasn't long before he was adding his own views to what Ali and his two nephews had to say about the unions.

"My fellow men, I ask you. Has anyone ever managed to save

himself, if he's weighed down with family? Even when there's a fire or flood, people put themselves before their children, to save themselves."

He pronounced his k's like g's, this man.

"Whoever does that, deserves to die," said Ali. His eyes on Hasan.

"What can a hand ever achieve on its own?" Mustafa said. "Without a second hand, it can't even clap!"

"Did the rich get rich by sitting on their haunches? It's the captain who saves the ship! The *captain!*"

"In the world of business," said Ekrem with a grin, "there's no room for all this talk about workers, or even Turkishness!"

"Some men are coming up to our door!"

This was little Hasan. No one paid him any attention. Around the table things are tense.

Mustafa was glaring at Ali. What had he been thinking, to bring this new guest into their midst? But Ali showed no sign of annoyance. Ekrem was his guest. It was the job of the host to keep the mood light. He didn't want Hüseyin and Mustafa laying into Ekrem. But the two brothers seemed happy to have found someone new to argue with, and so they lay into him. As if his sole purpose in joining them was to rub them the wrong way. And it heats up. Ekrem says that unions were invented by swindlers who were only interested in making more money for themselves. He himself would never dream of putting his money in the hands of others. Workers who gave their money to unions were suckers; they deserved to stay poor. In Hüseyin's view, Adana's union leaders were no better than landowners. But he met Ekrem's words with such fire as to make himself out to be a corrupt lawyer working on their behalf. He said his piece, and then it was over to Mustafa.

"Why waste time kicking up the dust?" he asked Ekrem. "Last time I checked, that was how the rich got richer."

The stone hits its target and sits there.

"No, no, no. You mark my words. One more year of gritting my teeth and . . ."

"Oh yes, grit those teeth why don't you. Who do you think you are, anyway? Do the rich get rich on saliva? You say it's the captain who saves the ship. Do you have any idea how much these captains you so admire back each other up? They might not clasp each other to the chest like we fools do with our families and our neighbors, but the rich know full well how to unite against the working class!"

Raising his hand to his narrow forehead, Ekrem smoothed back his brilliantined hair.

Then he turned to Mustafa. "What's your line of work?"

Oya took a closer look at the two men's moustaches. Ekrem's was thin, and just above his lips. She knew the type: always bragging about how no German woman could resist him. While having to settle for a fifth-class prostitute. She didn't like him being here. He only added to the tension, and to the unease Oya had felt from the very beginning. And now he was looking straight at her. Glaring. As if to say, What's this woman doing here, with all these men? As if to add, Is this any way to do business?

From the moment Ekrem walked into the room, the gulf between Oya and the women of the house grew wider still. From the moment they set eyes on her, they saw her as belonging to another breed. Without a moment's thought, they thought her breed to be superior to their own. Oya didn't like that, though she knew such attitudes were hard to change. Ali meanwhile, had welcomed her as Hüseyin's guest. For Ali she was neither a man nor a woman. She was simply an extension of Hüseyin. With no identity of her own. No gender, either. This, Oya thought, was only to be expected.

What Hüseyin made of her, on the other hand. That was a question she'd prefer not to dwell on. It didn't particularly interest her. He took her for a friend, probably. Unless? Either way, it's not important. All she wanted to know was what Mustafa thought of her – not what he thought of her presence here, but in general. She sensed a certain affinity, even if he didn't like her, and found her lacking, whatever his reasons.

Ekrem, on the other hand. Things being as they were, Oya knew exactly what was going on in this man's coarse mind. From the moment he'd walked into the room, he'd been giving her filthy looks. Flashing his filthy pencil moustache at her. Taking

Oya to be one of those little opportunities that he saw as his right to claim. Here she was, a woman drinking in the company of men. Available, in other words. Ekrem knew what to do next!

The filthy looks he'd been sending Oya's way while lecturing the assembled had not been lost on Mustafa or Hüseyin. They'd added to Mustafa's fury. Which made Oya more nervous than ever. She regretted a thousand times over that she had not stayed in that taxi and gone straight back to the hotel.

"I'm a teacher," said Mustafa. "And what's it to you?"

Soon they would come to blows.

"Ali told me you just got out of prison. So tell me, what landed you inside? The teachers' struggle?"

"The people's struggle. Teachers are not a class. Even so, the Teacher's Union helped my wife while I was inside."

Güler. His anguish, blotting out the anger that Ekrem had provoked in him. Here I am, having this pointless argument with this idiotic brute of a man. And still no idea where Güler is, or how she is.

Just in time, Gülşah and Ziynet provided a distraction. Rushing in with the tray of food. Placing it on the center of the table. Ali had made it known that supper was to be served at once. He wasn't happy with the way things were going.

All he wanted was to entertain his guests. It grieved him, to be denied this simple pleasure. He glared at his wife and his sister-in-law, as if it was their fault.

But never mind. The food was ready. The guests were feasting now on köftes, salad, ochre, and all the rest. And Ali was cheering up. Time, he thought, to draw Mustafa out a bit.

"So where do you think we're headed, my boy?"

Mustafa is done with this conversation. But he can't control his anger.

"Until the day you people claim your rights, we're headed nowhere."

Now, for the first time, Oya notices Zekeriya at the end of the table, eating in silence. At around the same time, the door gets kicked in. So many things, happening at the same time. She won't think about Zekeriya until later.

Zekeriya is Ziynet's husband. He's a graduate of Adana Motor Arts Lycée. Even as a student, he pinned a grey wolf badge to his collar. When the door crashes in, he shows no reaction. And maybe that's because he's living with his in-laws. It's not for him to interfere with the household's comings and goings. He hasn't said a word all evening. No. He had said one word. Handing his wife his glass, he'd said "Water!" A handsome boy, with hazel eyes and skin the color of wheat. Oya thinks Ziynet might be quite in love with him. She can imagine him roaming the streets of Adana with Ziynet's dowry in the back of his open truck. And Ziynet, amid the satin quilts, the cotton mattresses, and the pillows she herself had embroidered. Tossing care to the winds. Raising her hands to dance. While the young ones at back of the truck pounded on their drums to the beat to the rhythm of their pounding hearts. These dowry trucks pass in front of Oya's hotel every day. She loves watching them from her window. All those young men, all those young girls. Belly dancing at the back of the truck, to the rhythm of the drums. Poverty's answer to the world. We know how to celebrate. We take joy where we can.

But she's got it all wrong. The young men who parade through the streets with their brides' dowries – they're the haves, not the have-nots. The ones who have land in the outlying villages. The shop-owners. People who own their homes and fields, at the very least. Villagers turned burghers. Next to the Adana rich, they might look poor, but mention the word wedding, or circumcision, or association, and they find the money to furnish whatever tradition calls for. They lead simple, unostentatious lives, these people. To people like Oya, that implies modest means. Oya knows only that other world, where those with much less money lead much more ostentatious lives.

The laborers who come pouring into Adana, leaving behind them the towns and fields that can no longer sustain them – they can't afford to keep up with such traditions. No one loaded Ziynet's dowry onto the back of a truck to tour the city. She didn't have that kind of dowry. All she had was a roll of calico that her sister Gülşah had somehow managed to store for years on end in some corner of their two-room house. Plus a few scarves, pillowcases, quilt covers. A few odds and ends, in other words. A few throw pillows edged with crocheted lace. Add to this the wedding gifts from their Maraş relations. One gave them money for quilts, another for a mattress. They have in mind to pool all this together, to set up house in Iskenderun.

Ziynet must be practical, this she knows. Working only with what she has. That said, she is not about to give up all her dreams. And where has her mind not traveled? Yes, Zekeriya is handsome, but that alone is not enough. There's that quilt she saw in the window of that shop in Kuruköprü Meydan: yellow satin, with beads sewn into every square! A nylon mosquito net decorated with artificial flowers and pearls! A quilted, intricately embroidered bed cover! She's set her heart on them all. Every bit as much as she'd set her heart on Zekeriya. Oh, what she would give, to be able to decorate their marriage bed with these treasures! But she has nothing to give. All she has are these dreams to entertain her when she lies down at the end of a long day of housework. Dreams that excite her far more to her than the prospect of being with Zekeriya. Gülşah thinks her silly. "What do you want with rags like that?" she says. "If you had any brains, you'd be dreaming of a refrigerator." Killjoy. But what else could an old wife like her be? What use would she and old Ali have for a beautifully made bed?

Ali and Gülşah sleep on the divan where all their guests are now seated. On winter nights, when they're very tired, they don't even take off the coverlet, don't even put on a sheet. As soon as supper's over, they just lie down to make the most of the heat coming from the stove.

Ziynet and the children sleep in the side bedroom. The light in there doesn't always work. So Ziynet stays out of that room until she's ready to fall asleep. Instead she carries on with her knitting, while Ali and Gülşah sleep. Hasan does his homework. Ziynet wonders if the old couple has ever made love. They're no place for that in this house, no time either. And Gülşah is still only thirty-eight. Ziynet hasn't the faintest idea how old Ali is. In her eyes, this scrawny man with sloping shoulders is old. And Gülşah's dreams would never take her to a shop window in Kuruköprü Meydan. She has no Zekeriya. She dreams of refrigerators instead. To make it easier to feed all the mouths it is her duty to feed. You can cook meals several days ahead, and put them in the refrigerator, to sit pretty until you need them. How could anyone dream of more?

"I'm going to make Zekeriya fresh meals every day," Ziynet told her.

"You do that. Go ahead and inflame his balls. Then watch him give you a belly as big as Mount Hüt once a year."

They'd had this exchange that morning, while they were cleaning the okra, waiting for Zekeriya to get back from Iskenderun.

Ziynet the newlywed, lecturing a sister who spent so many years chopping onions, peeling potatoes, kneading flour and minced meat.

Her knees are giving her trouble again. When Ali called to say Mehmet was coming to supper, she was curled up on the divan. That's when Zekeriya turned up. Gülşah was so glad to hear about Mustafa that she'd hardly noticed him. She and Ziynet got straight to work getting the house ready. After pacing the room for a few minutes, Zekeriya left the house. But not before combing back his shiny hair. Whatever was on his mind, it wasn't Ziynet's satin quilted dreams. Nor was it the longing to which Ziynet gave his name.

Gülşah doesn't care what Ziynet longs for. Satin quilts, mosquito nets, she thinks. What foolish dreams. Gülşah can't even bring herself to care about the pains shooting from her waist to her knees, and from her knees to her brain, each one stronger than the last. For all her moaning and groaning, she'd given the stone floor a good clean. She'd shaken all the mats. She'd lost patience with Ziynet, who was only pretending to help, and doing everything by half measures.

"If you clean your own house like this, don't expect any satin quilts from your man. Expect a beating!"

Ziynet didn't bother to listen. In one ear and out the other. Zekeriya was besotted with her. What would a worn rag like

Gülşah's husband know about passion, or the taste of a man's beating?

By the time the cleaning was done, and the okra were cooking on the stove, it was all too much for Gülşah. She collapsed onto the sofa she'd just cleaned.

"A nice bumbar! That's what I'll make my Mustafa!"

She'd done her bit for Mustafa over the years. Never forget the woman's part in such things. Whoever she cared for, she loved.

"Mustafa's turned anarchist."

Zekeriya was in the room, just back from Iskenderun, when Ziynet said this. It was jealousy that made her lash out. There was her sister, so exhausted she could barely stand. But she was getting up to make her nephew a beautiful bumbar.

"Watch your mouth, my girl. Stop spouting nonsense. Mustafa is Ali's flesh and blood, a Maraş boy through and through. He's one of us. So how could he be an anarchist?"

"That's what Zekeriya says he is."

"What does that boy know about our Maraş people?"

That was the last straw for Ziynet. Zekeriya's people are not from Maraş so her sister counts him as an outsider. The two women didn't say another thing to each other until the guests arrived. As she went about her drudgery, Ziynet let her thoughts sail back to her Zekeriya, her everything, and the house in Iskenderun that she had already built in her dreams. Zekeriya came back late.

By then all thoughts of satin quilts and Iskenderun love nests had vanished, and Ziynet was in a sulk. She'd give him the cold shoulder tonight. Or so she thought, until the raid.

Gülşah brought in the bumbar. As if to make him feel even guiltier. To remind him of the last thing Güler had said to him, that last morning: "Shall I make you a nice bumbar?" Just before he'd let his pregnant wife go to the door to let in the soldiers. Urfa a gigantic question in his mind. A question magnifying all the wrongs he'd erased from his mind. A question to which he could find no answer. A question he'd not even found the courage to ask. And after all that. Ali's unconditional love. His abiding interest in him. It was all too much. Too much for any man of conscience. And now, to top it all off, this bumbar. To arrest the wave of emotion welling up in him, to stop the tears, he snapped at his uncle.

"Until the day you people claim your rights, we're headed nowhere."

Where did *you people* come from? Since when has Mustafa given himself permission to lecture to *you people*?

He'll think about all that later. Not just the raid, but the secret sins and thoughts that rushed out the moment that door crashed in, spilling its filth across the room. The whole nauseating evening.

When his father told him to run out and ask Uncle Ekremgil to join them, Hasan did just that. There, beneath the broken streetlamp, he saw four men. As he was running past, he bumped into one of them. But they paid him no notice. Hasan, though, was used to being cursed on such occasions. Sometimes people even threw stones at him. In fact, he'd been at fault. There'd been no need to run. Uncle Ekremgil lived just next door. But Hasan had in mind to check in with Hüsrev's gang first. To tell him that Uncle Mustafa was back, that he'd brought a woman with him, too.

He got to the water pump and waited. His father and Hüsrev's father didn't get along. Some sort of argument, some sort of resentment. That was all he knew. "Fucking Arab. Fuck him, and his religion." Hasan had heard his father say that. Hüsrev's family were Arabs. The Maraş people were often at loggerheads with the Arabs who shared these streets. Quarrels that sooner or later ended up in the police station. Whereupon the police would give both sides a beating. Even so. These beatings only served to deepen the divisions.

Hasan whistled. Hüsrev knew at once it was him. They sat next to each other in school. They ran around together after school, too. They're children, after all. All play, all day long.

Hasan stood at the water pump, holding the toy gun Uncle Mustafa had bought him as a present, having managed a quick detour to the American market on his way to Ali's. It looked almost real, this gun. Hasan couldn't believe his eyes. When Hüsrev sneaks out of his house, Hasan is hiding behind a tree. He jumps out.

"Hands up!"

"Huh? Who's there?"

"Martial law."

"Where'd you get that gun?"

"I said hands up, anarchist!"

". . . ."

"Don't move! This is a real gun!"

"Are you sure? What if it goes off?"

"Of course I'm sure. My uncle gave it to me."

"Is your uncle a policeman?"

"No, you idiot. He's an anarchist. He's friends with Deniz Gezmiş and Yılmaz Güney. They're the ones who gave him this gun."

"You're making that up."

"I swear. It's true. If you don't believe me, come back with me and you can ask Uncle Mustafa yourself."

He was about to do just that when he heard his mother calling him to come back inside.

Hüsrev knew from experience that the best way to avoid a beating was to tell his parents something that would surprise them. So he told them that there was an anarchist over at Hasan's. Later, after Ali's house was raided, a rumor circulated that Hüsrev's father had informed on him, and that they'd even asked the police to pay them for the information. But according to the men Hasan had seen on his way over to Hüsrev's house, that was just idle Arab gossip.

What's clear, though, is that there would be more bad blood between the two families at the end of it. Bekir, Hüsrev's father, had genuinely considered going to the police that night, but in the end he'd given up on the idea, because he was too tired, because he couldn't face the prospect of the beating Officer Necip would give him, if the denunciation turned out to be false.

Hasan went running home. Picking up Uncle Ekrem along the way. As they headed inside, they both noticed the four men in the shadows next to the door. This before Hasan saw one of them listening at the door itself. The man looked none too happy to see Hasan and Ekrem. He scuttled off. The other men scattered. When they got inside, Hasan said nothing, expecting that Ekrem would take care of it. Then his mother filled his plate with food. Children forget fast, but they remember fast, too. Fingering his gun, he thought about Hüsrev, and then he remembered what he'd seen at the door coming in.

"There are some men outside!"

No one seemed to hear him. Ekrem had seen the men, too, but he wasn't saying anything either. Later, after it was all over, Oya would wonder about this, as would Mustafa. Just then, his head was still spinning with memories of bumbar. He paid Hasan no attention. He could have called Urfa from his brother's office. Their neighbors had a phone. He could have found out how things were with Güler. But he'd not made that call. And now, for the first time in his life, he couldn't bear the sight of bumbar.

Oya, meanwhile, is nibbling on white cheese and radishes, both of which she has cut into tiny pieces. She's passed on the okra. She hates okra. Seeing Mustafa pick at his bumbar, she wonders if perhaps he likes it as little as she does.

Gülşah is worried. Seeing him pick over the dish she'd made for him specially, despite being so tired and in such pain, she wonders. Did I cook it wrong? She'd only wanted to cheer him up.

"It's good, my boy. I made it with my own hands. Eat a little, why don't you."

Mustafa's mind is elsewhere. He doesn't hear Gülşah. If he had, he would certainly have wished health to her hands and told her how good this bumbar was. But with his mind full of dark thoughts, he'd broken his aunt's heart. His first mistake. The first of many. He'd not even managed to respect his aunt, who'd given him everything, expecting nothing in return. After all his fine talk about founding all relations in respect. Pushing away the bumbar, and blind to the tears welling up in his aunt's eyes, while

Güler loomed up in his mind like an incubus, Mustafa had eyes only for Ekrem. The stand-in for all his foes.

Zekeriya takes Mustafa's share of the bumbar. He loves this dish. To get back at her big sister, Ziynet piles his plate high. He's relishing every bite. Ziynet's not sorry. Let her sister suffer! To think that she'd passed over a man as youthful and handsome as Zekeriya, just to lavish her attentions on this Mustafa, this anarchist who would bring his family trouble for seven generations. Gülşah, meanwhile, is distraught. Here is Mustafa, fresh out of prison, and I've failed him.

Ziynet is standing behind her husband, watching his strong jaw move. When he eats, his ears wiggle a bit, too. The way donkeys' ears do. The thought makes her smile. When in fact, watching Zekeriya eat usually makes her stomach simmer with desire. But why in her stomach, and only when she watches him eat? Truth be told, she doesn't desire him the way a woman familiar with desire might. And she doesn't know why that is. It was just that, every once in a while, at the oddest times, it feels like something hot is simmering inside her. Or bleeding. It has to be Zekeriya making her feel like that. She has no way of knowing. Whatever is simmering inside her, it's Zekeriya who lit the flame. That's what she thinks, anyway. She stands there now, watching his jaw go up and down, and it sets her steaming. In bed, on the other hand, she doesn't feel much at all. The passion she feels watching her husband's great jaw is worthy of a Tarık Akın film, but it turns to snores in bed. Beneath the heavy quilt and her husband's heavy panting, her own desires sail away like poplar fluff. She's just guessing, though. If it's not Zekeriya bringing fire to her cheeks, then what is it?

When they got back from city hall on their marriage day, Zekeriya had a long face. He and his sister were both glaring at her brother-in-law. Zekeriya had wanted an imam to marry them. Ali had refused. "I wouldn't even let a donkey's imam in here." Most people in Maraş are Alevi. They have no time for imams.

Ali being a man of consequence, Zekeriya could not bring himself to talk back. Ziynet, though. That was another question. What did they think they were doing, upsetting her husband? When her sister said, "Tell your husband to go sulk somewhere else," Ziynet had been furious. At the same time, though, she could see her sister's side. Truth was, Zekeriya had nowhere else to go, and therefore no way of insisting on the sort of ceremony he had in mind. When it came to money, they depended on Ali's generosity.

Ziynet had first set eyes on Zekeriya while attending sewing school. On Independence Day. Just outside Motor Arts Lycée. A green scarf around his neck. White trousers. Not the sort of person you'd expect to be depending on a shriveled man like her brother-in-law Ali. She'd willed away that fine holiday memory, but then one evening, while she was hurrying home, she could hear someone following her. Just the sight of this handsome the boy was enough to remind her of the green scarf he'd been wearing when she first spotted him on Independence Day. A week or so later, they were engaged. Zekeriya had no family. He'd lost his parents while still in primary school. The headmaster had taken him under his wing. Even after Zekeriya graduated, he'd continued to look after the boy, making best use of his connections. It was with the help of the Adana branch National Struggle Association that Zekeriya was able to enroll in Motor Arts Lycée. The grey wolf badge that he wore on his collar was his everything. He never took it off. Not even on his wedding day. Two old men from the Association attended the ceremony, wearing brown kalpaks. Independence medals on their chests. "They were injured in the War of Independence, these two." So Zekeriya proudly told his wife. When it came time to say his vows, he took no notice of the wedding clerk's strange looks when he placed one hand on the Koran and the other on his gun before saying yes. When Ali, infuriated, asked him to explain what he thought he was doing, he'd silenced him by saying, "That's our ritual."

Whereupon Ali, who had covered all the costs of this wedding, from the sweets to the bride and groom's clothes, had whispered into his wife's ear. "I'm guessing that another of their rituals is freeloading."

How Ziynet pitied Zekeriya, for having nothing. His helplessness was her consolation. "He has nothing to give!" And that was the truth: apart from the grey wolf badge on his collar and the National Struggle Association that had supported him for so long, but no longer, he had nothing. This because he had chosen an Alevi girl for a wife: that was why the Association had refused to help cover the cost of the wedding. Actually, Zekeriya knows none of this, and neither does he stop to consider why this Association supported him in the first place. Or why that assistance had now been withdrawn. He'd never thought much, either about the meaning behind their fervent chants at meetings. "Where have we come from?" "The Altay Mountains!" "Where are we headed?" "To Greater Turkey!" To tell the truth, he had every reason to be grateful to these people who had supported him throughout his education. They'd sworn to support Turkish youth, these men, and they'd kept their word. He was in their debt. He did as they asked. But Zekeriya's secret strengths had turned out to be a thick skull and a mind lacking in vision. A disappointment, then. And so they'd given up on him.

But not before setting him up in Iskenderun. They'd arranged for one of their contacts, an Adana factory manager, to put in a call to a friend in Iskenderun, to recommend him for the job. Saying, "It's the least we can do, sir. Let us help our nation's youth." So let them come to Ziynet with their gossip, let them mock her husband for being the ward of his wife's relatives. Nothing can stop them now.

Zekeriya has important people looking out for him. And Ali?

He can't even make himself heard at the police station. Can't even call the city where he works a home. You can't go around asking everyone where they're from. Such disrespect! One day soon, Zekeriya's pockets will be full. They might be empty right now, but there are men of consequence opening doors for him. What could be more important than finding work? What's more, he has an education.

As she thinks about all this, her stomach starts heating up again. As she stands behind her husband, she does her best to extinguish the flame brought about by his grinding jaws.

In Iskenderun, everything will be different. Their first night together, he didn't even take Ziynet's clothes off. First he groped her down there, groped her hard, and the moment he pushed his way in, he'd ejaculated. And then he'd said, "Move over a little, girl." And pushed her aside to examine the blood on the sheet. Thinking that this must be how the thing they called lovemaking began and ended, Ziynet had not given much thought to her aching perineum. She wasn't in the habit of agonizing over such things anyway. But then, in the middle of the night, when Zekeriya's snoring woke her up, and she'd told herself she'd better get used to the way a man snores, she'd felt her cheeks go hot, as if she'd had a dirty thought. Hearing a man snore – for some strange reason, it lit the flame of desire. Same thing when she watched him eat.

And if Güler isn't in Urfa – then what? I've been banned from teaching, for sure. Knocking back the rakı Hüseyin had just poured for him, Mustafa turned back to Ekrem.

"You think you'll get ahead, but you'll never be your own man. By turning yourself into another country's service, you've swindled your own kind."

"We're all somebody's service," said Ekrem. "You're in service to Moscow. Ali's in service to Mediterranean Industries."

Oya imagined herself on a plane to Ankara. When my exile's over, I'm definitely taking a plane. When she was in Yıldırım Military Prison, she'd watched the passing planes with such longing. Planes equaled freedom. If there was one thing she was sure about, it was that the people up there in the sky had no idea there were prisoners somewhere below them, kept in place by submachine guns and barbed wire.

She saw Mustafa rise to take a swing at Ekrem.

"Work for the police, do you? Whose idea was it, to bring this sewer rat into this house?"

Before Mustafa could take a swing at Ekrem, the police kicked the door in. One look, and it was clear that was what they were. Three surly, scowling men, bursting into the room.

Before Oya could get on that plane.

Ekrem could probably tell that Mustafa was about to swing

at him. And maybe he was hoping to distract him, or fend him off, when he turned to Ali and said, "There were some men at the door." This at the exact same moment those men kicked the door in.

This, in any event, was how Oya would remember how things played out in the moments just before the raid, when she thought about it later. If she could trust her memories. There had been so much going on, and so much to puzzle over, and her mind was in a fog.

What every last person in that room would remember about the moment those three officers from Adana First Branch Police Station came bursting into the room: the one called Abdullah. Or rather, his gruesome scowl. He probably didn't always look so ferocious. He could have lost his temper because an argument had kicked off inside before he'd finished what he was here to do. In other words, he would have liked to spend more time with his ear against the wooden door before breaking it down. Add to that his chronic stomach problem, and the fact that he'd had no time to eat, and some light might be cast on the dark fury in his eyes. Deep lines on the sides of his mouth. His moustache so heavy as to make any smile impossible. But anyway, he was here to do a job. Put him in front of nasty people, and he's going to give them nasty looks. If he'd had any idea how much every last person in that room would be marked and crushed forever by the way he'd looked at them, he would have felt vindicated. He would have thought: job done.

No one but Oya would remember anything about either of the others. She'd seen one of these men at Hacıbayram Police Station, where she went every evening to sign in. Fairish hair, grey-blue eyes, every bone in his body crooked. His name was Sezai. And it was probably his crooked bones that had marked him out from all the other officers, watchmen, and undercover policemen she'd come across during those visits. Oya had assumed him to be one of the many unfortunates who were always getting in trouble with the police. She even remembered smiling at him once, to give him courage. And now here he is again, this Sezai, right behind the scowling Abdullah.

So he's an undercover policemen, she said to herself. Reporting to Hacıbayram Station. Which means that they've raided this house because of me. Sezai knows what she looks like. That's why they've sent him after her. But what would a little neighborhood police station have to do with a raid like this? A raid led by this Abdullah. Unless this is a coincidence, this Sezai must be here because he knows her.

Oya looked at Gülşah, who was looking at the door. As if that door was accusing her of burning all that food she'd prepared with such care and love. As if all this were her fault. If only Oya could set her straight. The words were on her lips. "Don't look like that. They've come for me. Don't look like that. I'm the only one they want. Ellerinize sağlık! Health to your hands! It was a splendid meal." But before she could say a thing, Abdullah barked: "You, and you, and you. Come with me."

Mustafa, Oya, and Hüseyin. The scowling Abdullah pointed at them each in turn. Gülşah's three guests, in other words. Mustafa, for whom she'd spent the whole afternoon making bumbar, even though her back was killing her. Gülşah, who was looking in despair at her hands. Blackened by all the onions and potatoes they'd peeled. Reddened and swollen by water as cold as ice. There may be other Gülşahs in the world, Oya thought. But with this one, I've lost my chance.

When Abdullah pointed at him, Mustafa jumped to his feet. He took one step, then stopped, to ask himself: *Where exactly am I going?* It shocked him, to see how quick he'd been to follow an order. He remembered the first raid. The first time he'd been taken off. He'd been just as accommodating then. Which must mean he thought himself guilty. Even though he'd done nothing. Unless he was being found guilty of the "crime" he'd wanted to commit? In those days, he would have done whatever was required of him. But why had he slunk away like a criminal? To repudiate the cause, to distance himself from its ideals. That's what. Not for a second could he say he had any real choice to make. But when they'd rung his doorbell, back in Urfa, and he'd hid himself behind his wife's swollen stomach, what had he been doing if not acting like a criminal, and for the flimsiest of reasons? Thinking back now on what became of him later – after he was taken off blindfolded – he could understand why he'd collapsed under torture. Yes, it was true. His body had reached its limit. But he'd already embraced defeat by then. His faith in the movement weakened. We fell short, me and mine. Those ideas we'd spent so many years debating – we never put them into action. We thought we had, but we were wrong. And then, before we had achieved anything, we fell at the first hurdle. We fell apart. Became the criminals they thought we were.

That's how Mustafa made sense of the speed with which he obeyed Abdullah's command. Where did I think I was going? At that precise moment, what was I was doing? I was eating supper at my uncle's house. That's all. I was doing nothing wrong. Nothing. The real crime – it was inviting this friend to come along. To take her with them to their uncle's house. But what was guilt. What was innocence. In his mind, he could no longer tell the difference. Right or wrong, he was ready to be judged. Resigned to it. He'd thought prison had made him stronger. But had it? "To rise up and resist!" Ahmet had said. "These are not just beautiful words! They speak of class consciousness. And it is only those who embrace class consciousness who can rise up, who can resist in the true sense of the word and take a stand. This is class war. Socialism is the ideology of the working class. So it is not enough to embrace the words, or to see the beauty in them, or the justice. And not enough to live up to them, either. In times of oppression, it's your class ideology that presses down on you the hardest." Or words to that effect. But didn't Mustafa come from a working-class family? "Forget what it says on your identity card." That was Ahmet's reply. "You teachers, for example. You're typical of the petit bourgeoisie. Your attitudes. The way you live. You chose to become a teacher. Chose to join the petit bourgeoisie. But at the same time, you wish to acknowledge the ideology of the class you came from. And that's impossible. You can't choose the two at once."

Ahmet, on the other hand. His father was a deputy in the National Assembly. And perhaps that was why Mustafa didn't take his words too seriously. If Ahmet were here in his place, would he resist? He didn't hand himself right over. He didn't fire. But he didn't die, either. They'd just laid low for a while. There were others who died, though. "Death is not a beginning," Ahmet would say. "It's a result! It's an act of resistance. Of struggle! Death has a part to play in the struggle." But it seemed to Mustafa that death could be a beginning, too. After death, or rather, after people died, those coming after them could learn better how to resist. First to take that risk. To die, and then to take the risk.

Banish these thoughts. Was this really the time? He'd never risked a thing. What risks had there been to take? But here he was, handing himself over, in front of everyone. Ready to be taken away.

Furiously he sat himself down again. To make as if he'd not heard Abdullah's command. Hüseyin, meanwhile, is trying to work out what Mustafa is thinking. Or rather, he is looking to Mustafa to tell him what to do. As if Mustafa were older than he was, as if he had no choice but to defer to his older brother. But he's the older brother. That afternoon, in the office, Mustafa had been throwing his weight around. Time now for him to practice what he preached.

"What's with this get-up?" he'd said. "These sideburns. And this fancy overcoat. Trying to rise in the world, are you? Knick-knacks everywhere, too. Have you put it all behind you, then?"

"No," Hüseyin had said.

"So you say! But what does it mean when a man not born bourgeois apes his ways? This is exactly the sort of thing that weakens us. Aping the bourgeoisie, even though we come from the working class. After all those years of trying to overthrow them. Years of struggle. We discover the ideology that speaks to our condition, and the moment it is revealed to us, we falter. What's happening here? Is it that we struggle only to give up what we've invested so much in? After struggling so long to change our conditions, and finally seeing an opportunity to do so, we're wavering, even if that's the last thing we want. Only workers with no wish to change their class can be true revolutionaries. And they are the only ones who can change that class, in the name of a working-class ideology."

"You're kidding. Not those bourgeois bastards again!"

"You know Ahmet. He turned out to be tougher than me, even. We used to make fun of him. Call him the 'Beyoğlu baby.' And why was that? Because he understood the conditions of his own class through and through. He could see it was on the verge of collapse. He'd put his faith in the future of the working class instead. He knew better than any of us how degenerate his own class was. He could see its days were numbered. So he switched his allegiance to the stronger side. He's ready to adjust. And that means he is far more of a revolutionary than you. Or even me. Every time we try and improve ourselves, or change the way we live, even just a little, we move that much farther from the people we truly are. And where do we end up? We collapse into our new comforts. We close our eyes to degeneracy. Open ourselves to betrayal."

Betrayal. Where had that word come from? It was early yet, for Mustafa to be thinking about betrayal. Early even for Hüseyin. But how long would it be?

Hüseyin, meanwhile. He could feel his tongue getting blacker and blacker – his whole mouth going black. So much so that he almost welcomed the idea of following Abdullah to wherever he would take him, almost had convinced himself that wherever that place was, it would help to cure that ulcer.

But there was more to come. Because Ali had his own ideas about these men who had kicked in his door and were now proposing to cart off his guests. He was their host, after all!

"What makes you think you can come into my house and order us around? These people are my guests. You come sit down, too, my brother. Mustafa, Hüseyin, come on now. Shuffle over. Who ever heard of leaving in the middle of a meal?"

What gave Ali the courage to say that? Maybe it was that he'd recognized Abdullah. Another man from Maraş. So he'd turned into a policeman. So what. The important thing was that he was from Maraş.

But Abdullah is not even looking at Ali. While Ali examined this man more closely, wondering if he'd been mistaken, if Abdullah was not from Maraş after all. And that was when a chill went through him, as if he were up against a dread disease, a terrible calamity that might blot out the whole world. The worst thing was, Abdullah seemed to have smelled his fear.

"And now he's asking me to explain myself," said Abdullah. "All right then, that settles it. I'm taking you all in."

"Taking us where?" asked Ali. "My dear fellow countryman, what is our sin?"

"I'm a police officer," snapped Abdullah. "I take who I want, where I want." Those few words were enough for everyone in that room at that moment to bow to his will. So he mustn't be from Maraş, Ali thought.

"The women and children can stay. As for the rest of you – in the car! Now!"

So I don't count as a woman, Oya thought.

"Are you sure you want me to come in too?" they heard Ekrem say. "I'm not one of them, as you know." But Abdullah piled him into the police car with the others. This is not the time for making distinctions. The more men he brings in, the better. And so that is what he's doing. Abdullah would have been happy even to add these two undercover policemen to his catch. He loved nothing more than to see criminals multiplying. Or so Oya thought. If only just to think something. She needs to keep her cool. To be ready to face whatever lies ahead. To behave herself. And not to let this ludicrous nightmare get the better of her. All she wants, really, is to be back in her hotel sleeping, to never have been here. But it's much too late for that.

She looked over at Hüseyin. Perhaps because she knew him best. "What's happening?" she asked. He gave no answer. Not that Oya expected one. Too early to know what was happening. That's when Ziynet cut her finger. When she saw Zekeriya being carted off, she started slicing bread for no good reason and cut her finger. Ziynet's bleeding finger. Oya would remember this detail last. When she thought back later, on the evening's first chapter.

The neighborhood boys chase after the police car's blue light. Abdullah speaks into his radio:

"A nest of anarchists has been raided in the Independence District. Six anarchists have been seized!"

The Interrogation

THE BRIDGE party's heating up, all right. Or so it seems to Colonel Muzaffer Bey, (retired) Director, Mediterranean Industries Manufacturing. It's so smoky in his salon that he can barely see beyond his nose. The crystal chandelier has stopped sparkling, even. The shafts of light just hang there, as if frozen by all the evil eyes his wife's guests have warded off. He'd had this precious piece smuggled in all the way from Beirut. The maid had polished the whole thing only this morning. But what with all this man-to-man combat at the tables, Nurten Hanım has hardly noticed this sorry turn of events. And the chandelier is the least of his worries. Muzaffer Bey and Necmettin the cardiologist are losing. Muzaffer Bey is pouting, having lost patience with his partner, who is talking up a storm instead of concentrating on the game.

"Yes, sir. These parapsychologists. They've established that two people in two different places can communicate by brainwaves."

The more Necmettin Bey chatters, the better it suits Zekai Bey, Chief Constable, Adana Police. To increase his chances, he throws the man another line.

"How interesting," he says. "I've read something about this too. In Reader's Digest. They claim that a woman living in Chicago was able to communicate with her son in Korea, when he was over there fighting the war."

"It could well be, sir. As for this argument that the soul never dies. . ."

Muzaffer Bey glares at the waiter who is standing by the door. Whenever Muzaffer Bey loses patience with his partner, he's quick to find another target for his rage. The waiter, who is just as quick to read his master's expression, makes a quick retreat, ferrying out the half-empty trays of dried and crushed canapes and returning soon after with a new tray full of glasses. Whiskey on the rocks.

Zekai Bey reaches out eagerly for a fresh glass. He's enjoying a run of luck tonight. He returns to the subject.

"It's amazing, isn't it, what people can perceive."

"Especially white people. That's because white people appeared on this earth long, long before black people, maybe even millions of years earlier. Over time they became highly advanced beings. Then came the yellow people. The black people came last. These primitive beings were so impressed by their white superiors that they bowed to them like gods."

"So you're saying that souls that keep coming back to life are more developed each time they do?"

"There's no doubt about it, sir! We can go so far as to say that genius is nothing other than the evolution of an eternal soul as it travels from body to body, fulfilling its mission."

"You're wanted on the phone, sir."

Neither Zekai nor Necmettin Bey seem to take in the waiter's words. It is Muzaffer Bey, eager for a pause in the game, who snaps at him.

"Speak louder, son!"

The waiter steps closer to Zekai Bey.

"You're wanted on the phone, sir."

Zekai turns to the waiter, vague and reluctant.

"Who's calling?"

Even though he knows who it will be.

"I don't know, sir!"

"Is it from Police Headquarters?"

"They didn't say, sir. They're probably waiting to tell you."

Zekai Bey is about to say, "Why are you disturbing me, when you haven't even bothered to ask who's calling?" Then he remembers where he is. And his host has just scolded the boy. There's nothing to be done. With a sigh, he rises to his feet.

Everyone at the station knows that Zekai Bey plays bridge three nights a week, every week of the year, and always in the same homes. They know the phone numbers, too. "If anything happens, call me." He's told them that a thousand times over, but he usually manages to give them the slip. And then, in the morning, if it did turn out to be important, he showers them with curses. That's why his men have stopped telling whoever answered the phone that they were calling from Headquarters. The wily cuckolds! He might still have given them the slip, but tonight he really is expecting an important call. *They could be calling from the Koza Hotel,* he tells himself.

"Who's calling?"

"This is Abdullah, sir."

They all call him sir. Just like in the army.

Zekai Bey lost his patience.

"Why are you disturbing me?"

"We've raided an anarchist nest. Caught them meeting in secret."

"So what? Lock them up. Inform Martial Law Command. Do I have to teach you your own job? Begin the interrogation. Tomorrow I . . ."

"The Martial Law Command has been informed, sir. The Colonel is with them. They're waiting for you to join them."

At once, Zekai Bey pulled himself up.

"Why didn't you tell me, you fool? Make the Colonel a coffee! Where did you put him? Oh for God's sake. Open up my office. Put on the electric heater. I'm coming right away."

"Yes, sir!"

Zekai Bey makes his excuses. Everyone shows understanding. They've known for some time that Zekai Bey has become a very important man with many demands on his time.

Muzzafer Bey is pleased that the game he was losing will have to be cut short. Zekai Bey not so much. Did they really have to call him in, just when he was winning? They're always asking him how much longer martial law is going to last. But who bears the brunt of it? He does. Does Ismet Bey care? If it were left to him, it would be martial law forever. Ismet Bey, his bridge partner, is the Chairman of the International Industrial and Commercial Bank. He's not even bothered to lose his partner just when they were winning. Of course not. Playing with money is the man's sole occupation. Zekai Bey hurries off to his official car, not even pausing to adjust his coat.

"Stop right there! In front of the Koza Hotel!"

His chauffeur rushes out to open the door for him, but by the time he gets there, Zekai Bey is already at the reception desk.

"Is Abuzer Bey here yet? The Lebanese fellow, I mean."

"They haven't arrived yet, sir."

"The moment they arrive, they should call me at this number . . . Just a minute. Best to give him this card. I've written down all that's necessary."

Zekai hurries out of the hotel, just as fast as he came in. The man at reception chases after him.

"Sir! Just a moment . . ."

But Zekai Bey keeps moving. Casting just a glance over his shoulder. Jumping back into the car, he signals to his driver to wait. Huffing and puffing, the receptionist holds out a package.

"They left this for you, sir."

Sezai Bey takes the package, no questions asked. As the car moves away, he gives the receptionist an absentminded wave.

In the package are two cartons of Kent cigarettes. Removing the cellophane from one of them, he takes out a cigarette. Lights up. Before putting his lighter back into his waistcoat pocket, he passes his fingers over it. Such a good feel to it. As smooth as a leaf. Best lighter he's ever had. What is it that these infidels can't make?

Turgut Bey gave him this lighter, to thank him for various services rendered during the election for the association. Knowing how much he'd appreciate it.

The car stopped in front of Police Headquarters. Zekai Bey hurried inside. Hoping he'd not kept the Colonel waiting too long, he raced down the corridor. Abdullah ran alongside him, trying to tell him something. But he pushed him aside.

He opened the door to this office. "I'm so sorry to keep you waiting, sir," he said.

Then he stopped. The room was empty. He wheeled around. Only to bump into Abdullah.

"Where's the Colonel?"

"They've left, sir."

"What?"

"It wasn't anything important. I mean – it was, and then it wasn't"

"What's that supposed to mean, you fool?"

"I have no idea, sir. First they told us to do the raid, and then they lost interest."

"Dear God. So tell me. What exactly did the colonel say?"

Abdullah scratches his head. Whatever he says, he'll be the one taking the blame.

Zekai Bey explodes.

"What is this, a three-ring circus? Who's in charge here?"

He pulls himself together, the better to vent his rage on this Abdullah.

"Who said you could raid a house without my say-so?"

"A denunciation, sir . . ."

"Who denounced who?"

"I don't know."

"So you went in knowing nothing, did you, fool?"

"We got the address from Martial Law Command. We tried to call you . . ."

Zekai Bey now remembers that someone had tried to reach him at Muzaffer Bey's earlier in the evening.

"Enough! So you went off on this fool's errand. And what did you bring back? Whatever it was, it doesn't seem to be what Martial Law Command had in mind."

"I don't know, sir."

"Then what *do* you know, you fool? Beyond calling me in here in the middle of the night."

"We went to the address they gave us, sir. First I listened at the door."

"And?"

"We didn't get to hear much before the children spotted us. What I mean to say is, we were obliged to raid the house before we'd heard enough."

"What *did* you hear, god damn it?"

"One of them . . . one of them was talking about the bourgeoisie, sir . . ."

"You goose brain! On the phone you told me you'd raided an anarchist hideout!"

"That's what the informer told us. According to the order, that is. They said it might be . . . could be . . . important."

Abdullah always waffled like that, when he was confused.

"All right, then. What else did the colonel say?"

"He said to put a little pressure on the woman."

"What woman?"

Then he waved Abdullah away. "Go on then. Get started with the interrogation."

He needs some time to pull himself together first. Time to

smoke another Kent. He's left the package in the car. He presses down on the bell.

"Bring up the package I left in the car! Stop! While you're at it, make me a coffee, no sugar."

The telephone began to ring. He waved the janitor away.

"Hello? Oh, yes! Abuzer Beyefendi! How good to hear from you!... No, of course not. No, really. It's my pleasure. No need for excuses... Yes... Yes... Splendid... I'll take care of it tomorrow. No, I'll come myself . . . We've agreed to the price, sir. And it's more than you expected. Tomorrow ten o'clock it is, then . . . I'll be there, sir... May I ask for your room number? Are you pleased with the hotel? I was the one who recommended it, sir. Three of my men will be at your service. Until then, Abuzer Bey . . ."

He waited until the other party had hung up before setting down his own receiver. Now that was more like it. He rubbed his hands. He picked up the open carton the janitor had left on his desk. Pulled out a cigarette and lit up. He sat back in his chair.

He stared at the statuette of Atatürk on his desk. The great leader was climbing Kocatepe. Then suddenly Zekai Bey frowned. He pressed on his bell.

"Send for Abdullah!"

Entering the room, Abdullah bore little resemblance to the scowling menace who had just raided a house. Instead he wore the simpering expression of man reporting to his superior.

"You call yourself a policeman, boy?"

"Sir . . . with your permission . . ."

"Shut up . . . Bring me the woman! Stop! This woman, who is she?"

On reaching Police Headquarters, they'd taken Oya off separately, thrown her into a dark cell. Before closing the door, Abdullah said, "We'll talk to you later." This with the ghastly scowl to which she was now accustomed.

A shitty look for a shitty business, she thinks.

She doesn't want to think about what might be in store, what dread meaning he wants her to take from the word 'talk.' Better not to think at all, she tells the walls. But because it has always been her habit to probe every situation from every angle both before it has happened as well as after, she knows she can't stop herself. Even if she knows full well that it serves her no purpose here. She just needs to stay focused. Fix her eyes on the here and now. Face whatever she has to face. Keep her mind from straying beyond these limits. She must use that mind to get herself through this, to keep herself strong.

To stop it throbbing, she stretches her hands around her head. It's pitch dark, this cell. The size of a beach cabin, by her reckoning. She goes back to her silly habit of smoothing the dust she can't see from her trousers. Is she afraid? It's much too soon for that question. She's confused. Can barely carry a thought. Her insides are tied up into one big knot. It doesn't know how to untie itself. It cowers at the very thought.

She was sitting on something that could be a wooden bench or could be a bunk. Whatever it was, it had no need of a name. She had a pain in her lower back. She took off her sheepskin cloak and spread it out on the wooden bench. Tried to lie down, knees up against her chest. Curled up like a woodlouse. Just think, if Abdullah comes back to me and finds a woodlouse in my place! She imagines Abdullah stomping on that bug. She shudders. Already she has begun to terrify herself with her own metaphors.

She longed to make a shell for her thoughts and climb inside. She noticed now that she had her fists clenched, as if they offered just such a shell, a refuge that no one and nothing could ever breach. Loosen up a little, stop, try to relax. No, that wasn't right. No sense trying to relax in a place so uncomfortable, when she had absolutely no idea what was ahead. She turned up the collar of her pullover, to cover her ears. She closed her eyes.

"You're a worker, aren't you? Then why did you let that prostitute into your house?"

She wakes up to this question, or rather to its echo, from some point far away. I must have dropped off. No way of knowing if she dreamed it, or if it was real. Then the echo repeats itself. There follows a strangled cry.

She shuddered. Jumped to her feet. That's Ali. Hard to know if he's crying or screaming. Hard to give any meaning whatever to that sound. So how does she know it's Ali? Suddenly she realizes. It's Abdullah asking the question. She is the prostitute in question. And it was Ali who'd let her into his house.

The pain in her lower back is getting worse. Is it her period? Damn. Why does it always take her by surprise? Even women who lead blameless lives make sure they won't get caught out. They take supplies with them, just in case. Oya, though. She tends to forget she has a body. After all I've been through over the past eighteen months, I'm still the same absent-minded Oya.

And if my period comes on tonight? More than anything, it's this that Oya most fears. It's how we've been conditioned. If we see our own bodies as shameful, if its untold secrets are mysteries even to us, if we censor our thoughts, lest they be judged evil, how are we ever to stand up for our beliefs? If my period starts tonight, then what? What if it's already started? She tries to check her trousers. She can't see a thing. When time comes for Abdullah to pull me out into the light, I'm going to disgrace myself. In front of this man who has called me a prostitute. I'll be too ashamed to defend myself.

Suddenly she is in a panic. What to do, to avoid disgracing herself — that is her one and only thought. Maybe there's a guard outside the door. A guard with just a bit of compassion. Maybe I can get him to bring me some cotton. She pounds on the door. Somehow forgetting that it's the middle of the night, that no one is going to find cotton to buy at this hour, even if they want to.

She has no idea how long she goes on pounding on that door. All she knows that the more she does, and the more the pounding hurts her arms and fists, the less shame she feels at the prospect of facing Abdullah with blood on her trousers.

She stopped. How strange, she thought. To be seized by this one thought, when there were so many other ugly things she might be facing. She took a breath. Sat down again on the wooden bench, no longer caring about the pain in her lower back.

A bad idea to relax. For now she had to confront the fact that Ali was being beaten. She could almost see Gülşah standing before her, looking at her hands, looking at her hands forever and ever. *Your husband is being beaten, Gülşah, and all because he welcomed me into his house. After you'd spent all afternoon cleaning and cooking for your guests, even though your back was aching. Look at your hands, how swollen they are. You slaved away all day, just so your husband could be beaten.* Oya recoiled at the sound of her own voice. She closed her eyes, to save herself from the sight of Gülşah. Where did it come from, this idea that they were beating Ali solely on account of me? Ali is a worker. An outsider, from Maraş. Any time he falls into the hands of the police, he'll get a beating. So I'm not the only reason he's getting beaten right now. How foolish, to imagine myself at the center of every calamity.

As for prostitutes. That is just what you are, Oya. You're acting as if you didn't hear what Abdullah asked while he was beating Ali. "Why did you let that prostitute into your house?" Put aside the word itself for now. Fact is, he was talking about you. In Abdullah's eyes, you couldn't be anything else. And even if you could, you're up against a man who has made it his business to scowl at you like you're the devil incarnate. Why wouldn't he use the worst word for you he could find?

I am the prostitute who's responsible for Ali's beating. That's just how it is.

This is what should be giving me pain right now. Instead I'm shaking in shame at the prospect of standing with blood seeping through my trousers in front of a man who thinks me a prostitute. When really you should be feeling shame about something else entirely. So now they're calling you a prostitute. Just think what might come next. But whatever degradations they have in store for you, none of it should matter to you. The only thing you need to fear are the degradations you visit on yourself. Against yourself. And also. The shame you should be feeling about all those others. Gülşah, for example. And Ali.

She stopped her thoughts there. It was enough that she had panicked. She could not afford to wallow in guilt. The beating they're giving Ali at this moment is not just about me. Or not at all about me. I shouldn't be tormenting myself like this, it will only wear me out. She's speaking out loud again. This is not the time to be letting such thoughts into her brain. How is she going to stand up to them, if she has already accepted their view of her?

Suddenly the door flew open. And there he was before her, Abdullah of the gruesome scowl. Catching Oya in the midst of praying that her period hadn't started. What could be more pathetic? When do I pray, if I'm not praying for that? Forget the man's questions. March! Stop! Wait!

Now Oya is standing before Zekai Bey. Trying to hold her head high, trying not to blink. Fogged with fatigue, eyes still struggling to adjust to the light. Hard not to blink in such circumstances. Feeling her eyes well up, Oya curses herself. She can't let this man see any tears in her eyes. He'll take that to mean she is frightened. But what is she thinking? Hasn't she decided to give no importance whatsoever to what these men think of her? Time to stop thinking about where these men get their ideas. From now on she must confine her thoughts to her responsibilities. That's why it's so important to stand straight. Maybe the only reason. Since the moment she got here, she's done nothing but worry about what these men thought of her. She can't help it. It's a habit she can't break.

For a while Zekai Bey acts as if she is not even in the room. While sizing her up, from the corner of his eye. There she is, standing before me, back straight. But I'm the one who decides for how long. I'm in charge of time here, and who's in charge of time, wins. If I wanted, I could keep her standing there for hours on end. The decision is for me to make. To make her wait. One more small way to tire her out. You won't be able to keep that pose for long, my girl. No need to stare straight ahead for no reason. We're not on equal footing, we two. You've lost before you've begun. The sooner you accept defeat, the better. For a moment, Zekai Bey's thoughts glide back to the bridge party he was forced to leave too early. He likes to think of everything in life as a game of poker. Right now he sees this woman standing before him as his opponent across the card table. Never mind that this is a game he knows he'll win. For now there is the pretence that they are on an equal footing. Play with the woman, trip her up. Make her wait for the blow that is mine to make, in the manner I decide, at the time of my own choosing.

"You're married, I understand."

"Yes."

"And you have children?"

"Yes."

"Excellent. Please sit down."

Oya takes a moment to decide whether or not to obey this man's instruction. Every bit of her wants to repulse him. Him and his fake courtesies. But in the end, she judges it best to rest her legs, which have begun to ache. Keeping her strength is more important right now than making a show of it. For a moment she's even tempted to sit back in her chair. But then she decides against it. She would never be able to forgive herself, if she let herself relax too much. She must do her best to strike a neutral pose – neither tense nor relaxed – and keep her thoughts within the same bounds. This will help her play the long game, she hopes.

Suddenly Zekai looks up to fix his eyes on her.

Oya is glad she hadn't sat back. Had she had lowered herself that far, she might as well have been looking up at this man from a bed. He would have had the upper hand from the start.

"So tell me, Hanımefendi, how is it that you, a married woman, a married woman with children, no less, ended up at a table drinking raki with the scum of the earth?"

He's addressed her as Hanımefendi, but he's spat it out like a curse.

"I wasn't drinking."

Oya blushes. For God's sake. What does it matter, if I was drinking or not? What a fool I am! Trying to defend myself, even though I know what this man intends to do. Trying to show myself a woman beyond reproach! Even when I know he's out to crush me. I sound like a schoolgirl trying to justify herself to an unsympathetic teacher. What does my drinking or not drinking have to do with any of this? And anyway, it's only by chance that I didn't have a drink tonight, I could just as easily have been drinking. What difference would that have made? Would it have stopped those scowling men from barging into Ali's house? She lifts up her head again, to meet Zekai Bey's eyes.

"So you say you weren't drinking. But we know the whole story."

"It doesn't matter if I was drinking, or not drinking."

Zekai Bey pauses. He is beginning to lose interest in this pretense of an equal footing. It might be fun, he thinks, to go straight in for the hill. No, he decides. Pull yourself together. Take a deep breath and start again.

"What business did you have, in a room full of men?"

"There were women there too."

There she goes again. Defending herself. It makes her so angry, to see how quick she is to defend her bourgeois honor. Even when that is the last thing she wants to do. Oya feels her cheeks reddening. She resolves, once again, to cast off this senseless shame. She knows it for what it is, after all. So she takes a deep breath, to exhale all that antiquated shame in one go.

"Or are you with the morality police?"

Zekai Bey doesn't like her lip.

"Out every night whoring, are you?"

"Are you a police officer, or are you a sex maniac?"

Oya is on her feet. Shouting. One punch to the face, though, and she has crumpled back into her chair.

Zekai is breathing through his nose now. I'm not letting this whore ruin my game. He's already tired of it. Foolish to have entertained the idea at all. Striding to his desk, he lights himself a Kent. Then he reaches out to offer one to Oya.

"Cigarette?"

With horror Oya sees herself reaching for the cigarette packet. As if she's on automatic pilot. That punch must have addled her brain. She pulls back her hand, as if from a flame. No, let's not smoke his cigarettes.

"Take it. Please. You'll enjoy it."

"No, I won't."

"Don't worry. We're not going to poison you."

"You're the one who should be worrying. You're responsible for keeping me alive."

Zekai Bey turns his back to her. Bitch. What difference does it make if she smokes or not. She's addicted. He knows that from the way she reached out. She's going to have to go without a cigarette till morning now. She'll soon be very sorry that she turned my cigarette down.

"We're responsible for upstanding citizens. Not for traitors."

"You're responsible for everyone in your custody."

Oya stops there. The pain in her cheek is making her tear up. Why am I bothering to speak to this man? Next thing I know, I'll be telling him about the Declaration of Human Rights.

"Now wait. We haven't touched a hair on your head so far. And here you are, squealing and squirming, spouting nonsense about the law. But I'm not having it. No constitutions or penal codes in here!"

Furious that her eyes have teared up, Oya shouts:

"So you're saying there's no constitution? In that case, you're the one who's trampling on it. You're the traitor."

"Quiet, bitch! You know full well that martial law is allowed under the constitution. Don't you hear that on the radio every day? It was to protect the constitution that they declared martial law. Our job is to enforce it. And why do we do that? To protect the constitution! Day and night!"

"Why bother? Who's forcing you?"

Oya's not sure if she should be talking back. She's wearing herself out. It's a little soon for her to be wearing herself out.

"We're cleaning things up. Getting rid of all you perverts. This nation will never fall at the feet of whores like you. You know why? Because we're here, that's why. God is with us. And the Turkish race! This nation's pure-hearted youth! Bless them to the heavens! We're going to hunt you down like bedbugs. Smoke you out. Until our nation is as pure and clean as heaven itself . . ."

Zekai Bey's cigarette goes out. After lighting it again, he blows his smoke into Oya's face. She's more beautiful, this bitch, with her cheeks red. It might, he thinks, be fun to provoke her again. And then he could seize her by the hair and . . .

Oya falls silent. Zekai Bey can see the fire in her eyes. Suddenly, Oya shudders. She is determined not to speak. She can see that this man is trying to provoke her. And anyway. What's the point of speaking? Foolish and pointless to engage in any conversation whatsoever. No, she does not need to convince this man of anything. She should say nothing to him beyond the absolute necessity. All she should be thinking about is how to get out of this godforsaken place as soon as possible. That and only that. This is not the place to stage a fight. You can't win. You've already lost. Oya looks around the room. Her eyes fall on the brass bust of Atatürk on Zekai Bey's desk.

"Take a good look at him, why don't you? Look at Atatürk and feel your shame! Did he save our nation for degenerates like you? Tell me. Did he save it so that you could sell it off? Tell me!"

Oya doesn't answer.

"I asked you a question, whore!"

Grabbing her by the hair, he knocks her head against the wall.

"Am I to understand that this is the Directorship of the Struggle Against Prostitution?"

Another punch.

"And this bitch thinks she can make fun of me! You answer my question. You answer it or else."

Oya is glad to hear herself speaking with a calm voice.

"I have yet to be told what I am being charged with."

"Listen to this bitch now. Pretending she doesn't know. You

didn't think we were going to fall for that, did you? We're only just beginning here. We know everything. Do you understand?"

"In that case, could you kindly tell me why I have been deprived of my freedom?"

"And now she wants to talk about freedom. Who do you think you are, bitch, to talk about freedom? You have no freedom. You're here in this city to serve out your exile. Every move you make, you have to report to us. But I can see that even this was not enough to set you straight. But you wait and see. We can knock sense into anyone. We do it night and day. And when it comes to a miserable whore like you . . ."

"Is that what you're charging me with? Prostitution?"

Oya likes the sound of her voice. She likes seeing this man redden with anger, too. He wants to do the same to me. But now he's the one blowing his top.

"I'm the one asking the questions here. Got that straight? I couldn't care less about your whoring. Thank the Lord for keeping our nation's girls safe from you. We're not about to let them fall into your hands. We're cleaning out the pimps, every last one of them."

"So what is the reason for my being detained?"

Zekai Bey explodes.

"The reason? Our nation is in jeopardy. Our nation! What reason could matter more than that? I was civilized enough to show you some respect, but since when does that mean anything to the likes of you? Why should we treat shameless criminals like human beings? Why even bother with an interrogation? Better just to line you up against the wall and mow you down."

Sensing that he had gone too far, Zekai Bey slowed himself down.

"But even with all that, I told myself. She's a woman, a mother. Let's interrogate her nicely. Let's not turn her over to others . . . You do understand, don't you, how things would have played out, if we had?"

He sucked hard on his cigarette. Then he stopped to cough.

Oya was trembling. But she wasn't scared yet. She wasn't even sure if she had any reason to be scared. It was her nerves making her tremble. Time had a way of wearing on her nerves. Worried that Zekai Bey might hear her voice trembling and assume from that that she was scared, she enunciated each word:

"So I can assume that you have legal authority to interrogate me?"

"Listen. We are the law. Get that into your head, will you? What is it with you people? You think nothing of our nation's laws, until the shoe is on the other foot! Have you no shame?"

"Am I to understand from this that my interrogation is to take place outside the legal framework?"

For a moment Zekai Bey paused. Listen to this bitch. Still asking questions. Time for her to learn who asks the questions in this place, and who gives the answers. He pressed on his bell.

Stemmed his rage. This was a good time to end the game. The martial law people had yet to find a way to arrest these people. He stared blankly for a few moments at the janitor waiting in the doorway.

"Get me Abdullah."

He gave Oya a cold glare, to let her know how little she mattered to him.

"You are now going to answer all of Abdullah's questions nicely."

He sat back in his chair.

"I don't have any more time to waste on you."

He wheeled around his chair to give his back to Oya. Best way to humiliate this woman, he thought, was to treat her like someone of no importance. But he couldn't keep it up. As Oya left, she could hear him saying:

"If she doesn't give straight answers where they're taking her now, she'll soon be longing to be back in this office."

A chill goes down Oya's spine. Suddenly she can't move. Me too? Well, why wouldn't they? There'd be no point to it, though. They don't have anything on me, after all. Most likely, they detained us without any real reason. Would they know already how little she'd have to give them? Why waste their efforts for nothing? Those questions have left ice trails all across her brain. She can't help it. She can't push Zekai Bey's threats from her mind. Nor can she brush away the stories she heard while in prison: what happened to others might soon be happening to her. In those days, it was other people's stories she carried. Now she would be living them. She's not so foolish as to not know the difference between sharing a burden and living it. No. Zekai Bey only said that to scare me . . . and, well, he succeeded. I'm scared. Idiotic. Absolute nonsense. Evil, to finish off this evening's raid with torture. Don't even imagine it. Don't be such a fool. If worse comes to worst, I'll be arrested, no more. At the very least, there must be some genuine reason behind all this. From the moment she began her sentence, she'd been so careful, so correct. And now they bring her in? What is to be gained from all this commotion? How she hates herself, for losing herself in explanations and excuses. *What's become of you? Did any of this make any sense, ever?* And still she's trying to make some sort of sense of it. But for them, torture always does have a meaning. For instance, when the Romans were hunting down Christians, they'd sometimes throw one to the lions, just to lull the spectators in the arena, just to amuse them. There's no big shake-down going on here. No brilliant spectacle. No hectoring crowd. When all is said and done, there will be just the one headline: *Police raid house in the Independence District where a secret meeting was underway*. It might be fear that has her going through all the possibilities. Or she might just be doing this to stay calm.

Abdullah walks beside her in silence. His evil looks don't scare her as much as they did before. What can this man do to me? He can beat me, he can curse me. He'd never go so far as the deliberate, systematic kind of torture she's heard about, thousands of times over. When she thinks about that sort of torture, and then thinks about what Abdullah could do to her, Oya is almost relieved, almost amused. But Zekai Bey had said something else. He spoken of her being taken somewhere. Oya had heard of other *somewheres* in Ankara and Istanbul. She'd heard there were places like that in Adana, too. Those things she'd heard about in such horror – they can happen here too. Close enough to touch. They're almost there. Electric wires, attached to all your fingers and toes. Hearts beating so hard they might burst. Begging to be killed. Deliberately kept alive, but only just. Lying in a pool of blood and vomit, no longer a woman, no longer human. Rolling down and down and down . . . And then, the worst a man can do, but with a truncheon . . .

Suddenly she notices the truncheon in Abdullah's hands. Is that what he beat Ali with? At just that moment, she looks down the corridor and sees Ali crumpled up on a bench. One of his eyes is shut. Bruised deep purple. The soles of his feet are swollen up like drums. He's moaning. She pauses, then walks over to Ali's side.

"I'm sorry."

He stares up at her blankly through a sightless eye. Then he turns away, to moan some more.

He didn't even recognize her. No, he did recognize her. He was just shocked by her asinine gesture. What exactly am I apologizing for? What sense is there in apologizing to Ali at this moment? She can sense Abdullah smirking at her. Even he knows what an idiot I was to do that. Maybe while I'm at it I should apologize to Abdullah as well. This man who brought us in. Who beat poor Ali to a pulp. It would have been bad enough if she'd wished Ali a quick recovery. But no. She'd had to apologize.

I didn't apologize on behalf of Abdullah, the police, and their headquarters. I apologized for getting him and his family into trouble by visiting their house. I'm still putting myself at the center of everything. I'm too quick to assume it's all about me. I don't know why they raided the house yet. It could have been because of Mustafa, or Hüseyin, or even Zekeriya. Or Ekrem. Yes, Ekrem. Someone seeking some sort of advantage might have denounced him. Or could it be Ali?

After all. Do I know anything about this man? Maybe he got himself mixed up in something. It could be a coincidence, that they raided the house when I was there. No, my dear. If that had been the case, Abdullah would not have singled out Mustafa, Hüseyin, and me at the outset. Not that I know much about these brothers either. Maybe all this was a trap. They'd turned up so suddenly. Her suspicions, her guilt. That about sums it up for people like me. Yet another mixed-up little bourgeois lady!

Abdullah's job now is to give her a beating. This will do her some good. What she needs now is physical pain. Otherwise she'll keep babbling and quarreling. In these days of struggle, is it too much to expect us to give up fighting with ourselves, or worrying how people see us?

Abdullah is smirking. He's in no rush to take her wherever he's supposed to be taking her. He's trying to humiliate me, Oya thinks. Still, she's thinking it's all about her. How ugly or beautiful she looks. What all this means. God damn it. They leave Ali behind to continue down the corridor.

"You're apologizing to this man? There's nothing he didn't say about you. Nothing."

Oya stops.

"If you beat someone like a dog, they'll tell you anything."

"If I'd known who that woman was, I would have knocked her down and kicked her. That's what he said."

"He never said that. Our people are kind to their guests."

Even as she utters these words, she sees how ridiculous they are, and stops. Our people. Referring to Ali as our people. Choosing a moment like this to discuss our people. What gives you the right to use this term? Because for some stupid reason you've landed yourself in this police station. What was I doing at Ali's house anyway? Trying to raise their consciousness? That's not why I was there. Hardly the time or place. And even if it were, you can be sure that our people are not about to let their consciousness be raised by a woman so starved of company that she has no idea if she's coming or going. You went to that house because you couldn't bear another evening alone with your darkest thoughts. If Hüseyin hadn't come to fetch you, you'd be at the hotel right now, in bed. Still in exile, but safe in your little shell. Nothing to boast about, nothing to regret. So long as it didn't end up here. But here you are, in deep trouble. Why is anyone's guess. No point thinking about what happened before, or what might happen next. They might have judged you as important. They might be giving you a hard time. That won't change a thing. For you, this night holds no significance whatsoever. You might be able to fool everyone else. But you can't fool yourself.

Abdullah opens a door and walks through it, head high. This room does not look like a torture chamber nor does it seem to lend itself to beatings, falakas, or what have you. No, this is just your standard brightly lit office. A wardrobe next to the door. A wastepaper basket. Three formica tables. Pleather chairs. There are even two vases. No. In a room like this, even Abdullah would struggle to give someone a beating. There's a huge window here, besides. The curtains not even drawn. Oya stands in the middle of the room. Abdullah rummages through the drawers until he finds a notepad. He throws it onto one of the tables. With a ballpoint pen.

"Sit here and write your statement."

A standard request. Like "pay at the cashier." They're trying to confuse me, Oya thinks. Even Abdullah. Still the same grim face, and the same terrifying moustache, but his voice is neutral.

"What am I meant to write? I don't even know what I'm accused of."

"You know. Of course you know. A clandestine meeting."

"What meeting? There was nothing clandestine going on. We went there for supper."

She's losing her grip again. Offering Abdullah useless explanations. The room had thrown her off.

"You'll confess to being an anarchist. You'll write it all down."

"I have nothing to write."

"You might not now, but you'll write up a storm, I assure you, in the place you're going next."

So now it's Abdullah's turn to scare her. And now Oya can see it. Whatever balloon Zekai Bey and Abdullah had been taking turns inflating – it's burst. Otherwise things would have been happening differently. Sooner or later, a balloon is going to burst. They have nothing on me. How could they have? Even so, they've given me a good scare. So fine. Let's imagine that this were not the case. What if they had something on me? No point in thinking about that now. Abdullah leaves the room. Forgetting his truncheon on one of the other tables. Or maybe he didn't forget it. Maybe he's left it there to scare me. To say, you write your statement, or else. So there it is. Time to get to work. Like everyone else. Until they can find the strength to sign their names. As always. Pushed to the brink of death, but no further. They know full well that I have nothing much to write about right now. But if they want to arrest me? She can hear Abdullah talking out in the corridor.

"I didn't hear much, sir. We searched the house. We found nothing."

She's sure now they'll release her in the morning. All they want is to ruffle her feathers for a while. Having brought her this far. So why did I fly off the handle like that? I was close to committing an offense. I'm so inexperienced. What if I really did belong to an illegal organization? I'd have been a disgrace, an absolute disgrace! Let this be a lesson to me. I need to act like someone who knows she's going to be released at the end of all this: cool, indifferent, observant.

She notices that her eyes keep returning to the truncheon sitting on the table across from her. A committed activist behaves differently from an indifferent bystander. If she were an activist, how would she be acting? Like this? No, I'd be a totally different person if I were an activist. A bystander is one thing, a revolutionary something else entirely. She has no idea what she'd be like if she were a revolutionary. They would have treated me differently, too. That's for sure. The conditions would have been different, too. The way they used that truncheon, too. I wouldn't have given that truncheon such a fearful look. I would have given it a casual glance. It and everything else. While remembering that I was surrounded by weapons, always. My whole life a drawn gun. Such a different life from my own. But this truncheon. It's not even a weapon, really. It's just a vile and ordinary tool. An instrument of evil. Nothing stylish or dashing about it. Nothing heroic either. To be hit by a bullet – that could be a noble thing. Even a beautiful thing. But to be beaten with a truncheon? For a revolutionary, that could count as a humiliation.

Before her eyes, the truncheon takes on revolting new shapes. So evil, this instrument. Turned by sick minds into the ugliest phallus ever seen. So she has been told. They defile even nature! Turning a truncheon into the ugliest, vilest travesty of their own penises.

She remembers Sema. Here she is again, waking up crying in the middle of the night. Sobbing uncontrollably. Oya takes her a glass of water and sits down beside her.

"I've suffered so many humiliations, and so much pain. You know all this. But there is one thing I haven't forgotten."

"Let it go, Sema. Try to forget."

"I can't forget it. I mustn't."

"Then tell me, Sema. It might give you some relief."

Putting aside all the other degradations she'd suffered, Sema told her about the truncheon.

"You must put it out of your mind, Sema. It's nothing more than a crude instrument of torture. The evil is in what they add to it. The evil is in the hand that wields it. It didn't reach you.

The evil stayed in those ugly hands. The instrument itself means nothing."

Sema isn't listening to Oya. How empty my words are, Oya thinks. How empty my thoughts on so many other things I've never experienced. I'm a typical well-heeled intellectual. Standing on the sidelines, grazed by a hunter's bullet but otherwise unscathed. Sema is crying. She can't sleep. It's shame keeping her awake. While Oya feels another sort of shame: too deep ever to overcome.

"Look, Oya," Sema says. "I've always been comfortable with my sexuality. Until recently, I never overthought it, never made a fuss. I saw it for what it was and moved on. I didn't hide myself away. I'd not been overly conditioned. But from the moment those three brutes rammed that truncheon into my anus, I've been haunted by my body. By my sexuality, too. They fill me with such horror. As if there were nothing more profane. Were I not a sexual being, they could have beaten me, yes, they could have given me electric shocks, pulled out my fingernails.... done anything at all. They could cause me deadly pain. Drive me mad with pain. I could have survived all that and put it behind me. I wouldn't feel the disgust I feel now. I'd feel no shame. Three men. Well maybe I shouldn't even call them men. Three of them, goading each other on. Ramming that truncheon into my anus. The pain was insane, but even stronger was my disgust, my shame. The worst of it was the sexism. To be a woman – it became the greatest betrayal of all. While the men – they had left themselves behind somehow. It no longer mattered to them who I was or what I was. All that mattered was the ugliest penis of the century. Using it in the ugliest way they dared. Rejoicing in it. And then, when they'd had their way. Before I fainted. I heard them cheering. And then one of them cried out, *TrunCHEON!* You know what I mean. The same way a frenzied crowd at a football match would cry out, *Gooooaaal!* The same way, exactly."

It turned Oya's stomach, to hear all this. She spent the rest of the night vomiting. But Sema stopped crying. Later on, in court, she spoke with great calm about the many months of bleeding that had followed.

The truncheon Abdullah had left on the table accidentally or on purpose brought those memories back to her. Best to avert her eyes. Divert her thoughts. Maybe they'd left her here to drown in her own worst memories. Because she doesn't want to look. Doesn't want to remember. But there it is, sitting right in front of her. Disgusting. And profane.

"Did they use the truncheon on you in military prison, big sister?"

This on the morning she is transferred to Ankara Central Prison. She is squatting in the stone yard. Head bowed. She wants to accustom herself to this new prison as fast as she can. Taking care not to take offense at the Gypsies' and carriage drivers' violent curses, and not to blush at their salty jokes. Even so, she's a know-nothing novice in this place. She has more surprises ahead, she can see. More shame, too. She has her head bowed so that no one can see her involuntary blushing. How the raucous laughter grates her nerves. The courtyard is full of toddlers roaming around without diapers. She imagines herself in a courtyard swept clean of the turds they have left in their wake. What she wants now is a freshly brewed glass of tea. She'll get up now and make herself some tea. This will be the first step toward making herself at home in this civil prison. Another lusty, raucous laugh. In her sleeveless cotton print shift, Menekşe begins to dance.

"How could there ever be a lover better than me?"

This is the first time she sees Menekşe. Later she'll grow accustomed to her fellow inmates' wild curses and wilder laughter, their violent quarrels and their belly-dancing. She'll grow to love these women who can create joy and fury out of nothing. But she'll always love Menekşe the most. She was the one who taught Oya how insignificant she was amid their feuds and their curses. From that very first morning, when Oya still had no idea how the prison kitchen worked, and Menekşe opened her arms to her. Offering her a glass of the tea that she'd just brewed, and that Oya so longed for.

"Have some of my tea, big sister!"

They sat down together on Menekşe's kilim. The tea was deep red, red as blood. It washed away all her painful memories from military prison, even the ones she'd thought she'd never forget. It was afterward, and with the same abandon she gave to laughing and belly-dancing, that Menekşe asked:

"In military prison, did they use the truncheon on you, too?"

Oya's tea glass was burning in her hand. She didn't answer. Nor did Menekşe press her. She just sat there with her tea, watching the gendarmes who were watching the courtyard as they walked along the tops of the walls surrounding it.

"You tasted good, little boy! As good as your truncheon, or almost!"

How it shocks Oya, to hear Menekşe urge them on like that, to make as if she liked it. It makes her blood crawl, as much as the image of a truncheon-turned-penis. She says as much to this new friend of hers:

"That tells me you've never been done by a truncheon. Do you have any idea what they do with that thing? Hah! Well, let me tell you. No one knows as much about truncheons as I do."

Oya stands up and goes inside. Suddenly she can't bear this Menekşe. She decides to forget her, think about her own needs instead. She needs to find a place to lay out her bed, find a toilet that's not plastered with baby crap. There are a few things she needs from the canteen, and then she'll need to hunt down a place in the kitchen for her stove, her pans, and her supplies. She turns away from her strange new surroundings. No longer hearing the shouting and the cursing. Her only thought to make some sort of nest to get her through her time here.

That evening, she returns to the courtyard. Sits down on one of the few remaining scraggy patches of grass. From her little island, she looks out over the sea of screams and shouts and curses. It's too soon for her to know this place. She must learn to train her eyes on it without wincing. Brush away her prejudices and just observe. Here, then, are the people they talk so much about. The people about whom she'd formed so many ideas. Turns out I knew nothing about them, nothing at all. So here they are, a few of the women I've never met. A few of the people. It's not enough to observe them, not enough to find out why they're here. I need to put myself in their midst. Get along with them. Live with them, in short. Time to get going!

She can no longer remember how many women she introduced herself to that day. All she knows is that she threw herself into it. Never playing the lady, never showing shock. At sunset, the warden and his team shooed them all inside like chickens into a coop. Time for the headcount. While she was standing there, waiting to be counted, she heard the women in line behind her whispering to each other. "They say she was a friend of Deniz Gezmiş." She let it go.

That night, as she was settling into bed, she found herself watched by a pair of grey-blue eyes. It was Menekşe, lying in the bed next to hers.

"Are you angry at me, big sister?"

"No, of course not."

"Because they said Deniz Gezmiş was your lover. I told them I'd ask you to your face."

"Where did this come from?"

"We heard you were political."

"What exactly is that supposed to mean?"

"Well, Deniz Gezmiş was political, too, wasn't he? So they think you must have been friends."

"So anyone political is a friend of Deniz Gezmiş?"

"Ha ha! Deniz Gezmiş was the leader of all the politicals. And they say he had lots and lots of lovers."

"There were lots of us women in military prison. Not a single one knew Deniz Gezmiş that way. And neither did I."

"So you don't have a fella right now?"

"A fella? What's that supposed to mean?"

"A lover. A fella is a lover."

"I'm married."

"Forget husbands. A friend is something else. So Deniz Gezmiş wasn't your type? They say he was like a lion. Didn't you like him?"

Oya can see she's struggling.

"The day they hanged him, we all cried and cried."

Oya is paying attention now.

"Do you mean you were mourning Deniz Gezmiş?"

"The Sunnis called him a Kızılbaş. It was just us Alevis crying for him."

"So you're Alevi?"

"Yes, we've always been Alevis. Just like you."

"What do you mean by that?"

"Kotan Ana said so. She says that all politicals are Alevi infidels."

"Is Kotan Ana Sunni?"

"That's what she says. But she's really Alevi. She just doesn't want anyone to know."

"Why?"

Oya sees the shock in Menekşe's eyes – that an educated person could be so ignorant. The same way we might when people feign ignorance about torture.

"When they condemned him to death I cried my eyes out."

"So it upset you."

"I was upset, and I was scared. Sister, he was going to swing."

Oya looked over at this woman in her faded cotton shift, this woman who went through the day laughing, who broke into a dance at least five times a day. She looked at her childish face and her grey-blue eyes.

"You're in for a capital crime, in other words. What did you do?"

"I chopped up my friend!"

". . ."

"I have a husband, too, you know. We did it together. So he'll swing too."

"Why? Because you had a friend?"

"No! He saw him on the way to the Needleman."

"What's this about a Needleman?"

"You know what they say about them – how lusty women flock to them?"

Now Oya was really confused. Much later, she would piece together Menekşe's story, as far as she could:

Menekşe was from the city of Sivas. She had a lover. Her husband hears about it. He decides to kill Menekşe and her lover with her. When Menekşe works this out, she tells her husband that the lover was never her lover. That he was just trying his luck. She incites her husband, to save her own life.

"Since we're all from Sivas, old lady. They ratted on me. Told my husband. So he tells the whole coffeehouse, I'm going to kill them both. So it got back to me. So I told my husband that Halil was toying with my honor."

"Who's Halil?"

"My man."

"If he was your man, why did you say he was harassing you?"

"Because he was my lover! My husband was going to kill me!"

"I understand. Love is one thing. Life is another."

"So this was the plan we made together. I tricked Halil into coming to the house. Said it was empty. The moment he was on me, I yelled help! He's trying to rape me! My husband and my brother-in-law and so on, they burst into the house. They were outside, of course, waiting for the sign. They chopped him up with an ax."

"And you?"

"I joined in."

"Didn't you love this Halil?"

Menekşe makes an obscene gesture.

". . . . . ."

"I thought he was your fella."

"So what. He was a donkey, and a son of a donkey, and a grand-son of a donkey, too. We shoved him into a sack, and then my husband and I buried him in a cabbage patch."

Oya's nerves are making her smile. This hard, cold story makes no sense to her. Little Menekşe, conspiring to kill the man she loves with the husband she doesn't love. Shoving him into a sack and burying him in a cabbage patch. Oya struggles to understand how it could have come to this.

"And then what?"

"We ran off to the city. Wandered around there for five days . . . And then we were caught."

"Didn't you think about Halil at all, while you were wandering around? Even if you didn't love him that much, he was still your friend."

"Who I am I supposed to love here? Halil? Give it up, big sister. I can't love a dead man, can I? That's a sin."

She looks at Oya. Nothing but childish, heedless innocence in those grey-blue eyes. Nothing but human kindness.

"Okay then. What happened after you got caught?"

"They took me in to the police station. For four days and four nights, they beat me. Knocked me down and dragged me across the floor. Had their fun with the truncheon. I said nothing. But that husband of mine, he kissed the policemen's feet, a little bleeding was all it took, and he told them everything. They dragged me across so I could see that for myself."

"Did you say anything after that?"

"God forbid! As if I'd spill a secret to the police!"

"But there was evidence, wasn't there?"

Menekşe hasn't the faintest idea what Oya means by evidence. Oya falls silent.

"He blabbed, but I said nothing. So they beat me again, in front of that pimp husband of mine. I couldn't walk for a month after that. I had to crawl."

Her eyes welled up for a moment, but then she burst out laughing. From across the cell came a spatter of curses from those whose sleep she'd disturbed.

"I spat in the face of the policeman's truncheon."

"So then why were you dancing for the police this morning, saying that word over and over?"

"I was dancing for Little Boy's penis. He's my fella."

"Who's Little Boy?"

"You know. The gendarmes. That's our name for them."

"I thought the Needleman was your fella."

"God forbid, abla, big sister! Never!"

With time, Oya finds out how Ahmet the Needleman is important. Ahmet is also an inmate, one of the privileged ones who work for the prison administration. Either he is a nurse or he just gives injections. It's not clear how he got this job. All she knows for sure is that the inmates call him the Needleman. Whenever a woman is due to see the doctor, there's a big scuffle about Ahmet the Needleman. They all accuse each other of sleeping with him. They curse him to hell and back. They tell stories about him, each more scurrilous than the last. "Go to Ahmet," they yell at each other. "Hang your ass there, why don't you? No needles for you today, I see!" Needles is code for their every carnal thought. Oya can't quite believe these stories to be true, she doesn't see how they could be possible under prison conditions, but it's clear that when he finds a chance, he takes it. Oya knows this from secret notes brought to her by women who don't know how to read. Whenever it's clear that Ahmet has given love notes to several women at once, that's when the fights break out. They tear each other's hair out. But then, in no time at all, they are back to making jokes about him, as they raise their arms to dance across the courtyard.

This then is Menekşe's Needleman story, more or less. One of her rivals seems to have got a message across to her husband, to let him know that the Needleman was her fella.

Oya is glad to have his story to distract her from her own troubles during that first night at Ankara Central Prison. The longer it goes on, the better. They get up and brew themselves a fresh pot of tea. Paying no attention to Kotan Ana who shouts at them to stop making such a clatter in the kitchen. Menekşe asks for some of the Birinci cigarettes that Oya's brought with her from military prison. It's clear she has no one on the outside looking after her. She probably gets along in here by doing jobs for other inmates.

"Can I be your kitchen friend, big sister?"

Oya will later come to understand that a kitchen friend is someone who works for you in exchange for food. She does your cooking and cleaning, and even your laundry. But she doesn't know that yet. So she says, "Yes, let's eat together." When Menekşe starts fawning over her, she assumes it's because she's just trying to help a recent arrival.

"I can wash you, too, big sister!"

Oya flinches. Even as a child, she couldn't bear her own mother washing her.

"I can do that myself, thanks."

"I can do your laundry."

"No, my dear. No reason for idle hands. I can do that myself as well."

"I can smash your nits."

This takes Oya by surprise.

"Do they have lice here?"

Menekşe lets out a loud laugh. How could Oya not know that crushing nits is what Gypsies do to kill time. She'll grow to find it so relaxing that she'll fear becoming too accustomed to it. A head massage, Gypsy style.

"Not many nits here, big sister. Here, let me show you. Put your head on my lap."

"No, no, I don't want to right now."

She scratches Oya's head as if she really does have lice. This is too intimate for Oya, and it shames her to be making her revulsion so clear.

"So why did your husband get so angry about the Needleman? He'd killed your real fella, after all."

"You know Döne? Well she gave a note to the warden who was on his way there and said give this to Menekse's husband. She's jealous because of me and Ahmet and . . ." Enough, Oya thinks. She longs to be asleep in bed, with Ankara Central Prison forgotten until morning. But Menekşe keeps talking.

She and her husband are in dispute over a bedroll. Later, when Oya understands why it is that women in this civil prison give so much importance to their bedrolls, this won't surprise her. There might be sewage leaking from the roof, the ground might be littered with baby poo, but these women's beds exist in another world. It's the only place in this prison that's kept clean. Their beds are their homes, in a sense. Step away from their beds, and they're outside. Clean or dirty, it doesn't concern them. They don't see it as their responsibility. They busy themselves only with the beds they know to be their homes. They're like housewives who keep a row of slippers next to the door, to keep the filth of the streets from their sacred homes. Whose relentless war against any speck of filth that might float in through the doors or windows does not spare the children. Who scold those children for coming inside and daring to touch a doorknob without first washing their hands, but who think it natural if those same children walk down the street cracking open sunflower seeds with their teeth and then spitting them out onto the ground. The women in this prison are just the same. Their beds are their homes, and everywhere else – the courtyard, the kitchen, the toilets – is the street outside. The street belongs to everyone. Or rather, it belongs to no one. They draw a line around their beds and stake their claim. Their only job is to keep their tiny kingdoms pure and clean, defending them fiercely against all intruders. It's each woman for herself. And each day these women wake up in Ankara Central Prison, they roll up these beds of theirs with the utmost care, covering them with embroidered cloths to protect them from dirt and mildew. Their beds are their treasures, their everything. Their dignity. The wealthiest prisoners have satin quilts, which they cover with silk carpets every morning. But even for the poorest prisoners, it's the beds that remain the thing of greatest value, and the beds alone that mark the haves from the have-nots. After rolling up their beds, they'll all go into the same kitchen to cook under a roof that's leaking sewage, and it won't bother them a bit. But in their eyes, this does not make them into equals. Beyond their beds, it's the wilderness.

"I didn't send him my bedroll. That's why we're not speaking."

What difference does that make? Oya wonders. They're both facing death sentences, or life in prison. Unless lady luck smiles on them, and they get twenty-four years apiece. So what does it matter, if they're on speaking terms or not? Oya wants to go to bed. She wants to sleep. Lose herself in dreams without a cabbage patch in sight. But here is Menekşe again, standing right over her. She reaches into her blouse and pulls out a chit.

"Take a look at this song Ahmet wrote, big sister."

Maybe Menekşe is afraid of sleeping. Maybe she sees cabbage patches in her dreams. But there is no fear in her eyes. Only curiosity. She has eyes only for Ahmet the Needleman's words. In the dim light of the single naked lightbulb hanging from the ceiling, Oya struggles to make sense of Ahmet's song.

> *I didn't wander, didn't tire,*
> *Didn't die in vain,*
> *Nowhere in the world did I find*
> *A love like yours.*

Menekşe is happy. Menekşe is pleased. She pulls out another crumpled piece of paper from underneath her pillow. "Look, big sister, he gave me this one, too, and I kept it."

I write to you on April 23rd
I cannot feel remorse for our love
If you don't answer my letter
Remember this: love conquers all.

But I thought the gendarme was your fella, Oya almost asks, not Ahmet the Needleman. But she loses the will. She gives up, too, trying to find remorse in Menekşe's beautiful eyes, or imagine her haunted by nightmares full of cabbages that turn to gravestones. In her own dreams, she'll see three torturers sitting on Menekşe's naked back, pushing a gigantic truncheon into her anus. Oya wants to scream, but then Menekşe looks up at the gendarmes patrolling the courtyard from the top of the wall. She begins to dance, singing, "Do me with your truncheon." The gendarme jumps down from the wall, a truncheon in his hand. No, it's not a truncheon. It's a cabbage. Oya wakes up covered in sweat.

The formica table just across from her becomes a cabbage, with body parts buried inside it. The truncheon becomes the penis of Menekşe's lover. Ahmet the Needleman's syringe becomes another penis. There on the formica table, the truncheons – no, the ugly organs – begin to multiply. All wanting the same thing: to rape Sema's beliefs. It is all Oya can do to keep from screaming.

A door opens. But not into a room. This iron door leads into a military prison that was once a stable. Zafer the policewoman steps inside. Her gun in one hand, her truncheon in the other. With her pale green uniform and her black socks, she is the only one who blends in with her surroundings. All the other women – the ones who don't fit in with them at all – are standing in line in front of the beds. At the end of the line is Çiğdem. Holding up her right arm, which is in a plaster cast. How white it is, Oya thinks, next to those black socks. This could be a horror film. After she came back from torture, when she was only half conscious, convinced that someone was trying to kill her, Çiğdem had jumped out the window. She's still not fully recovered. As she stands there in line, her blank-eyed face is as white as her cast. Whatever Zafer commands, in a bark that Oya can barely believe has come from a female larynx, Cigdem obeys. "Attention!" "At ease!" These are not just commands. These are kicks and blows, squealing. The truncheons they used on Sema and so many others.

"Attention! At ease. You! I said at ease."

But Çiğdem cannot lower her arm. Her face is as white as a face in an open casket being lowered into a grave. Her gaze emptied of all expression, as only those suffering deep pain can do.

The arm inside her plaster cast is festering with sores. Sores that bear witness to her days of torture, and the marks it has left on her young mind. Silently, making no complaint, she holds up her festering plastered arm for all to see.

There she stands, silent, determined to travel through this time of doubt and confusion alone. And now Zafer is walking toward her, wielding her big black truncheon. As if to locate the one part of this innocent creature's body that has yet to be broken.

"At ease! At ease I said!"

Çiğdem shows no reaction. She stands there as if she hasn't heard Zafer's command, as if she hasn't even seen her. As if there is nothing in the world but her beautiful heart. As if everything they wanted to break in her is now encased in plaster. There she stands, silently waiting to be repaired. And it's as if the truncheon in Zafer's hand and the gun on her hip are not enough for her. As if it wasn't in Zafer's power to turn her key in the lock and shut them all behind that iron door. As if there were no barbed wire fences outside, no guards patrolling them with submachine guns. She still must vent the full force of her fury on Çiğdem. She wants to beat her, tear her up, wipe her off the face of the earth. As slowly, very slowly every other woman in this barrack, moves toward that truncheon.

Once again Oya looks at the empty sheet in front of her. So far she has written just one word: TRUNCHEON! No wonder. A blank sheet of paper, and then the police, and then a truncheon. She tears up the sheet of paper. What can she write? Does she need to write anything? Should she try and prove her innocence? But who here is the offender? What is the crime? Maybe she should go back to the beginning. Start with the truncheons, and the barbed wire. The submachine guns, and Zafer. Build it up from there. But she still has to defend herself. Speak up against this ridiculous and unjust raid. Stand up for human rights. Pointless! Abdullah and Zekai will find any number of justifications for the raid. And any number of crimes to charge Oya with. What should she be defending under these circumstances? What should she be denying? The more she thinks, the greater her confusion. She considers listing all her splendid connections for Zekai Bey, before giving up on the idea. They'll say she was trying to provoke them, she'll only be playing into their hands. The best thing is to leave the page blank. But why should I shy away from defending myself, why am I not standing up for my rights, why am I not doing everything I can to regain my freedom?

I was only a guest in the house that was raided for unknown reasons this evening. Of those who were present in the house at the time, I am only acquainted with the lawyer, Hüseyin Başgör. He is not a close friend. I met up with him in connection with my case at the Adana Court of Justice. Because I knew no one in Adana, he offered to help me with a number of minor matters. This evening he invited me to supper with his relatives. I have nothing else to say . . .

Even as she writes out these sentences, she has to laugh at them. This is only making the whole thing more ridiculous. She tears up this sheet too. Tears it into tiny pieces and puts them all into the palm of her hand, before blowing on them. Off they fly, all across the room. One or two white shreds landing on top of the truncheon. Black and white. Zafer and Çiğdem.

There is it before her, Çiğdem's face. Plastered on the wall before her, like a poster, to give a face to all the ugliness, all the injustice. The posters and the walls begin to multiply. The more space they take, the less there is for the ugliness. The baleful menace in Abdullah's face shrinks and shrinks until it's as small as an insect underfoot. A sewer fly, fetid with microbes, but small enough to fight against. Small enough to destroy. The faces of every policeman she's ever known – they seep into Abdullah's face. While Abdullah's face seeps into the face of every other policeman she's ever known.

And then, they all merge, and there before her is Güllü the Professional's policeman lover.

Asuman Yemez, the leader of the gang, has her hands on her hips, the gold bracelets on her fat arms sparkling. "Prostitutes! Adulterers! Let Asuman bow to your needs. Today all your teas are on me. You'll never find another like me . . . You'd have a hard time finding anyone else in this place who knows the value of a little pussy." Asuman Yemez is a nightclub owner. She is the protector of unregistered prostitutes and their bread and butter. She's found ways of using them in Ankara Central Prison, too. She reaches out to every girl and woman charged with prostitution or adultery and takes them under her wing. Her racket is to feed them a little, protect them a little, and then use them to her own ends. They are all indebted to Asuman Yemez, and because they know they might need her one day on the outside they try to stay in her good books. Asuman is a big woman, even by their standards. Standing beside Asuman, who answers to no man, and who can make even the most troublesome waiter tremble, a working girl can feel safe. Even if she feels herself crushed and cheap and reduced to nothing, Asuman's attentions let her hold her head high. Asuman's inside because she shot her lover after finding out he wanted to leave her. She tricked him into driving out to the dam and shot him there. He survived, but the case ended up in military court: he'd gone to Martial Law Command and denounced her. Asuman struts around the courtyard in her purple velvet pantaloons, hands on hips, jangling the golden bracelets on her fat arms.

"Can there ever be justice in this world, dear girls? Give a little pussy and it's sorted. If Martial Law Command hadn't interfered, I could have sent my waiters after the family of that brute who put me in here." Asuman Yemez talks about her waiters as if they're her personal army. The prison's hapless, hopeless working girls listen to her transfixed. They're at her beck and call, making her tea, scrubbing her back, doing her laundry. The only one who doesn't defer to her is Güllü, the registered prostitute. She knows she'll never need Asuman. She's not even bothered by how strong she is. This greatly annoys Asuman, who is of the view that all the prison's prostitutes, registered or unregistered, should defer to her in all things.

"Güllü, my girl," she says. "This whoring nation is never going to thank you. It's only big sisters like me who protect girls from falling prey to wicked men. Instead you go and put your trust in drivers, waiters, or the police. Since when have the police had any love for us prostitutes? Sit. Sit. With God's will, you can spend another twenty years inside. And look. I'm writing it down. In a week, I'm out of here. I'm never coming back, and neither are any of my girls. Even if they've been at my nightclubs for just three days, I'll keep them safe. As for that lover of yours, the policeman you wish was dead . . ."

Güllü springs to her feet, wraps her hands around Asuman's neck:

"Don't you dare, God damn it! On Abdullah's life, repent!"

Güllü is doing time for shooting her lover, Abdullah the police-man. Be that as it may, she's not going to let Asuman kill her love. If anyone kills him, it will be her. She's not going to bow down to Asuman and her purple pantaloons. She might be a state-registered prostitute, but she knows a thing or two about the underworld. She has tricks up her sleeve.

Asuman turns her chafed neck towards Ulviye:

"This woman is getting horny, now that she can no longer prac-tice her profession!" Her gang of helpless little prostitutes and adulterers laugh with her.

"Think of the men your Abdullah reports to, and then think the rest of your way up the ladder. Those are the police officers I know. Those are the ones who kiss my hand. All I have to do is send over two girls and their doors swing wide open! They even get me permits for my waiters' guns!"

Güllü draws away, leaves the courtyard to sit in the dark bar-rack inside. Silent, like Çiğdem. Asuman shouts after her:

"Didn't anyone tell you that pussy makes the world go round? Or not to waste your youth on a fool policeman? Find someone to stick a truncheon up your pussy while you still can!"

Truncheons everywhere. In Zafer's hand. And Asuman's curses.

Truncheons . . . and police.

At the far end of the dormitory, amid all the stink that women's bodies can emit, Güllü sits rocking on her bed. "She's keening," the other women say. To Oya its sounds like a poem. Why can she be nothing to the world but a registered prostitute? Couldn't she be a poet as well? There probably was a time – no, definitely, there was a time – when this woman wasn't a prostitute, but she might have been a poet from the very start. One thing is sure. She wasn't always a state-registered prostitute. Just as Çiğdem didn't always have a broken arm. And Zafer hadn't always been wielding a truncheon. But right now, she's at it again. Swinging that truncheon and yelling. Right now, Çiğdem's face is ghostly white. Sema is no longer crying, she's over her shame. In court, she will find the strength to swing her bloody underpants at the so-called cornerstone of justice, screaming "I was tortured!" Shaking the shame she'd wanted to hide away like dirty laundry. Sending it back at them, like a boomerang. But Güllü . . . Güllü is a registered prostitute who's in jail for shooting her policeman lover. Her future is easy to read. No boomerangs for her. She'll be in here until the next general amnesty, and then she'll go back to working at a state brothel. She could well find herself another policeman lover. But if she does, she can be sure that he will treat her like dirt while going through her money, until she'll want to shoot him, too. She can make all number of little changes to start over again, over and over. This Oya knows. When Güllü tells Oya her story, she tries hard to look as if she's hearing something new.

It shames her, to think that she'd taken Güllü for something so ordinary and static.

Güllü grew up in a village. What was so surprising about that? Had she really expected her to be the daughter of a civil servant? Her husband went to Austria as a guest worker. There was a second wife. And then, the usual. The family keeps the second wife, but not Güllü. Güllü picks up baby Menderes and hits the road. The road is long and full of obstacles, but it is clear it will end at a state brothel.

Here she is, in this office at Adana Police Headquarters, breathing in its bureaucratic fumes, looking at that truncheon, and thinking of Güllü. She longs to add something new to her story, but she can't. The most she can do is imagine her policeman lover's grave. Abdullah's grave. With a huge marble headstone shaped like a truncheon. Yes, it's hard to add anything new to Güllü's story, not without fooling herself. It was just Güllü's way. Rocking back and forth in that dormitory and keening:

You sent my love
To Austria
Dressed like a village
I lay down, bereft

The firmament turned to winter
My love left me, to marry another

My wicked brother-in-law showed me the door
Will the distance between us grow shorter?

No need for him to move mountains to reach Austria
But my wicked brother-in-law cast me off.
He gave me no help
Bereft and penniless
I had to sell all I had.

Tie your shoelaces tight
Set out on your journey
A brother-in-law can do this much at least
Instead the wicked man broke my marriage vows.

The mountains of Austria are far away they said
I let my hair grow, they said it was a trap
They pity someone who's away for six months
But if you are away more than a year, they say homesick

A dress of water cannot fly
My yellow boots are shining
Why are you crying, Menderes my son
Your father will be waiting for you in Austria

Actually this lament isn't original either. It's just one of so many Oya heard in Ankara Central Prison. She'd seen so many women like Güllü. Women branded as thieves or murderers, rogues or Gypsies. Women whose painted fingernails seemed best suited for reaching into shop windows and men's wallets. In the dusty, dull yellow light of the dormitory, she'd watched them write their laments on the tear-soaked pages of their cheap notebooks. All of them as ordinary as Güllü's. Like most real-life heartaches. *Why are you crying, Menderes my son. Your father is waiting for you in Austria.* In the valley of heartache, it was, in truth, an ordinary tale. She imagines Güllü holding little Menderes to her chest as she walks across the fields, which even if they are as fertile as the fields of Çukurova, will do nothing to lessen an ordinary heartache. No shoes on the boy's feet. No, he's wearing those standard orphan shoes, made of horsehair and cut-up tires. While I wait in this office at Adana Police Headquarters, I can send Güllü down any road I wish. As I can do for myself, if I get out of here. No, when. I'm getting out. That's definite. Just as definite as Güllü's not taking the road I've designed for her, just as definite as her ending up back in a state brothel, if they release her from Cebeci Prison.

Why am I thinking of Güllü right now? Or Çiğdem? Or Sema? Oya is desperate for a cigarette. Is that why she's thinking of them? How shameful, to think that she's not really thinking of Güllü or Çiğdem or Sema, but about cigarettes. But she has no cigarettes with her. Once again, the office expands to become a vast plain. Her thoughts flow down the middle, like the Menderes River. A noisy band of women arrives from Çukurova, spreading across the fields, picking cotton. They have tattoos on their faces. They're speaking Kurdish and Arabic. This time she makes them look like extras in a film. We always fall back on the same things. But how wrong it is, to shape memories to suit our own purposes, to do the same with living people. Oya tries to form a human bond with them, to be there with them, sharing their hopes and sorrows. But no, she can't. She can't connect with these women whose gold teeth will be their only reward for their summers under the murderous sun. Each and every one of them is a vehicle, there to help her bear this office, which is becoming harder to bear with every moment. As she sits back in her reasonably comfortable plastic chair, she can almost imagine she is watching a documentary on television. Thinking that this scene might be cut, and that scene made sharper. But she is overcome by a very ordinary, frustrating sadness: Güllü never makes it over the finely drawn mountain. She walks along the Menderes River. Walks and walks, maybe even as far as the Danube. Why are you crying, Menderes my son. Your father is waiting for you in Austria. At the road's end is a mountain. An insurmountable mountain. A mountain, at least, that Güllü can never hope to climb. She stands there before it, with Menderes in her arms.

Oya is crying. Rocking back and forth in her chair, like Güllü. Who am I crying for? For myself? For Güllü? Back in Ankara Central Prison, Oya's soft, unscarred heart had been so deeply touched by Güllü's lament that she'd burst into tears. Whereupon Güllü had asked, "Why are you crying? Because they hanged your friend Deniz Gezmiş?"

Taken by surprise, Oya said, "I'm crying for you."

Same as now. She's crying. She doesn't want to ask herself why. She's crying, and while she cries, she remembers all the things that made her cry before, and she cries about them, too. For them, and for herself. But most of all, she's probably crying because instead of being in her hotel, asleep in the bed that suddenly seems so lovely and comfortable, she's sitting here, waiting for an uncertain dawn.

The teardrops falling onto her hand are become steadily smaller. She waves that hand back and forth, just like she did when she was a child, until the teardrops are all flowing into each other. Maybe Güllü's story isn't true. Couldn't she have invented a past for herself, like every other prostitute? But what importance would that have? So she's a prostitute. This story is as true as the little beaded lace embroideries she knits to sell. Even if Güllü didn't walk with babe in arms across a plain, even if she didn't search the mountains of Austria for some sign of her husband, that changes nothing. She's inside because she shot her policeman lover. And isn't Oya playing the same trick on herself?

To prove to herself that her current plight will pass, she's pinning her hopes on immutable fate. Using Güllü's voice to suppress her own fears:

"So you know there's that place called Germany? No husband to be found. And then I started to crave men. Show me a good-looking man and there was no resisting him. I fell bigtime for the factory manager. The man wouldn't give me the time of day. *Nicht schoen*, he kept saying. Not pretty enough. *Du schwartz.* Which means, you're black. I wasn't thinking straight. During recess I cornered a man, pushed him behind the door. *Kuss,* I said. That means kiss me. The man pushed me . . . And I wounded him."

Güllü, whose heart is more wounded beyond what any switch-blade could do. She won't hide behind a man. Instead, she attacks. "I spent time in prison there in Germany. They placed Menderes in a home. It was good for him. They fattened him up a little. I thought I was in there for life. It was nothing like this place. That place was like a hotel. There were showers. A cinema, too. But they didn't keep me. They threw Menderes into my arms and said off you go. Put us on a train. With a ticket to Ankara. I had no one in Ankara. For a week, I walked the streets. You know where Gençlik Park is? Well, I was sitting there. And then, you know that scoundrel I was talking about? The late lamented policeman."

"Abdullah?"

"Yeah. Abdullah. Well, he came up to me. He put me in a state brothel, God bless him. Fed me and the boy both. Over two years, he got ten thousand lira out of me. For our food and drink, he said. But never mind. I would do it again. If he hadn't gone off with that woman . . ."

Suddenly Güllü goes mad. She tries to kiss Oya on the lips.

"One kiss! One *kuss*!"

Güllü lunges at her. Remembering another story they tell about her – that she tried to strangle another inmate in a fit of jealousy – Oya pulls away in fright. She legs it to the stairs.

But there is Güllü, barring the way. Oya darts into the toilet that is filled to the brim with baby shit. Just the sight of her fills Oya with terror. There she was, trying to help this woman, trying to understand her. She doesn't even have the stamina to be near her, to accept her existence. So much for trying to change this woman, or make a new life for her . . . And this Oya who's gone to hide in the toilet, how can she ever hope to change? Or remake herself? This is a difficult question. An important question. It must be asked. It takes more than one person to change someone. It takes a whole new order, she tells herself. A new society. A new country. Powerlessness. Such a bad place to hide.

Oya's stomach is churning. She's eye to eye now with the hairs on Güllü's upper lip. To suppress her revulsion, for Güllü and for herself, she dries her tears.

Back there in Esen Park, when Güllü caught Abdullah the policeman with another prostitute on his arms, and shot him on the spot, she was, despite all the ugliness in her, also beautiful. Oya searches her brain for an old photograph of a woman with that kind of beauty, but she fails. Her stomach is churning. That's all she can think about. That, and the hint of lust in Zekai Bey's anger. I didn't have anything to eat tonight. That explains it. What she would give now for a cigarette. She can see it before her eyes now: the cigarette Zekai Bey offered to her. If only I'd accepted it. If only I'd taken the whole pack from his hand. Or even that carton sitting on his desk. Grab it! No, it's good she didn't accept that cigarette he offered her. Her will is weakening, though. Time is Oya's enemy. And that's a fact.

The door opens.
    "Can you find me a cigarette?"
Oya is shocked. That these words came out of her mouth before she even knew who it was coming in. It's Abdullah. So there we have it. Güllü might have killed one Abdullah, but she didn't get around to killing all the others. Did Güllü's Abdullah have the same filthy scowl as this one? Suddenly she has no desire for a cigarette. Even if Abdullah brought her one, she'd wave it away. It does her good to think of all those other Abdullahs. Especially the Abdullah that Güllü shot dead. It does her good, to imagine each new Abdullah bleeding into the next. To see their truncheons multiplied and shared.
    "You're from Diyarbakır, are you?"

Now it's Abdullah's turn to be surprised. Even though he's used to people asking him where he's from. What's your country? It's the first thing he asks people, too. The first step toward friendship. But he has no wish to get to know Oya, let alone befriend her. Abdullah has no interest in knowing where people like Oya come from. They come from a different sort of place, these types. They have no country. He knows this from his time in the army. If a shout went round – "Anyone here from Maraş? Anyone from Siverek?" – these were the ones who turned around and asked, "Why do they want to know where I come from?" He'd stand there, wondering how to answer. In those days, he still had a lot to learn.

But Oya knows exactly why she's asking. She's wants to multiply him. Dilute his hateful features. Take some pleasure from that, relax, and take a deep breath, before curling back into her shell. And then, as if in response to the answer Abdullah has yet to offer, she asks another question.

"Do you know Firdevs?"

She doesn't expect an answer. Abdullah has already left the room. In his hand are the sheets of paper on which Oya has scribbled her words.

She has eyes as dark as grapes, this Firdevs. She's a Kurd, and she's been doing odd jobs in exchange for cigarettes and food for the past two years. At this moment, she's wearing shalwars and nothing else. Her two-year-old child is sucking from her naked breast, which is wrinkled as if she'd been nursing babies since the dawn of time. She's standing at the door of the toilet where Oya has gone to hide from Güllü. She's here to sweep it clean.

Firdevs is serving a 24-year sentence for hashish smuggling. It's hard to understand how a woman so poor, helpless, and unprotected could ever have been involved in a big money operation like drug smuggling. Where are the real smugglers? Oya wonders. Not to mention the Abdullahs of the world, who take their cut? They're nowhere to be found. Just Firdevs, serving out her twenty-four years. They caught her somewhere in Diyarbakır with her son Cevdet, who is now four years old. The reason: a denunciation. The baby now on her breast was still in her womb then. In the sash around her swollen belly they found many kilos of hashish. The police were almost going to take the baby out. More hashish in there, they must have thought. She had nothing else to give. And now? She has herself and her babies, nothing else. No visitors. No one to negotiate for her. No money either. She keeps herself and the two children fed by working as a cleaner. She's resigned to her sentence, just as she was resigned to give birth amid the excrement of this toilet.

"I know nothing about hashish. I never smoked any – for the sake of Ahmet and Cevdet's health. My man's the one in the know. All the other men, too."

"Which men?"

"Men. Just men. That's all I know. The masters of the goods. My man is a bold one. That's why they made him a courier. He did that for them. That's all I knew. And then he said, Firdevs, the big guys know who I am now, you can be the courier from here on in, and I'll get you brought over to Syria."

"Didn't you ask him to explain things a bit more?"

"It's wrong to ask a man any questions! One question got me five blows from my Abdullah. He's that kind of man . . ."

The kind of man, Oya thinks, who sees trouble coming and so offloads it onto his wife. Who, when she's caught with one baby in her arms and another in her belly, makes himself scarce. It shocks her, this brand of masculinity, as much as this helpless woman's acceptance of it. Firdevs blames her Abdullah for nothing. He may have beaten her for no reason, left her penniless with two children and no one to speak on her behalf, to waste away in a prison so far from home. But still she feels no rancour for the men who put her inside.

Who knows. Maybe Abdullah found his way across the minefields. Made it across the border, with his heart in his throat. Saved his skin by using his wife and children as a punching bag. To live a dog's life on the other side. But what about the real smugglers? The money men? The ones Firdevs calls the masters of the goods?'

They got what they wanted, by hook and by crook. And now they've gone back into their lairs. Oya wants Firdevs to understand this evil story.

"I don't know who they are, these masters," Firdevs keeps saying. "I never met them."

Fine. But what about the men who caught this woman who was brave enough to wrap all those kilos of hashish around her swollen belly? What about the men who sentenced her to 24 years? Did they really not know she was part of a larger network? Did the thought never even cross their minds? They must have known nothing, seen nothing. Here was Firdevs, poorer than the poorest woman in the poorest village, who'd wrapped that hashish around her belly, maybe out of love, maybe to avoid a beating, but most probably to feed her children. Who had not a clue as to what hashish was worth or what sort of trouble she was getting herself into. When they sentenced Firdevs and her children to 24 years in jail, these fine men probably thought they were doing their job.

Then they forgot all about her. But they should have been here to watch Firdevs waking up every morning at five to clean the toilets. And Ahmet, sucking hopelessly on his mother's breast. And Cevdet, who learns to speak in this prison, who knows nothing of life but the wet slaps he gets from everyone he passes in this courtyard. Like all the little ones in here, Cevdet knows how to wheedle and beg, to a degree that leaves Oya shaken. For two years now, he's been pulling at his mother's legs and crying. "Bubaa! Bubaa!" After Firdevs finishes with the toilets, she goes on to tackle the courtyard, the stone floors, and the sewage that has leaked from the ceiling onto the kitchen floor. When he isn't clinging to her shalwar, Cevdet is emptying the bins and rolling around in the rubbish. A little later, the warden comes in with the bread. Firdevs gets into a scuffle with the Gypsies after trying to cut slices for her two children as well as for herself. Cevdet starts crying, loud enough to be heard over the women's screams.

And what did Oya do, after seeing all this? She had good white bread coming to her from the outside. So she gave her ration to Firdevs. Only for the Gypsies to go after Firdevs again, to get their hands on the prize. With the same force they used on little Cevdet, when Oya gave him a piece of cake. They wrested it out of his hands and gave it to their own babies.

Abdullah has left his truncheon behind again. "Do you know Firdevs? The Firdevs from your own Diyarbakır? The Kurdish woman you left behind?"

This Abdullah could even be Firdevs's Abdullah. Abdullah the policeman. The real hashish smugglers, the ones who made Firdevs take the rap – maybe they'd got rid of him by putting him into the police force, to work alongside those who sang to their tune. Safely installed in Adana, he has put Firdevs and her two babies out of his mind. Oya felt herself dozing off. She rubbed her eyes. Here I am in a room that couldn't hold more than three officers by day. Look how many people I've pulled into it now. What am I really doing here? Trying to give my night some human interest. Trying, in other words, to imagine myself different from all my fellow citizens currently spending the night in jails and police stations across the nation. But all nightmares look much the same. At least if they want to frighten themselves. None of her diversions have worked. Not the chocolates and cakes she gave little Cevdet, or the money she gave his mother. Not the guilt that keeps growing and changing shape, every time Firdevs comes back to haunt her.

No matter how much she imagines Firdevs suffering, no matter how much she tries to make Abdullah worse than he actually is, the guilt won't budge. This Abdullah works for Adana Police Headquarters. He raided a house tonight and brought us all in. Oya, who can look forward to being charged with praising Communism, is a woman who gave little Cevdet the chocolates she'd not wanted to eat herself, for fear of getting fat. A woman who was happy to find someone like Firdevs to wash her clothes for a fee, and who as soon as she was set free, forgot all about that little boy who had no chocolate to eat, no father to care for him either. That's enough to make her guilty of a crime. More than enough.

Oya closed her eyes. She wants to lay her head down on the table and sleep. If she'd hoped her daydreaming would help her pass the time, she was wrong. It would have been better to concentrate on what was happening here tonight, and the statement she would soon be forced to make. Or on the streets outside, the Mediterranean, the palm trees. That could have strengthened her wish to be free.

Thinking about Zafer's hysterical cries, and her black socks, and Çiğdem standing in front of her, as white as a lily, and Sema, waving her bloody panties for all the world to see, and Menekşe, burying her lover in a cabbage patch, and Güllü, the state-registered prostitute, and Firdevs, and little Cevdet – these things only weaken her wish for freedom. How can she speak of freedom, next to people like this? How can she speak of guilt?

The guilt she has been carrying inside her tonight is heavier and more suffocating than anything they could think to charge her with, and more gruesome even than Abdullah's face. It presses down on her so hard as to make Zekai Bey's curses seem as light as poplar fluff, crushing her, sapping her strength.

"I must think about myself, and nothing else." She said this out loud. She set about pacing the room. One long stride after another. Why did they bring me here? No reason. Utterly frivolous, this raid. Have I done anything wrong? No. I'll be out by morning. Or by next week at the latest. My exile's almost over. I'll be extra careful during my final week here. I won't even pick up the phone. I can manage a week like that. And then it's on the plane and off to Ankara. And then? Pointless to think now about what comes next.

She stopped. Went back to her chair and sat down. Time

to write down something sensible. She paused. Remembered Abdullah, leaving the room with her pages. Damn it. What a fool she is! Did she really think she could get out of this without making a statement? I have no choice – I have to do this. Push away your crazy thoughts and sit down, write a proper statement. Get yourself out of this. Now! You must choose your battles carefully, very carefully indeed. As carefully as love. You must be open to all battles, see the beauty in the world and its importance. But you must choose the ones you wish to fight. If you just sit here refusing to write your statement – is that a battle worth fighting? Oooof. What use will beautiful sentences do me in here? Beauty knows no shadows. It has no place in here. She stands up, begins to pace the floor again. She remembers that she might be getting her period. She checks her trousers. Nothing. It's just anxiety. Nothing more. Grabbing the pages she'd not used for her statement, she pushes them down her trousers.

The office is wreathed in smoke. Zekai Bey stubs out his cigarette in the metal ashtray that was a new year's gift from Ismet Bey, the manager of the International Industry and Commerce Bank. He likes this ashtray. When he presses on a lever at its side, all the ashes fall into a lower chamber. Zekai could spend entire days playing with his lighter, his ashtray, and a good fountain pen. He prefers them to people, he feels more attached to them. But he needed to keep changing these little gadgets. To keep himself happy. The people Zekai Bey keeps around him are well aware of this, and they do what they can to keep him happy. But now, when Zekai Bey pushes down on the ashtray's little lever, nothing happens. And that annoys Zekai Bey to no end. Someone had broken his ashtray. He was about to ring the bell for the janitor and give him a good scolding, when he remembered that he'd brought his little daughter Ayça into the office with him that morning. And she'd been playing with the ashtray. Zekai Bey lost his frown. He doted on this little daughter of his, born after ten years of marriage. She was the only one in the world who could break his beloved gadgets and get away with it. He imagined her tiny little fists and smiled. Why fret over an ashtray, my dear? He remembered now that he'd promised to bring her a box of colored pencils. When she woke up in the morning, she'd be upset not to find them next to her bed. Because that was what she grown to expect: if she asked her father for something, it was waiting there for her when she woke up. It looked like this anarchist business was going to keep him here till morning. As soon as the shops open, I'll send out the chauffeur to buy them. He can drop them off at the house. But what if his wife is still asleep then? She'll be asleep, for sure. When does the lazy thing ever wake up when she should? The thought of his wife has Zekai Bey frowning again. His mother had chosen this woman for him because of the land she owned in the Karataş District. But in all this time, God be his witness, it's never brought him more than a tin or two of olive oil. In exchange for that olive oil, he had to spend his days with this stillbirth of a woman. Her pudgy round face. Her skin so dark it verged on purple. Always complaining of backaches or some other ache in that husky voice of hers. And oh, how she huffed and puffed when she got up in the morning. Thinking now of the thick, dark, oily hairs she left on her pillow, his stomach went sour. But they did still have relations once a week. This he still did. It had to be done, and with the same fury he gave to pacing his office on days when he decided his men were due a scolding.

Furiously, he rose from his chair. For a few minutes, he paced the room. Then he paused in front of the chair that Oya had occupied some time earlier. There was a spot of blood on it. For a moment he was afraid. Did she secretly cut her wrists. No, she's strong and healthy. Then suddenly it came to him. He smirked. A butterfly in his stomach. The whore! Sitting there right across from me! You're going to take her like this, by the hair . . . He pressed down hard on his lust rising up inside him. Before sitting down again, he rang his bell. When the janitor appeared, he told him to wipe the chair clean.

"Tell Abdullah to bring in the teacher."

At that moment it occurred to him that Oya and this teacher might have something going. As his mind filled with images of lewd coupling, his fury grew. He'd been fooled. Yes, he'd been fooled. But now he was going to show them what for. The whore and her lover. "They're headed back inside, these two." He said this out loud. When he saw the janitor gaping in amazement, he sent him away. The telephone rang.

"Yes, sir. Yes."

He stood up.

"We're investigating, sir. We'll be here till morning if that's what it takes . . . It's our duty . . . No sacrifice is too . . . Tomorrow. The culprits and the documents . . . I see, sir . . . Is it not necessary, sir? But . . . A meeting . . . If you ask me, sir, the circumstances are suspicious . . . That woman and the teacher . . . If we don't get anything out of them . . . of course . . . but still . . . to keep the investigation on a sound footing. Certainly. We can release them at any point we wish. We've not established any positive proof. Sir? We await your orders. Sir!" He put down the phone. One minute they say arrest these anarchists. Next minute they say let them go. His blood rushed to his head. What's become of us, damn it? Is this some sort of child's game? Did I leave my card game tonight for this? Did we get landed with this whore for nothing?

A knock on the door. Zekai Bey placed himself at the window, as if to imply he's expecting no visitors.

Mustafa's face is ashen. But he doesn't know this. His aim: to look strong, sound of body and mind. Like all revolutionaries everywhere. At all costs, to avoid the trap of humiliation. But still, his face is pale. From chain smoking in an airless cell holding six people. And indulging in the intellectual's most ridiculous habit: trying to separate the rational from the illogical. He's been down in that cell trying to figure out how he ended up here. So soon after being released. Before even seeing his family. Above all, without having done anything yet. *Without having done anything.* What a laughable phrase. Or so it seems to Mustafa. Here he is, giving substance to their very idea of crime. And what does that mean? It means that we too are slowly coming to accept ourselves as guilty on their terms. That it's a crime to have done something. That innocence is to have done nothing. Since when did we start thinking the struggle was a crime, and doing nothing was innocence and brilliance? He's all knotted up inside. Is he beginning to weaken? When he should be steeling himself for his next prison. For the next round of hard knocks. He must see what is to come as no more than happenstance. What is only to be expected in a war or on its outskirts. If they detain me now, I cannot call it an injustice. Think of yourself as a prisoner of war. You could be drinking water from a tap, and they still could take you in.

Injustice? He took a good long look at the man standing before him – at his tired, yellowed eyes, which carried the mark of his long nights of gambling. Hard to know what color they were. The bags underneath were deep purple. These were the eyes of a dog too old even to light up at the sight of his master. What can he expect from this man? Justice or injustice? How can he expect a dog to know the difference? To think he could expect justice from this man would be handing himself over to a dog. Blood rushed to his face. Zekai Bey could thank his many years of experience for picking up on this change in his victim right away. He was angry. This ruined Zekai Bey's plan of playing cold and condescending. But this was not an equal contest. He could use this opportunity to vent his hatred.

"You dirty dog. Having it off with your friend's wife, are you?"

At the same moment, he takes a swing at him. Mustafa is not expecting this. The insanity of it all throws him. He holds his hand over the cheek that took the punch. Zekai Bey is glad to see his victim rattled. He sits down and lights himself a cigarette.

Here he is again, falling into the old trap. Trying to defend himself. He stops rubbing his face and pulls himself together. Clenches his fists. In silence. Whatever Zekai Bey says, he'll be falling into his trap if he tries to defend himself. He thinks it over one more time. He makes up his mind.

Zekai Bey knows how to get under a man's skin. Through the corner of his eye, he watches Mustafa, waits for him to react. Few men can resist the urge to defend themselves when accused of eyeing up a friend's wife. This Zekai Bey knows. If he can get this man to ask for names, or times, if he can lure him into denials or corrections, he'll go a long way to wearing him down. The secret is to hit them where they least expect it. Wear the victim down by accusing him of crimes he's not committed. Scramble his brain. And then, at the very moment they expect the very worst from you, you start treating them well. Years of experience have taught him all this.

"Would you like a cigarette?"

Mustafa almost reaches out, catching himself just in time. A cigarette would provide an opening. An opening on the enemy's terms. Mustafa has no intention of falling for it. He knows the drill. These little mercies between beatings. He's been here before. In Istanbul, during his fifteen days of hell, they'd played the same game.

They'd interrogated him in pairs – one good, one bad. Though it would be more accurate to say that there'd been three bad apples for every good one. After the bad apples were done with their curses and their beatings, their falakas and their electric shocks, they'd disappear to be replaced by an interrogator who asked for nothing. Who'd just look into Mustafa's eyes, blinking as if to fight back tears. Who'd say, *my lion*. Who'd give him water. Is there anything you need? he'd ask. If you need me to pass on a message for you, don't hesitate to ask. It's the least I could do for you. I'm ashamed, he'd say. Today it's you. Tomorrow it could be us. And Mustafa had so believed in his new friend's troubled conscience that he had actually tried to console him. Saying, don't be so hard on yourself, my brother, it can't be helped. Later on, he mentioned this friend to another inmate in his cell. Saying, some of them are on our side. Pressing the point too hard, perhaps, in the way people do if they need to cling to hope. Talking then about this man who was ready to pass on messages for them to people on the outside. His cellmate had asked what his name was. Hearing it, he had given Mustafa a bitter smile. "So he's the one who's on our side? He's the one we're meant to trust? He's the one I've promised myself I'll kill one day. It's despicable, the way he does his job. He beat me, and stripped me, right in front of my fiancé. He . . ." His voice faded away, but his glare did not. It was as if he was blaming Mustafa for the same crimes. Mustafa spent the next days in some confusion. In those days of rest after torture, they offered him all sorts of food, but he couldn't touch a thing. It turned out that there was nothing to be confused about. After he had broached the subject with other friends, he found out that the identity of the good cop kept changing. The one who'd treated Mustafa the worst would turn out to be the one who'd treated a friend with kindness. Such were the rules of the game. They took turns playing the good cops and the bad. The interrogator who treated one victim well was the same one who treated another victim badly. All this in accordance with the rules by which they operated. And also, perhaps, to take a break. Whether they were being cruel or kind, it was endlessly exhausting work. This, in any event, is how Mustafa and his friends tried to see it when they were nursing themselves back to health. This must have been their way of distancing themselves from the ugly things that had been done to them. Their way of abstracting themselves from torture. To torture people, you need experience and you need knowledge. In his friends' view, these men had been trained for their work. The horror of what they were doing was lessened if they were going by the book, doing exactly as they'd been taught. Or they stopped seeing the horror altogether, Mustafa thought. The hardest thing is to be an amateur. An untrained torturer, a torturer drawing only from his own crude anger – he can suffer remorse, drive himself mad, even. But the professional torturer, the one who plays it by the rules – he'll never tire, will never suffer remorse. He will simply grow ever more confident in his work. This is his job, a job he knows well. Every new signed confession brings him satisfaction, and proof of his success.

Mustafa looked over at Zekai Bey. Next to those Istanbul interrogators, this man was an ignoramus. A policeman past his prime, a bigshot in his office, but nowhere else. For the first time ever, Mustafa is glad to have experienced hell. There's nothing this man can do to me. He can't confuse me or tire me out. He's certainly not going to fool me with the old cigarette trick.

"No cigarettes for me."

"Please! Take one! Listen, my son. You were only just released from prison. Do you have a child?"

"..."

"We happen to know you do."

"If you know, then why are you asking?"

"Can't you recognize fellow feeling when you see it? Of course, if you had really cared about your wife and child, you never would have got mixed up in this business in the first place."

Mustafa flinched. What does this man know about his wife and child? Or has something happened to Güler? Is that why he'd not heard from her this past month? Or had they . . . Why wouldn't they? Hadn't they been doing their best to make everyone's nearest and dearest feel unsafe? Suddenly he smiled. He looked up at Zekai Bey and smirked. No, of course not. If something had happened to Güler, I would have heard about it. Even where human rights and the constitution counted for nothing, news seeped in. Good news or bad, it had made its way through the prison walls. They had breathed it in and breathed it out, and in so doing kept their hearts beating. Mustafa relaxes. This Zekai couldn't touch Güler even if he wanted. His authority extends to the outskirts of Adana and no further. His hand cannot reach as far as Urfa, let alone Istanbul. The most he can do to me is to get me to sign some statement that will put me in jail. After that, I'll have all the time in the world. He looks at Zekai Bey, his expression neutral.

"I'd like to smoke now. But I'll have one of my own."

Before Zekai Bey can say anything, he reaches into his back pocket and takes out a pack of Birinci cigarettes. He lights up with a match. He inhales deeply, exhaling the smoke with force.

Zekai Bey longs to jump up and beat this Mustafa to a pulp. Even though he usually prefers to leave this job to others. It's dirty, exhausting work. And anyway, Zekai Bey knows revenge to be a dish best served cold.

"So you smoke Birincis, do you! The Communist cigarette!"

Mustafa glances over at Zekai Bey's Kents. Enough just to look. He opts to say nothing.

"Those who turn poverty into literature must be seen smoking the poor man's cigarette, it seems."

"Poverty is not literature."

"Glad to hear you say it. But let me ask you. What do you know about the people, huh? What do you know?"

". . ."

"Answer me, will you? You're a teacher, after all. The only thing you teachers know is arrogance. The people hate you, don't you know that, you fool?"

"Perhaps."

"What do you mean, perhaps? Shouldn't you be trying to endear yourself to these people you call the people?"

"That's what *you* should do. To justify the taxes the people pay. You take your wages out of their bread money."

"And who pays your wages, I wonder? Your father? Leave the people alone! Get off their necks, you lowlife!"

Mustafa says nothing. He tosses his cigarette to the ground and stubs it out with his shoe.

Zekai Bey looks with annoyance at the ash on the linoleum. It annoys him that Mustafa will not be drawn into an argument. It's getting late. He's too tired to continue with a one-way conversation. He needs a proper shouting match to keep himself awake. He's worked out by now that there is one thing and one thing only that would bring him true pleasure, and that would be getting a result from this interrogation. He suspects, though, that he's going to have to usher them out like little lambs come morning. First they crap on my evening, these scoundrels. And then they refuse to take me seriously. They should pay for it. And pay for it more. A night's not enough to bring them down. A day isn't either. I'm not letting any Communists out of here, and that's that. Guilty or not, they're staying.

Time to get another argument going. And when they're done arguing, he'll hand this dog over to two or three policemen who will give him a good beating. Having reached this decision, Zekai Bey relaxes.

"Where are you from?"

"Maraş."

"Good. I know the Southeast like the back of my hand. Its villages and its villagers. So let me tell you. Your ideas will never take root in these lands. The people are ignorant. They have no loyalty. Not to the nation. Not to its citizens. That's why we have to keep them under tight control. They'll do anything for money. Smuggle our national treasure across the border given half a chance. Blow themselves up taking sheep across the minefields. Night and day, we've been hammering it into them. Devoted our lives to teaching them loyalty to the nation. Its citizens. Its territorial integrity. Are we really going to close our eyes when you come here preaching treachery? Well, here is your answer. We never will. Understood?"

Mustafa's eyes are burning from fatigue. He's having a hard time keeping them open. He'd not slept at all on the night bus from Istanbul. It's like torture, this being half asleep and half awake. He would almost prefer Zekai Bey yelling at him and throwing a few punches. It would do me good to feel anger right now. Tomorrow is important. Güler is important. Whether they arrest him or not, tomorrow is important. He has to meet it with open eyes.

Zekai Bey won't stop talking. One singsong sentence after another.

"The nationnnnnnn!"

The vibrations he sets off by lengthening that word reach as far as Mustafa. His mind is swaying, like a cradle. Tomorrow. Tomorrow and Güler. Tomorrow he must not let himself be put inside. He has important things to do tomorrow. He tries to rouse himself. What happens at this moment might determine whether he goes back inside or not. He knows from experience that interrogations do not really determine that decision. Most of the time, the decision has already been made. From the suspect's perspective, an interrogation has little significance. But from the perspective of the interrogator, it does mean something. If there's something they wish to take or know, or something they wish to establish, a dossier they need to add to, an interrogation is important. A suspect under interrogation gives importance to something else entirely. Something far more important than freedom, or the prospect of losing it. What matters most is to protect their humanity under inhumane pressure. To hold onto their beliefs, in the movement and in themselves. To defend . . . Yes, that was the most important thing for a person in detention. To defend and stay safe. To protect. And then, to stay silent. To find the strength to stay silent. How hard it is, to stay silent. Even now, he's thinking he might have said too much. Silence. It serves other ends, too. Not to give anything away. Not to explain. Not to make the enemy's job easier. Not to point the way, and not to teach. Not to give the enemy the chance to learn from experience. If not for these reasons, silence would hold little importance for the one under interrogation. Last time, Mustafa had spoken. Said far more than needed. What he was able to say and what they forced out of him. They got so much more out of him than they'd needed.

To risk death. A phrase everyone knows. We used it often. And there were those who had indeed risked death. But to risk silence. We didn't dwell on that enough. Never tested it out. None of us knew how hard silence would be. We thought it would be enough to stay honest and courageous and true to our ideas. Silence would be something that came naturally. But then, all of us who ended up in that place – we all found out how wrong we were, and in the most painful way. It took more than honesty, courage, and commitment to stay silent. We talked about that a lot back in prison. We opened up about it, but not enough.

"Maybe this is the most important thing for us to be talking about." That was what Necdet had said one afternoon during Silent Hour. "Right now, we just skirt around it. Let ourselves off the hook. We shouldn't stay silent about why we end up talking. We used to take it for granted that a revolutionary never talked. Now we act as if it's natural for us to speak under torture. Wrong both times. Our new fatalism is just as false as our old romanticism. How should a revolutionary stay silent, and why? How can this be taught? How can we make this possible? It's why we all caved in: our refusal to accept that we would speak. And now, because we shy away from the subject – refuse to explore the reasons for talking – we're only setting ourselves up for new defeats. We learned how to risk death. Now is the time for us to learn about torture."

These words now seem as distant as childhood memories. We thought that to risk death was to risk everything. And that was our mistake. What made torture unbearable was wanting it to end. Wanting to be killed, in other words. His only wish had been for the interrogation to end in death. He'd wished that to the point of madness. There were those who'd seized the first chance they got. Did I really want to die? I don't remember. Most likely my fear of death was as great as my fear of torture.

Zekai Bey is looking at him. As if reading his thoughts.

"Actually, I see no reason why we should be breathing the same air," Zekai Bey says. "It's easy to make you talk. Why did you call this meeting? What was its purpose? You're going to sing for us now like a nightingale. Give us the whole story."

Best, Mustafa decides, to do my talking here and now, in this room. He doesn't think they're going to be able to spin this out too much longer. Otherwise, he'd have had to sit here until he melted like butter. This Zekai Bey wants to play cat and mouse with him. So let him.

"So let's begin. Why did you call this meeting?"

"It was a family gathering."

"A family gathering, you say. Shame on you. Fouling the institution of the family with your dirty ideas. What business did that Communist woman have at a family gathering?"

"She's our friend."

"Just one woman at the table with all those men? What were you going to do, have that prostitute dance for you?"

"She's not a prostitute!"

"Why are you getting angry? Because she's your lover? There's something going on between you, that's clear."

"I said she was a friend. Not a lover."

"So she's not a prostitute, and she's not your lover. So what business did she have there, with all those men?"

"Hüseyin invited her to supper. Because she was tired of being alone."

"Who's Hüseyin? Never mind. So she's this Hüseyin's lover."

"I said friend."

Mustafa is struggling to keep his anger under control. Every time this man calls Oya a prostitute, it's like he's cursing at Güler. Even if we're ready to risk anything, and commit ourselves body and soul, how will we ever reconcile ourselves to having our wives and sisters insulted? Just to think about it. It turns his stomach, just to think of what these men could do to Güler. The same foul things they've done to so many other revolutionaries' wives and lovers. The thought sends blood rushing to his brain. No, my man. I won't tolerate this.

"I won't tolerate this!"

He startles at the sound of his own voice. It must be the lack of sleep, he thinks. The upset. All that waiting. All those dark thoughts, knocking around my addled brain. The art of silence is hard to master.

He turns his head. Fixes his eyes on the doorknob.

"I have nothing to say."

To say this is to speak, though. What a pointless sentence. When I say I have nothing to say, I'm implying that I do actually have something to say but have chosen not to say it. He's getting tired.

"So you're saying you have nothing to say. But I know you'll find something to say. But it's pointless. Because we know everything. Why you called that meeting. As it happened, we were listening in. We have it all on tape!"

Now Mustafa remembers little Hasan telling his father that there were men standing outside the door. None of us paid him any need. But what about Ekrem? He'd come in with Hasan. He must have seen the policemen, too. So what did that mean? Why didn't he mention the men at the door? Ekrem must be with the police, then. He could have been recording them. But he doesn't quite fit the part of a secret policeman, Mustafa thinks. Policeman. Just the word is enough to make his skin crawl. More even than the thought that they'd been there. More than any crime, or any punishment. If Ekrem was with the police, what would he put in his statement? Would he need to put anything in writing, if it was all on that tape?

There was nothing to say, anyway. They'd discussed nothing. The frightening thing was to have let his guard down, little knowing that the police were listening. His fear of police had lost its shape and its moorings. It had become a constant anxiety, an obsession. Just as it had been in the old days. He pushed Ekrem from his mind. This was no time for unhealthy thoughts. Especially unhealthy thoughts that served no purpose.

"Which one of you used the word bourgeois?"

"I did. And what of it?"

He knows he should have smiled at Zekai Bey's question and let it pass. He should not have stood up to him. If Zekai Bey thinks it a crime to utter the word bourgeois, then why not make the most of his ignorance, why not show it for what it was, and have a bit of fun?

"I'm struggling to understand why the word bourgeois has to do with membership in a clandestine organization."

"So you take me for an ignoramus, do you? You think I don't know what is happening when the likes of you lecture workers about bourgeois this and bourgeois that? You're trying to provoke them to rise up against the bourgeoisie. You're trying to incite a revolution."

"The term bourgeois is a concept. In other words, the name of a thing. The scientific term for a class . . ."

Mustafa's voice trails off. As if it weren't already bad enough. He had to play the smart aleck. What's come over me? Since when is it my job to educate this man? I must think I'm back in the old days, in the coffeehouse in Kumkapı. It's as if nothing's changed between then and now. As if I'm back at university, talking up a storm.

Zekai Bey yawns. He rings his bell. Time to order himself a coffee. He has to make it through to morning. This game is beginning to bore him. Give me bridge any day. Bridge I know how to win. Nothing to amuse him here, though. He can't give this the concentration it needs. He can't even manage to get angry enough at this swarthy teacher's backtalk. He can't be bothered even to try. If he were sitting right now at that baize covered table in Muzaffer Bey's salon, he wouldn't be bored at all. He'd be roaring. Nothing would get to him. He'd forget it all. Forget. This was the word Zekai Bey used to measure the value of a thing. The more it allowed him to forget, the better it was. He never gave any thought to the things he wished to forget. But he went to a particular place, for example, and did a particular thing, then he needed to forget it all. "Listen to a woman's voice, and you forget everything. A man can forget everything if he stops to admire a view." Zekai Bey's only aim in life is to put himself in situations that allow him to forget. That's why he loves gambling. It helps him forget. Forget everything, until the new day dawns. But now here he is, with this swarthy little scamp who forgets nothing. Who's putting him on edge. Who's refusing to push him to the point where he could lose his temper and forget everything. He has to get angrier. Much, much angrier. If he fails at this, he'll be risking those who exempt themselves from the anger game. Things will go badly for him again. Like they did back at Muzaffer Bey's house, in the days when Turgut Sabuncu Beyefendi thought he could insult him.

Turgut Sabuncu Beyefendi is the owner of Mediterranean

Industries. He can count himself among the chief beneficiaries of the fertile Çukurova Valley. Much praised for his fine work in feeding and clothing the poor, Turgut Efendi is also Muzaffer Bey's boss. In his army days, Colonel Muzaffer Bey had been famous for putting as much pressure on the soldiers of Eastern Anatolia as the region's harsh climate. On retiring to take on his post at Mediterranean Industries, he'd made good use of the anger he'd cultivated in the army, venting it instead on the workers. Because Turgut Bey's family is refined and well-mannered. They've studied at Robert College, and in England, too. They don't like shouting or coarse behavior, and least of all brute force. They prefer to concern themselves with their charity work, leaving it to others to use whatever intimidation or brute force is needed to keep the workers in their place. But a point arrived when even Turgut Bey couldn't master his anger. Could no longer hold himself aloof. Zekai Bey remembers that evening well. That bridge party at Muzaffer Bey's, when Turgut Bey attacked him like a dog.

"You're not doing your job! Admit it. Admit it!"

Turgut Sabuncu Bey was foaming at the mouth. So much that he had to dab his mouth dry with his silk handkerchief. Forgetting the elegant manners that he wore like a tailored suit. Paying no attention to the other guests' efforts to calm him down. Flying into a rage because Zekai Bey had said that "unfortunately" the strike was "lawful."

The man had treated him like a dog. Proving to all that even here in Muzaffer Bey's salon, he was the boss. This refined gentleman who so disliked raising his voice. His squawks are still ringing in Zekai Bey's ears. "They came to me mumbling about the law. So tell me, why do we bother paying you? If the caravan is on the right path, what use are you dogs?" Later, when those dark days were well behind them, Turgut Beyefendi had regretted venting his rage on Zekai Bey, and had apologized. He'd sent his chauffeur over with two bottles of whiskey.

But for a long time, Zekai Bey had not been able to forget how the man had kicked him out like a dog. The memory kept returning to him. The only thing that truly erased it from his mind was gambling and winning big. But now, sitting here with Mustafa, it comes back to him: the evening when Turgut Bey attacked him, shouting in his face. Treating him like a dog. Actually, it was important to remember these things. That law business, it was bad. What if the workers started standing up for their rights again? If they walked out again, waving their arms? . . . Turgut Bey is hollering again, spraying spittle onto Zekai Bey's face. Spitting at him, almost. "Who's in charge of the law, I ask. Think about it. Who's the law for? They say they have rights under law! There's only one law. The law we know. The law that guarantees the social and economic order. How can a law be a law if it stands against that order? They were standing right in front of me. The ones the law should be stabbing were the ones holding the shields! Do I have to tell you your job, man? Use the sword of the law against the enemy! Since when is the law meant to work for all? The law belongs to us, or it belongs to them. And if it's ours – hear my command. Do your job. Use the law to do what the law's there to do. And if you can't, then get the hell out of here. Go join the other side. See how well you do with their law." More raving. More spittle.

Zekai Bey had always prided himself on living within the law. Enjoying the security it brought. But that night, he'd been shown that the law could not protect even him. Even worse, it had not saved him from being thrown out of that bridge party, thrown into the street like a dog. He wants to erase that lonely night. Forget shivering in that cold. He didn't go home. He'd gone straight back to headquarters, to order an instant raid. Thus to convince himself that he was a "man of the law." But even when the guards were making their ruckus, he still couldn't forget that moment when he'd been kicked out of law's comfortable bed like a dog. And after that, he'd done something he didn't often do: he'd beaten some Arab flunky who'd been brought in for smuggling. Usually Zekai Bey left the small fry to others. To every man his proper job. Every time he pounded the Arab's puny ribs, he could hear Turgut Beyefendi's screams echoing in his ears.

"Go find out what the law is for. Then come back and tell me. Every year I pay out a fortune in taxes to the state. If this state isn't going to protect my factory, then who is it there for – the looters?"

Of course, Zekai Bey knows full well who the law is there to protect. That's his job, after all. No one needs to tell him when to sharpen the blade, and when to blunt it. But he's not a magician. That's why he'd not done whatever the Turgut Beys of this world had been expecting from him. They'd done him wrong that night. So very wrong. What's the most a civil servant can do? He can pick up a phone to order an arrest or a release. That's about it. He can choose to slow down the paperwork or speed it up. In Turgut Bey's world, it was unheard of, to treat a man as he'd been treated that night. Was it Zekai Bey's job to change a law he didn't like? Did Turgut Bey not have better strings to pull? Was he short of friends in Ankara? Why doesn't he take his foaming mouth there for a change? Yes, let him rage against his fine friends in Ankara. It's their job to fix the laws that have Zekai Bey tied hand and foot!

It was because he'd not been able to say these things to Turgut Bey's face that he'd roughed up that Arab so badly. The half-naked tramp had been caught in one of the Hacıbayram coffeehouses with two cartons of smuggled cigarettes. He couldn't understand a thing Zekai Bey said.

"And right across the street from a police station. Ooooh, I'll show you what the law looks like, you little piece of shit."

The guards on duty had been shocked, to see the mighty Zekai Bey take this Arab on. They could not have known that Zekai Bey would have far preferred to work in a local police station, the sort of station where beatings like this were routine.

It was no accident that Turgut Bey had hired a famously ruthless army colonel to manage his factory. He had the strength to see off the unions and it didn't take him long to prove it. If he hadn't come to see that he'd done Zekai Bey a great wrong, would he have thought to apologize by sending over two bottles of whiskey?

And anyway. Zekai Bey had no wish to hold a grudge against Turgut Beyefendi. The more you take offense, the more you feel offended. The longer you hold a grudge, the angrier you get. He needs to find someone other than Turgut Bey to take it out on. If you leave your anger untended, you're also leaving your chair for someone else to fill. Zekai Bey has already been in his job for many years.

What he wants to do now is take the anger he's kept untended for so many long years and unleash it on Mustafa. Crush this vile excuse for a teacher. This he must do. If only he weren't so tired. He can't summon up enough anger. There's not enough evidence. Not enough legal justification. He remembers this, and then he remembers Turgut Bey. And being kicked out like a dog. Like a dog.

If he ends up having to release this Mustafa in the morning, he can be sure that Turgut Bey is going to get angry at him. Very soon. He'll kick him away again, like a dog . . .

Even a week ago, could this have happened? Whoever ended up in here, whether they were known Communists or just suspected Communists, would they have been getting out the next morning? No, they'd be doing forty nights inside at the very least. So what's happening now? Until tonight, they'd always said, "Arrest all suspects." But just now, on the phone, they'd started saying, "If you can't find anything, release them." Does this mean they're losing the will? Is there a reason behind this, or are they just too tired?

He rises to open the window, letting in the warmth of the Adana night. Mustafa looks as comfortable as a man can be in his situation. And Zekai Bey, as exasperated. Let us do all the heavy lifting, why don't you. While you idle scoundrels watch. He knows it, too. Knows my hands are tied. The prick! But nothing doing. I could . . .

This is the last straw. Why is this piece of shit looking so calm? He's sure he won't be arrested – that's why. What is it, that makes him so sure? Why did they just call him up to tell him to release these people, if they couldn't find anything? What's changed? All his life, Zekai Bey has prided himself on knowing how the wind is blowing, and how fiercely. Is he losing his touch? Is he no longer the man he was? Has something changed, without his picking up on it? Has he ended up on the wrong side of the seesaw? It's merciless, that seesaw. When it shoots up, you'd better be on the right side, or else! No one warns you. No one explains. But Zekai Bey knows how the game is played. He's used to racing towards a finish line that keeps on shifting. It's not the finish line that matters. It's knowing how to play on a football pitch that keeps changing shape. Without once conceding a goal.

It's not all that hard. Some things never change. And these are the things that give Zekai Bey his sense of security, that keep him living, running, and playing. One of those things is the power Turgut Bey enjoys. Which is why he must try to forget how Turgut Bey kicked him out like a dog. Or at least not dwell on it.

"Enough. Write down your statement."

He sets a notebook in front of Mustafa. And a ballpoint pen. He no longer cares if Mustafa writes anything or not. He just wishes for a night long enough for him to decide what to do.

Mustafa pores over the empty page in front of him. Does he really have to write something down? It's not as if there's anything he must not say. So he can write down something. Will this bring the night to an end? Must he describe the evening's events? Yes, he will. He knows that. If freedom awaits at the end of the string, then you've got to pull it toward you. He examines the ballpoint pen Zekai gave him. It's stamped with the words "Made in the USA." All at once, he's a child again. Looking at the paper and pens that one of his friends brought into school. All bearing the stamp of the Turkish Republic. Until one day Fadime the Teacher blew up all of a sudden. "If your father gives you any more of these, I'll denounce him." She said that to his friend Bülent. Mustafa never once had the chance to bring paper or pens marked as the property of the Turkish Republic. This was a privilege. Suddenly he remembers the classmates who'd enjoyed that privilege. All were sons and daughters of civil servants. Zeynep, who had special permission from the principal to use the teachers' entrance. She'd complained that the other staircase was too dirty. "I don't want to soil my shoes. With your permission, I'd like to use the teachers' entrance." The principal knew the family. She'd given the girl a special dispensation.

Putting aside the pen that was made in the USA, he sets to writing with his own.

"After my release, I set out for Urfa to join my family, stopping off in Adana, my hometown, to see my close uncle Ali . . ."

It irks him, shames him, to be writing all this down. Since when have we been under obligation to defend every last thing we do? When exactly did we come to accept this as normal? One set of clothes for being in the right. Another for being in the wrong. We've been changing in and out of them for so long now that we can hardly tell the difference. Zekai Bey presses his bell. Calls for Abdullah. Mustafa can hardly recognize the man he sees stuttering, bent over double, before his master. He tries to remember the face of the man who led the raid. But he can't.

"Who did you bring in from that house you raided?"

"Well, sir . . ." He coughs. "First of all, the blonde."

"Fine. Who else?"

"There's Ekrem Şahin. The fellow who went in with the boy, sir, while we were outside listening. That's why we couldn't listen too much longer, sir. So unfortunately, we have no definitive evidence . . ."

Zekai Bey eyes dart towards Mustafa. What is it with this Abdullah? Why is this idiot babbling about there being no definitive evidence with the suspect here in the room? You're supposed to come in here and give him a scare. With one eye on Mustafa, he clears his throat, before giving Abdullah what's coming to him.

"It's for the courts to decide what counts as proof."

He says this to inject a little anxiety into Mustafa. Make him think that this business might not end anytime soon, could even end in prosecution.

Abdullah can see that his boss is furious with him. He braces himself, knowing that he might have to bear the brunt of the fury that Zekai Bey would have preferred to vent on Mustafa.

"Who else?"

"Zekeriya Yaman. I've met him before. He's harmless. He was even thinking of joining the police at one point. He's a nationalist. The National Struggle Association put him through school."

Hearing Zekeriya's name and the word police uttered so close together, Mustafa flinches. His pen falls to the floor. He doesn't have it in him, to keep his calm. So Zekeriya is with the police. Which means that the one who arranged this evening . . .

Quickly he pulls himself together. This is the oldest police trick in the book and he's not falling for it. If Zekeriya was really with the police, they'd never say it in front of me. They're trying to throw me off. Zekeriya only got back from Iskenderun this evening. How would he have known that Mustafa had just been released, or that he would be spending the night in Adana? He was angry with himself for letting his mind wander. He should have been paying attention to this exchange between Zekai Bey and Abdullah. He was just so tired. When he needed to be wide awake, all ears. These men knew how to put a doubt into a person's mind. Their aim was to shake you up. Because that's what a single doubt can do: at a time when you need to have all your wits about you, it shakes you up. It makes you ask yourself: could the friend I trust most in the world really be working for the police? Until you get to the point where you can hardly trust your own beliefs. And come undone.

His brain was finally working again. He began to scribble down a few words, making as if he had no interest in what this Zekai was saying to Abdullah.

"And the man of the house?"

"Yes. The owner of the house where the secret meeting was being held . . . We brought him in too. They've roughed him up, of course. But there isn't much he knows. If he did have something to tell us, he would have done. We pressed him hard enough, to be sure."

Again Mustafa's pen slides from his hand. His blood is racing now. Fatigue pushed aside. All suspicions with it. He's on fire, and he needs water. Give me water, before I burn myself up.

His debt to his uncle. I'll put your son through school, Uncle. After that he set his heart on widening the circle. Bringing all the Ali's of the world inside it, and all their sons. Multiplying his debt. Spreading himself so thin. At what point can I say I've paid my debt? They gave my uncle a beating. Because of me. So far, this is the only thing I've been able to give him. Trouble. His tongue goes dry, and then it swells up. He crumples up the page he's been writing on. There is nothing to write about.

"Shut the window."

Zekai Bey has run out of things to ask Abdullah. How can he make it through to the morning, if he can't think of anything else to ask? He needs more questions. A whole truckload of questions. To fire up his rage. He can't do this unless he's on fire. Without anger, this game is hard to bear. To keep this going, he needs to outdo Turgut Bey even.

"Fine, then. Take this one with you. Put him back in his cell."

As he rises from his chair, crumpled page still in hand, Mustafa considers putting it back on the table. Why hadn't Zekai Bey asked for it? Placing it next to the ballpoint pen that was made in America, he leaves the room with Abdullah. Time to put Zekai Bey out of his mind. He'd overestimated this man. He lights up a cigarette without bothering to ask Abdullah for permission.

Abdullah is in a foul mood. He's on edge. He's not at all happy with the way this is playing out. And that's because his boss is not at all happy with *him*. He might be in the dark about everything else, but this one thing he knows. He casts a sidelong glance at Mustafa. Sensing his contempt. People like Mustafa intimidate him. In other words, teachers. He can't help it. Teachers make him feel small. He only barely made it through primary school. When he thinks back on that place, all he can remember are the beatings he got from Master Metin. Same for the army, and the beatings he got there. Lessons and beatings – in his mind, they're one and the same. That's how it was for him, anyway. In the end he learned that the best thing to do around those who set themselves up as your teachers was to watch your step. So he's relieved, not to have had to beat this Mustafa. That would have been like asking a common soldier to beat a colonel. Even if he deserved it, the man was still a colonel. You never knew, even with this luckless teacher beside him. He could end up in his classroom. The man could end up taking him by the ear and slamming his head against the blackboard. Bang! Bang! Bang! He gives Mustafa another look. No, my friend. This one's going inside. He's a Communist. That's for sure. When it comes to giving a Communist the beating he's been asking for, who's going to split hairs about rank? His mood lifted, if only just a little. He turned to Mustafa. Half vengeful, half mocking.

"I hear you just got out . . . Such bad luck . . ."

". . ."

"And with your family still waiting."

"They can wait. They're used to it."

"If only you'd had a chance to see them first, though. Such a pity."

Mustafa is furious, to have failed to keep this man from riling him. He grits his teeth. His left eye starts twitching.

Abdullah falls silent. In Muş, where he did his military service, there was a lieutenant whose left eye twitched just before he laid into an underling.

They're back at the holding cell already. He unbolts the door, and then unlocks it. He doesn't push Mustafa in this time. "Go on now. Inside."

The cell is thick with smoke. Mustafa can hardly see a thing. Their numbers have increased, though. Two new dark shapes, sitting cross-legged on the floor. He can't make out their faces. But never mind. In time, his eyes will adjust to the darkness. There's plenty of time for them to get to know each other.

Ekrem, thinking only of himself, lies stretched out on the wooden bench. Zekeriya has managed to find space for himself at its far end. The moment he sees Abdullah, he jumps up and stands at attention. Hüseyin is pacing back and forth smoking.

Five steps one way, five steps back. He looks at Mustafa, his eyes brimming with questions. But Mustafa ignores him. Instead his eyes search for his uncle. But Ali isn't here. He crouches down next to the two strangers, who are still whispering to each other, unfazed by Abdullah's presence.

Abdullah shakes the sleeping Ekrem. Startled, Ekrem jumps up.

"What is it, friend?"

"The boss says you can go."

As he says this, he casts Mustafa a sidelong glance. As if to say, Look, we're releasing the innocent parties. Once again, Mustafa makes him feel small. But who cares about him? He's thrown the stone, and it's Zekeriya who picks it up.

"Say, brother. Did you ask about me? I only got back from Iskenderun this evening. I had no idea about any of this. I don't approve of Mustafa, or anyone like him. They're not my family. They're my wife's relations. I didn't say a thing about Anarchism at the table. But when I get back home, I'm going to beat that wife of mine blue for letting that brute into the house."

Mustafa's stomach is churning. From hunger, from sleeplessness, and also, just a bit, from Zekeriya's words. If they come back asking for a statement, this is what he'll write. "Ekrem, Zekeriya and I decided to form a clandestine organization, with the aim of turning the workers of Adana into Marxist Leninists." Full stop. That would be enough to put the villainous Zekeriya in his place. But even policemen as clumsy as these wouldn't swallow it. They'd take it as an insult. An injustice.

Best not to think about it. Instead he gave his attention to the strangers whispering beside him. They were speaking Kurdish. He searched for the gum he'd stuck on the wall before going off to be questioned. Found it. Began to chew.

"You were going to find a way out for me, brother, weren't you?"

Abdullah's eyes are on Mustafa. Squeezed into this little holding cell, this teacher no longer scares him. But Abdullah still hasn't managed to scare this teacher. That bothers him.

"Don't worry. I spoke for you. He's an understanding sort, our Zekai Bey. Don't you worry. The boss is the real thing. He can tell a man's innocent just by looking in his eyes."

"Thanks so much, brother. Can you speak to him again? I have a new job waiting for me in Iskenderun. I can't be late."

"No need to panic. We just need to take care of these other ones first."

Again he glances at Mustafa. Then at Hüseyin. His heart stops. He forgot to mention this one to Zekai Bey. What to do? Zekai Bey's ready to explode as it is. How's he going to go back in there and tell him there was a man he forgot to mention? He knows what Zekai Bey would have to say to that. "Where was your brain when I asked you the first time?" He'd be fired, for sure. Or demoted and reassigned. Until now, he could have fallen at the man's feet and begged forgiveness. But after this – no, he'd never excuse this. First raid the house, and then give the boss the full list of the men I've brought in. His worm-eaten face goes dark. He turns his rage on Zekeriya. "What business did you have with all those Communists anyway, you prick? Look where it's landed you!"

He turns away from the anxious Zekeriya. Smoothing his jacket, he leads Ekrem from the cell. On his way out, Ekrem says no goodbyes. No one could care less, either. Except for Zekeriya, who's regretting his words now, wondering if somehow they have narrowed the distance between him and the true offenders. He curls up on the bench that Ekrem has just vacated.

Mustafa's jaws are aching. He'd thought the gum would help him keep his mouth from going rusty but it hasn't worked. He sticks it back on the wall. He lights another cigarette. Hüseyin has stopped pacing. Now he's standing right over him. Mustafa does not look up. He doesn't want to look up. He's thinking about Ali. Blaming himself. Hüseyin should be doing the same. He was the one who got them invited to Ali's for supper. He was the busybody who had to tell everyone that Mustafa was out of prison. Of course Ali was going to invite them over, the moment he heard. He should have known to keep his distance for a while. But Hüseyin had not given Mustafa any time to think. He'd been too busy complaining about Adana, talking like he himself had been sent here to serve out a sentence of exile. All afternoon, in that office of his. Not once had he shut his mouth. Babbling endlessly about what was revolutionary and what wasn't. Such and such was wrong. Such and such was bound to happen. Theories. Organizations. The people. People trying to hide their fear behind such words. Who had no right to criticize those who had attempted something, even if they'd not succeeded. Mustafa knows people like this. And there's no difference between those people and Hüseyin. How else to understand how he'd behaved this afternoon? Given half a chance he'd have continued through the evening. Criticizing him in front of Ali and his family. Trying to hide his cowardice by proving that Mustafa had taken the wrong path.

Mustafa sucks in on his cigarette. Fills his lungs with smoke. Until he starts coughing. Choking, almost.

Hüseyin is still standing there right over him. Watching Mustafa spew phlegm all over the hem of his fancy overcoat. Where did he get the idea for this coat? To idle in the cake shops of Atatürk Boulevard, no doubt. Playing the suffocated provincial intellectual. Twisting his moustache and drinking tea. Ogling the Ayas College girls who could just die for those cakes. Dreaming about making one of them his own. A flirtatious conversation, at the very least. He wants to be angry at Hüseyin. Right or wrong, that's what he longs for. And right now, that's easy. It gives him something to think about. It helps him forget Ali.

And no one else? He's thinking about his wife now, and his

daughter. The daughter is easy to pass over. He hasn't even met her yet. Glimpsed her just once or twice, between bars. In prison, it had upset him to think about her. But maybe he had just been giving all his other troubles her name.

"What did they ask you?"

"What was there to ask?"

The nerve of it. To stand there looming over him and ask him what they'd asked. He cares about himself and no one else. All he's worried about is what might happen to him. My wife, my daughter, everything we've been through, everything that might happen next – he cares about none of that. He couldn't care less about the revolution either. Mustafa wants to scare this man.

"Come on now, tell me. Don't keep me here waiting."

"There's nothing to tell."

Hüseyin leans over. Whispers into Mustafa's ear.

"If you're wondering if these guys next to you are with the police, don't worry. They're with us. I spoke to one of them. He's a tax accountant. They're doing him for weapons."

"Since when do you count gun runners as being with us?"

Mustafa is shouting. The Kurds next to him stop whispering. Hüseyin looks worried.

"What's come over you? It's not what you think . . ."

"What is it then?"

"They're not gun runners. The police searched their house and found a gun."

"And you're telling me a gun isn't a weapon?"

"What's got into you? He's a tax accountant. That's what he told me. And you know what it's like here when it comes to taxes. He got on the wrong side of some bigwig. Or maybe two. Anyway, someone denounced them. Said they were leftists. They had the gun in the house because there'd been death threats. So that was the gun they found."

"A gun's a gun. He got a weapon to watch his back."

"Stop spinning tales. He needed to protect himself. Isn't that so, Veyis?"

The man Hüseyin addressed as Veyis didn't seem too bothered. A tall, thin fellow. He's smiling. The rough looking man beside him is the one who answers Hüseyin's question.

"The weapon's mine."

Mustafa is curious now about these two strangers. About Veyis, who's been speaking with some urgency to his companion in Kurdish all this time. He looks to have some education. He must be the accountant. He seems to regret the answer his friend just gave Hüseyin. Maybe it's what he's been talking about. And he has more to say. Veyis turns away. His voice is musical, insistent. Like a lullaby, Mustafa thinks. It's all he can do to keep his eyes open.

Exasperated, Hüseyin goes back to his pacing. Then he gives up. Comes back over to Mustafa.

"Give me a cigarette, would you?"

"There's already too much smoke in here."

"It hasn't stopped *you* from smoking!"

"I just got back. But you're right. I'll stop smoking, too."

He stubs out his half-smoked cigarette with his shoe. No cigarettes for Hüseyin either. He wishes he would just disappear. That by the end of the night he might stand accused of forming a clandestine society with Hüseyin, or meeting with him in secret – of any joint activity whatsoever – the very idea offends him.

Hüseyin shrugs his shoulders.

"You've changed. Beyond recognition – do you know that? The slightest thing, and you go off. You're worse than an old rifle. It's like you blame the whole world for landing in prison. Like you think everyone's your enemy."

"Knock it off. I know who my enemies are. At least, I'm beginning to work it out."

Mustafa stands up. Takes out his cigarettes.

"Never mind. Here. Have a smoke."

Why is he giving Hüseyin such a hard time? He might not be a revolutionary, but he's an honorable man, is he not? No, he doesn't like his brother much. But how much does he like himself? Does he sincerely believe he's done enough? What's his real reason for picking on his brother? What good will it do? Be a man for a change. Be strong. Better late than never. Nothing else matters.

"When do you think they'll be calling me in?"

"I don't know."

"Did they ask you about me?"

"No."

"I know what's going to happen. They'll call me in last. They don't know much about you in this city, but they have a big fat dossier on me. I have that from a friend at the bar association. He told me to be careful. They've been bugging my office."

"Is that why you spent the whole afternoon pelting me with questions?"

Hüseyin falls silent. He's angry now.

What's the big deal here? Why won't Mustafa say a thing about his interrogation? It's as if he wants to put it all on me. As if I'm the one who got us raided. So he thinks I'm a provocateur. Maybe he should take a good look at himself for a change. Take some responsibility for his own part in this. Who's the one who got out of prison and came straight to us? Never thinking that we might be under observation. When you're fresh out of prison, you need to watch your step. Watch where you go and who you see. You need to remember that you're being followed. It's not my job to remind him of all that. He got out of jail, and he came straight here. What was I supposed to do, tell him to go away? The police got suspicious. What's the man doing in Adana? Why is he going to a worker's house for supper? How could they know that the man was a relative? If we'd told them, would they even believe it? And then there was Oya. They kept a close watch on her. So when she came with us – well of course. They were suspicious.

Oya. This is the first time he's thought of her since they got here. He remembers now that he was the one who invited her to supper at Ali's. She was in the hotel, with no plans to go out. Why did I get the idea to take her with us? She was in so much trouble already.

Remorse washes over him. For the first time, he feels a pang of guilt. He sucks in on his cigarette. He empties his lungs, as if to rid himself of the thoughts now plaguing him. No point in being sorry. It's not as if I had to twist her arm. I was just trying to do something nice for her. Because she was so lonely. A change of scene might do her good, I said. She almost didn't come. It was her decision, though. She's a grown woman, after all. It's up to her, to decide what's right or wrong.

He knows he's brought shame on himself. But while Mustafa was off being questioned, he'd heard his uncle's screams echoing down the hallway. And a terrible fear had overtaken him. He could be facing eight years in prison, fifteen years maybe. His whole life ruined. All he'd wanted from Mustafa was a bit of reassurance. A bit of advice on how to hold that fear in check. Or at least, contain it. But what does Mustafa do instead? He messes up his head even more. Until he's fear personified.

"What did they ask about me?"

Mustafa is angry.

"Nothing."

"What do you mean, nothing?"

"I mean nothing. What do you want me to say?"

"Tell me. Please! Tell me, so that I can say the same!"

"You can say what you like."

"You know what? You're a coward."

Mustafa smiles. He can't help it. But it lifts his mood. That's all that was missing. Hüseyin calling him a coward. So insulting it was funny. No. Too ridiculous even to count as an insult. That Hüseyin would get this frightened. And then accuse his brother of cowardice. Nothing surprising here. He can count on Hüseyin to exaggerate a problem and then blame everyone but himself. Mustafa feels angrier with Hüseyin right now than he is with Zekai Bey and Abdullah. He's has no backbone, this fool. He could read forty tons of books. But the most he would ever dare would be to cast a vote for a party on the left. In secret. Put him under a bit of pressure, and he wouldn't even do that. He'd have all manner of learned reasons to back it up with. He has it in him to change sides overnight. Turn into one of those glib traitors. He's going to have to keep an eye on this brother of his. Mustafa turns away. Sweat is pouring down his forehead. But what if . . .? Wasn't he the one who arranged for them to go to Ali's tonight? Hüseyin. Maybe he's one of them already. Working for the police. Someone like Hüseyin, with family ties like his, in a city like Adana. With intellectual pretensions, and an interest in Marxism. Who could be more perfect? They'll make sure to send him the tastiest lawsuits. Next thing you know, he'll be a deputy in the national assembly. He might even have been working for them as a student. Didn't he always have one foot in and one foot out? Back when they were all making hard choices, joining groups that didn't compromise, and putting themselves on the line, Hüseyin was only a just a Socialist. Could he afford to trust him, just because he was a blood relation? Who wasn't a Socialist in those days? You just assumed it. You didn't even ask. There were so many other more important questions to ask. But this one – always one step behind, always hemming and hawing and calculating his risks.

Not for nothing that Mustafa's friends had gone after him. Who knows? They might have heard rumors that he was working for the police. I should never have saved him.

He wiped the sweat off his forehead with the back of his hand. He knows he's wrong to be thinking all this. I'm the one responsible for this fiasco. I wasn't ready for this raid. It threw me. As did my doubts about my wife. That's the first thing that happens when you start to crumble. You let your doubts eat you alive. He turns back to face Hüseyin. Attempting a smile.

"They didn't ask about you. To be more accurate, the Chief Superintendent of Adana Police didn't ask about you."

"Who did?"

"No one. He was the only one who questioned me."

"When it's my turn to be questioned, what should I say?"

"Nothing. What else is there to say?"

"The ones who see torture – I've heard they hold nothing back."

"What is there to hold back, you idiot? The most they could get you to say – the very most – would be that we'd been holding a secret meeting. In the end this would be proven false, too. Get over it."

"You have no idea, though. What they do to people."

He can't even feel angry at Hüseyin. Even though he can see this boy is ready to do anything to provoke him.

"We have no choice," Mustafa tells him. "At the end of the day, we'll have to sign statements."

"Are you crazy, or what? You can get eight years for forming an organization."

"What choice do we have, dear brother? You're the one who brought us all together, after all."

Now Hüseyin is terrified. So much so that he doesn't even realize that Mustafa is mocking him.

"You say I'm the one who brought us all together? Please. All I did was suggest we go see Ali. Actually it was Ali who insisted that I bring you. He wanted to see you."

"Fine. But what about Oya?"

Hüseyin falls silent. As if he'd been caught red-handed.

"They'll be thinking you're our organization's man in Adana."

"Stop tormenting me. What organization are you talking about? There isn't one!"

"You said it yourself, didn't you? They can get you to say anything they want."

Hüseyin looks to be in a panic. Zekeriya is lying on the bench behind them, snoring. Mustafa wants to laugh. He wants to let out a laugh as primitive as this man's snores.

"Even this Zekeriya has more backbone than you do. He's decided to relax – get himself some sleep, at least. Instead of spending the whole night blabbering, like you."

No. This is wrong. He shouldn't be taking it out on Hüseyin. He offers him another cigarette. He no longer wants to frighten his brother, or mock him. It's too easy. It serves no purpose.

"Don't worry. He didn't ask about you. Didn't even mention your name. My guess is they're not even going to question you."

"Why do you think that?"

"The interrogations are over."

"But they haven't called me in yet."

"Either they counted you out or they forgot all about you. It's all the same to them."

Hüseyin goes red. After the initial relief comes the rage.

"Why would they forget about me? In their eyes, I'm the third most important person. At the very least."

"Important how?"

"When they did the raid, you and I and Oya were the first ones they pointed out. That makes us the most important."

"Really? Are you serious?"

This time Hüseyin can tell his brother is mocking him. He's angry now.

"In the beginning, they were going to take just us three. If Ali hadn't put on that little show, it would have just been the three of us."

No time now for lethargy, hopelessness, or sarcasm. Just anger, pulsing through his body. Mustafa grabbed his brother by the collar.

"How dare you talk about our uncle like that?"

Hüseyin has been confused since his brother got back from questioning. He's starting to stutter.

"What's come over you? Dear brother . . . If he hadn't talked back to the police . . . I mean, if he had kept his mouth shut . . . They would never have taken him in otherwise. We were the ones they wanted."

"We were, were we? And who are *we* exactly? What are you? Who are you? Why did they want you, I wonder? You can't even start a fire. You'd only end up burning yourself, you fool!"

"I'm not sure I can say."

You could frighten Hüseyin to death, but you'd never shake his faith in his own importance.

"Can you get this into your thick head? The interrogations are over, I told you. Such a shame, though, that they beat up men like Ali, and leave wise guys like you untouched."

"Did Ali get a beating?"

"Are you the only one in here who didn't hear it?"

"How could I know it was Ali? It could have been anyone. Let go of my collar."

Mustafa lets go of Hüseyin's collar. He settles back down on the floor. He doesn't want to see his brother's face. The nerve of him, to talk to me like that in the first place. And then to try and blame me for what they did to Ali. He wishes the rogues upstairs would keep it up, give Hüseyin a taste of what they could do to a man. But no. There's no point in wishing Hüseyin something he hasn't earned. He doesn't deserve torture. No, he does not. Not everyone gets to be tortured. No, it's not something you can count on experiencing. It's a test. A test that only some can pass. To which only the most studious and committed have earned the right. There is nothing casual or generic about the pain. It has a nobility to it. A significance. Why do we love our factions so?

The longer this night goes on, the more I'm unraveling. Best, thinks Mustafa, not to think at all. Best if they did not take Hüseyin off to be questioned. The worst punishment would be to let him out in one piece. If they do end up taking him upstairs, just imagine what sort of story he'd tell about his little interrogation. He'd brag and boast about this shitty little night forever after, as if it was the worst thing that any man had ever endured.

He's wearing himself out trying to pin the blame on his brother. What does he have to say for himself? Aside from landing himself in a cell in Adana Police Headquarters for some ridiculous reason and laying into Hüseyin. Aside from obsessing over details.

To obsess over details is to deviate from the cause. That's what Doğan had said. "Why are you so eager to think like a bourgeois intellectual? After all we've done to set ourselves free. I've shrugged off the details." Doğan was always saying that. He aspired to purity, and simplicity. The son of an Istanbul industrialist. A man of letters, so to speak. Back in the day, he'd written poetry. Those who'd known him then had plenty of stories to tell about him. A degenerate. A hopeless drunk. Maybe this was why he was so fond of talking about "changing people." There were a lot of people in that prison who couldn't stand him. They said that he was glad prison had toughened him. That he wished conditions to be even tougher. And also, he was against their pooling money to buy fruit and milk and such. He made so much of it that a fight broke out in the dormitory. Nuri of Sivas put him in his place.

"You know what you are? A dilettante. We're not interested in playing at misery like you. Pain, hardship, hunger – we've known these things since infancy. We didn't come here to get educated.

We're not overjoyed to be here, either. The more we can do to improve our lives in here, the better. Do you hear?"

Maybe that was unfair of Nuri. Maybe he should have been giving Doğan his due for trying so hard to overcome his bourgeois ways. But Nuri was right, nonetheless. Doğan had no right to lecture them on righteous deprivation. Doğan had accused Nuri of lacking revolutionary consciousness. Sending all Nuri's blood rushing to his head.

"Hey. You. You know nothing of our world. You have no idea how little it takes for us to land in jail. We don't have to surround ourselves with the collected works of Marx and Lenin to end up behind bars. All we need is to step on someone's toe. Rub someone the wrong way. One wrong move and it's over. We're inside."

"What are you trying to say here – that someone denounced you? I honestly can't see why they would bother!" Well, Nuri wasn't going to let himself be mocked. So that was when he'd leapt down from his bunk and grabbed Doğan by the collar.

"So you think you're suffering, in this nice little political prison? Let's see what you'd do if you had to spend time in a slap-dash lockup made of horsehair! No one's there unless he's been denounced. As I was! I want my freedom back. The moment I'm released, I'm heading straight back to Sivas. I have five people to support there. I have no wish to sit here starving and doing embroidery, or get my sentence lengthened by doing something stupid. If we take what's left of the money we've pooled and spend it on milk, or tomatoes, that's fine by me. It's what we need. End of story."

"Fine," Doğan replied. "But where, may I ask, does that leave the movement? Any extra money we have should be going outside, to support the movement."

"What an idiot you are. Since when are movements bankrolled by prisoners? The money we have in here – doesn't it all come from your fathers? The same fathers you so long to destroy? All that being so, why don't you just ask the suckers to stop financing the movement by devious means and just pay them directly?"

"My friend. Please listen . . ." But Nuri had not waited to hear what Doğan went on to say. He just turned his back, and turned on the police radio, to listen to Aliye Akkılıç singing folksongs.

They had both gone too far, Mustafa thought. Each might be right about some things, but they were wrong about others. He did notice, though, that there was one thing they shared: fear.

Doğan feared the nearness of the world he'd turned against and now wished to put behind him. He feared it might sink its hooks back into him. It's this that put him on the attack. He was like an alcoholic who could not risk drinking a single drop. He was on the run from his old habits, knowing they might still catch up with him. He spoke harshly because he was trying to break his class ties, make the cut so clean that those ties would be irreparable. Always knowing how hard those ties were to break.

And Nuri? He was afraid of life itself. Afraid of the hardships awaiting him. Of not finding a job. Of leaving those who depended on him in the lurch. Of having taken an already blighted life and burned away any chances he had left on pointless revolutionary action. He didn't like taking chances. Risk being a luxury for people like him. He had yearnings, and they were hard to suppress. A beautiful woman. Good food. Nice clothes. These were not blessings he was willing to push away.

"It's like this," he would say. "All the things Doğan wants to fucking throw away – those are the things I want. Understand? There's nothing wrong with that. The things we never had – the things we saw others getting, and getting the lion's share – isn't that why we became leftists? He shouldn't expect me to applaud him for giving up his lion's share. If that's what he wants to do, then fine. But he shouldn't expect the same from me. Tell me. Why should I have to give up my share?"

Outside, the sky was rumbling. Mustafa jumped. Thunder! Why had he been thinking of Nuri and Doğan and their secret fears? The obvious answer: to distract himself from his own. Mustafa was frightened. Of being arrested again, and for no good reason, before he'd even had a chance to see his wife. Of ending up back in prison, without having had a chance to sleep with a single woman, after all that time inside. So long since he'd last slept. So deep the gloom descending. He wants to sleep with a woman.

Any woman will do. By putting it like that, he can diminish his wife's importance. His wife, whom he's missed so very much. Whom he sanctified in his dreams. He can't afford to think about her right now. He must use all his powers to imagine someone else. A tall, blond woman. That's what he wants. A woman like Oya. Mustafa shudders. To be thinking like that about a woman like Oya, a woman he doesn't even know, a woman he shouldn't be thinking about in this way. Proving Zekai Bey right. His wife was dark. And fairly short, too. Since the birth, she'd started to grow a double chin. He'd noticed this when she visited him in prison. And now, no matter hard he tries, he cannot remember a single time they'd been together physically that had brought them pleasure. Maybe because it had never happened. How much time had they had together, anyway? All those months, when he gave everything he had to the movement. And to his wife? Her mind had always seemed to be elsewhere when they made love. She'd endured in silence. Just as she'd done during the suppers they'd shared, month after month. The teas they'd sipped at breakfast, while reading the paper.

What would it be like with Oya? What *could* it be like? Hard to know what her breasts were like, beneath that thick pullover. Her legs were muscular. She'd have stamina. Push him hard. With a woman like that, you risked shame. You risked looking clumsy. He tried to imagine her naked. Naked beneath him. But that image, too, remained distant. Indistinct, and out of reach. He could remember her neck, though, and the curve of her ears. As much as it appalled him, to give her name to his lust, the desire he now felt for her was greater than anything he had ever felt for anyone. Shame, man. Shame. The night had begun as a farce. If he went on like this, where might it end? He was going around in circles. This needed to stop. Best to give his attention to his surroundings.

Looking over at Veyis, who was still deep in conversation with his rough-looking friend, he noticed how well-dressed the man was. As if he expected every Kurd to be swinging a cartridge belt from his shoulders. They were sitting cross-legged, just next to him. Veyis had round black eyes, and a gentle gaze. Aside from those eyes, there was nothing round about him. His wiry frame was all sinew, all nerves.

More thunder. The gathering storm sends the plain's humid air through the bars of the barred window above them. Mustafa can barely breathe.

"Did the thunder frighten you, my friend?"

I must have gone pale. Why has this Veyis stopped talking to his friend and turned to me?

He takes a closer look at the man. His round eyes are not black, but light brown. And gentle. He's looking at Mustafa kindly. He's trying to reach out.

"Yes, my friend. The thunder frightened me. And many other things, too."

Suddenly he wants to confide in this man. Share all those fears. Tell him about lusting after Oya. About his wife. His child. How he dreaded seeing them again. The mistakes he must not forget. And then back to Oya – how he didn't know the first thing about her. Or, to be perfectly honest, about love itself. He wanted to tell this man that he didn't even know how to have sex worth remembering. Even if he wasn't all that interested, even if he bored the man to death. He wanted to explain how he'd spent his time in prison believing himself to be preparing for something, even believing himself to be prepared, only to discover that he'd prepared himself for nothing whatsoever or, rather, that being prepared, in the abstract, had no meaning.

"Even the bravest and most brilliant know fear."

He's smiling now. As if he'd heard everything that Mustafa had wanted to tell him.

"Your name's Veyis, if I'm not mistaken?"

"Is that what he told you?" He nodded in Hüseyin's direction. He let no mockery into his voice, while making it clear that he'd formed a clear opinion.

"Yes. He also told me you were in because of a gun."

"Yes, I heard that. That's what frightened me. When they found the gun."

"The gun's mine."

This came from the older man sitting beside him. Just down

from the mountains, by the look of him. Veyis looked at him in despair.

"There it is, then. That's what's frightening me right now."

We all have someone we fear for, Mustafa thinks. It's Ali I fear for, and my wife, and for the Mustafa I might become, after the true dawn.

"We all have people we fear for. All of us."

These fine words seem to fit Veyis like a good suit.

"What evil most concerns you?"

Mustafa is suddenly exasperated by this stranger.

"Ugliness."

With that, Veyis falls silent. He turns back to his older, rougher looking companion. It's the same old story, Mustafa decides. With that one meaningless word, he has ended the conversation. Infuriating man! He's not having it.

"Ugliness? On its own, that word doesn't mean a thing."

"There is ugliness in situations," says Veyis. "In relationships. Ugliness is the status quo. The unborn. The tree that never knows leaves. It's tyranny. It's the circle that never expands. It's being caught inside that circle." He looks up, gestures in Hüseyin's direction. "Like your friend over there. He's afraid for himself. That's what ugliness is. Fear whittled down. If you let it grow instead – it can be beautiful. Beauty can never exist inside narrow confines. The same holds true for human happiness. The more it grows, the more beautiful its essence. The less it mixes with ugliness and evil."

Mustafa is surprised. He wasn't expecting this man to launch so suddenly into philosophizing. He examines his face more closely. It truly is beautiful. Cheekbones sharply drawn. Dark skin, forehead tensed and glowing. His hands, never still. His long, thin fingers always gesturing. Tracing a statue in thin air. Sculpting beauty itself. They'd look good on a weapon, these hands. That reminds him of the gun.

"You like weapons, I take it."

"Whatever can help us confront ugliness, I like."

"And killing?"

"It's not a question of killing. What matters is to refuse to bow to ugliness. What's important is who holds the gun. The one who's on the side of beauty? Or the one on the side of ugliness?"

Mustafa doesn't know what to make of it. How this man has turned the whole business into a struggle between ugliness and beauty. Nevertheless, he seizes on it like an amulet that might help to save him. From fatigue, if nothing else. He needs to stay awake.

"I wasn't expecting such poetic words from an accountant."

"Am I right in thinking you're one of those people who confuse a person's profession with his essence?"

Mustafa does not reply. To keep himself from saying something stupid. Even so. Each profession has its own characteris-

tics. Each attracts its own kind. Inspectors, consultants, brokers
– they can all be put in their own categories. He's about to say so,
but Veyis doesn't give him time.

"What does a teacher make you think of?"

That catches Mustafa off guard. But he sees nothing threaten-
ing in Veyis's large round eyes.

"So you know I'm a teacher."

"Actually I didn't."

"Then why did you ask me what a teacher makes me think of?"

"To explain how you can change your associations with a particular profession. It's never possible to get to the truth through
our associations and definitions. So you're a teacher. When you
say the word teacher, I think of shalwars crawling with fleas."

"Are you from Tunceli?"

"Yes, from a village nearby. We're mountain people, in fact."

Mustafa is having a hard time seeing a connection between
this well-dressed man and a shalwar crawling with fleas.

"I used to wear shalwars, too, when I was little."

"Perhaps. But that was not what I wanted to say. For years, I
wore the same black shalwars. Every so often, my mother would
wash them and hang them in the sun to dry. But we never got rid
of the fleas. When the shalwars were clean, they were that much
easier to see. I'd look at those fleas. I wanted to ask my mother
how they'd managed not to drown. But I never did."

"Why not?"

"So as not to speak Kurdish. My mother could speak only Kurdish. But I was afraid to speak to her in Kurdish. That's why we didn't ever really speak, for many years."

An idea came to Mustafa.

"Is she a teacher?"

"Maybe she thought she was being progressive, that she was doing something important. Actually, we children thought it was the right thing for her to do, in spite of all we had to endure. She banned us from speaking Kurdish."

"Maybe she was just complying with some directive."

"Perhaps. No. Certainly. Even so, she could have allowed for the fact that our family spoke only Kurdish. Like my mother."

"They probably thought you'd teach her Turkish."

"How were we going to do the state's job for them? With our scrawny legs swimming in shalwars that were too big for us?"

Enough, thinks Mustafa. He doesn't want to be grouped with that foolish old teacher.

"They put spies in the classroom. Our own classmates. They would eavesdrop on us at night and the next morning they would denounce the ones who'd spoken Kurdish at home."

"And then?"

"It was pretty straightforward, actually. Because we all had no choice but to speak Kurdish at home. So they'd just denounce anyone they were angry at. The teachers would use a falaka on the offenders."

Mustafa looked away. What he'd seen in those misty eyes was not hatred, but something else. Something much harder to bear.

"Do you still hate that teacher?"

"I just feel sorrow, for never having talked with my mother, when I so wanted to."

"You could still have found a way, somehow?"

"I was too afraid. Afraid of the beating I might get. Afraid of the teacher, too. He was like God to me. So I sacrificed my ties with my mother."

No point in pushing this any further. Mustafa lights himself a cigarette. But he can't stop himself from asking.

"Is your mother still alive?"

"She died when I was still wearing those black shalwars."

"I understand."

"No, you can't. You can never understand how vile I find that fear now."

"Why do you blame yourself? What could you have done? When you were so weak you couldn't even defeat a flea?"

"It's not just the fear. Do you know what? My mother was shot."

"Murdered?"

"A murder, or an accident. Call it what you will."

"Who shot her?"

"What a pointless question. As if we had any chance of finding out."

That was Veyis' rough-looking companion.

Mustafa falls silent. He's all knotted up inside. Zekai Bey might not have found grounds to charge him. By the time this night comes to an end, he'll still end up guilty. All he wants is to smoke his cigarette in peace. But Veyis's friend keeps talking.

"The police kidnapped our brother's fiancé. Our brother went after them. He caught them in the stream bed."

"Be quiet, Teberdar. He's not interested in hearing this."

"No, he should know. You shouldn't murder your own kind."

"I don't want anyone . . ." Mustafa has no idea what to say.

"He's talking without acknowledging my pain, this one."

Veyis turns to reason gently with his friend Teberdar, who says, "Tell him how our grief knows no end." The sorrow in the cell so thick now that Mustafa can almost reach out and touch it. It's that heavy, that close. There's something Teberdar wants to tell him. Mustafa holds back, doesn't want to hurt him without meaning to.

"My brother shot the gendarme."

"Good. So he took his revenge and restored his honor."

At once he sees he's said the wrong thing. Daggers from Teberdar.

"Even death will not bring justice."

Veyis intervenes.

"There was more than honor at stake here. That night, just before dawn, the army surrounded our village. There'd been a denunciation. Someone had told the authorities that there'd been a rebellion, that they'd fired on the gendarmes, and wounded a soldier. It would take too long to tell the whole story. The long and the short of it is that the village refused to hand over my older brother. It's unclear who shot who. But that was the night someone shot my mother. They also shot this one's brother. We two have been together ever since. He took me under his wing and became my mother and father both. When we came down from the mountains, he worked the fields while putting me through school. I won a scholarship for university, but that didn't stop him from going without food and drink to send me money. In the end I became an accountant, so I could look after him. But he never let me. He never comes to visit without a big basket of food. But there is something he expects from me. Something he's never put into words."

"Maybe he wants you to call the murderers to account. As they should be."

Suddenly Veyis is on fire. He jumps up, eyes flashing.

"Stop trying to simplify this! I just told you . . . how many innocent people died because they used weapons to restore their honor . . . My mother . . . Stop reciting platitudes. We carry our grief, our mother's lives, on our backs. So you go right ahead, chewing up words like that gum you just stuck on the wall. We know the value of what we carry on our backs. Nothing you say can change that."

Mustafa regrets having offended him. What a night. Outside the sky's still rumbling. If only it could rain and wash this night away, and all his past mistakes. He looks into Veyis's eyes, seeing fear and anguish.

"Try and calm down, my lion. I didn't mean that. We who fight against injustice, we all carry that obligation, and that weight."

"Every blade of grass has its own roots," says Veyis.

Then he falls silent. Mustafa offers him a cigarette. He's even smiling at Hüseyin now. Veyis sits back down to smoke in silence. "It's like this, my friend. Before we enter a fight, we count the dead." Leaning over, he whispers: "I'm not angry at you. But you know how many people there are out there, judging us from their armchairs. I'm angry at them."

"He who judges from an armchair brings a great shame on himself."

This is Teberdar. Mustafa is taken aback. He wasn't expecting aphorisms from a man like this.

No one speaks. Zekeriya's snores grow louder. Hüseyin is pacing again. Mustafa turns his head. He wants to shout at him, tell him to keep his eyes on where he's going. No point in adding to his guilt and sorrow. He turns around to Veyis instead. He wants an answer from those deep brown eyes.

"I understand why Teberdar has decided to take the blame. Why he's saying the gun's his."

And then he falls silent, as together they await the dawn.

Dawn

A NY MINUTE NOW, Adana's greatest bounty will be rising over
the far hills. The jewelers along Bankalar Avenue have their
shutters tightly barred against it. Only wallets fattened by the
wealth of the Çukurova Valley can open them. Only the rich
with their thick necks, rowdy jargon, and big cars. With their
fat, dark-haired wives, who insist on the largest refrigerators and
the grandest front doors. Who ride over their maids like tractors,
but who might warm to a gold bracelet, if only as consolation for
all the money their husbands have wasted on their broad-hipped
bar girls. It's not quite morning. Behind the shutters, the light-
less displays of charms, chains, and gold bracelets have longer
to wait. So too do the banks that are their next-door neighbors.
There is only one sign of life on this avenue of banks, offices,
and tightly locked shutters. And that is the crowd gathering on
the pavement just outside Küçük Saat. They've floated in from
the outskirts of the city, these shadows, and from the towns and
villages just beyond them. From the city's Karaköprü District,

too. They've come in search of their own dawns: any job that will pay for the day's bread. They crouch down on the pavement, and on the stairs of the avenue's shuttered businesses, pinning their hopes on the dawn. The sooner the sun rises, the sooner their hunt for work can begin. All they want is their share of Adana's great bounty. If they can find just one day's work as a field hand or a laborer, they can look forward to eating a flatbread piled with tomatoes, peppers, and red radishes under the noonday sun. What more can a person want? In a city like Adana, dawn is worth the wait.

The sun will be peaking up over the horizon any moment now. Any moment now, the foremen will arrive to pace up and down in their fedoras and their flat caps, searching the crowd for the people that suit their needs. Testing the gold in their teeth, almost. Those left behind will then be shooed away to make room for the morning papers. As the women head home empty-handed, their calloused feet in thongs, and their faces covered in tattoos, they must jump over stack after stack of newspapers, each one topped by a color photograph of a sobbing Salih Güney kissing his daughter Arzu.

Off they fly to their shantytowns, clearing the way for the office workers, shop assistants, and bank clerks who will soon be filling these sidewalks.

The guards on duty at Hacıbayram Police Station are exhausted. Yet again, their incident books are full. It's always like this when it's getting around time to clear the city of Arab illegals. The back streets are still empty. The city still sleeps. The bar girls have only just returned to their hotels. Their canary-yellow wigs have slipped. Their jet-black locks are showing. In the shadow of their artificial eyelashes, the rings under their eyes look even darker. In their struggle to be as fair as their customers like them, they have ended up making their skin even darker, with tinges of green and yellow that look like vomit. The businessmen who stopped off at the Koza Hotel on their way to Beirut are now back in their cars. They pay no heed to these women with whom they'd shared their nights and their whiskey. All that matters now is the dawn. Hitting the road before sunrise. Getting that all-important early start.

It's dawn now even in the buildings still under construction along Inönü Avenue. The workers have rolled up their beds and lined them up along the base of the brick walls they built only yesterday. The soup is on the stove. The foreman will be here any minute to put them back to work. Plenty comes to those who start work at first light.

Adana's sweet, warm autumn sun is rising now behind the twelve-story apartment buildings of Atatürk Boulevard. It finds no greeting here, though. There is nothing in these tightly shut-tered rooms that needs the sun's caress. It finished its work in the Çukurova Valley some time ago. The workers have swept its cotton fields clean. Their masters are still asleep, behind shutters through which not a ray of light can pass, but already they are galloping toward the dawn. Soon, very soon, they will be piling into their Chevrolet Impalas to inspect their cotton. Like addicts. Besotted lovers, brushing all fatigue aside. Because the soil calls for passion. Only a constant, burning jealousy can harness its fertile promise. This the masters know. This is the madness that consumes them. Even their villas, with their lush gardens and their orange groves, even these luxuries cannot quench their thirst. Their hearts belong to the soil that yields to their will, season after season, year after year. To their betrothed, who multiplies each new seed by a thousand. She must stay hidden from all eyes, and all things, even the delights of morning. She is never to be shared. She must be guarded. Shielded. Treasured more than life itself for the millions she yields in pure profit. And no matter how late her master has gone to bed, dawn will find him rushing back to her side, to protect her from the brutish, loveless, godless, workers who will never know her worth. While back in their villas, their wives and children sleep on. Their shutters are closed. It never dawns inside.

Last night's downpour has turned Atatürk Park into a sea of mud. The night watchman is having a hard time wading over to its namesake's statue. The mud that's seeped into his boots is also lapping against the great man's pedestal. The surrounding grass is ruined. The watchman is exhausted after his night of geometric patrolling. He's walked this park's paths so many times by now that he can tell you the exact distance between its palm trees. From one palm tree to the next it is always ten paces. In his mind he folds the park in half, the way a tailor might a length of cloth. As he plods from tree to tree and path to path, Hayati folds the park's two halves over in his mind. Now and again, he stops for a rest, curling up beneath the Atatürk statue the park's center. As a young man he watched over gardens thick with orange and tangerine trees, fig trees and rose bushes. But now he's old. Too old to be in charge of Ömer Sabanci's villa. Instead he's in charge of this park, and this Atatürk statue looming over him. It doesn't take much out of him. It's easier to guard a statue than it is to guard a villa. And Hayati guards this one well. When the day dawns and the park begins to fill, he won't let anyone climb Atatürk's statue. Or anyone else's, either. Not the statue of Mehmetçik the Common Soldier, and not the naked man holding the ear of wheat, God forbid. This naked man offends him. But he still protects him. Even if he does not have the first idea who he is.

Hayati was born in a village near Karataş, but in all these years it has never occurred to him that the naked man was intended to represent a villager. As the day dawns, Hayati begins to feel more wakeful. He turns into the path on his right. Gazes gloomily at the palm trees and the autumn flowers. He'd be happy to see the whole park covered in concrete. He knows how hard it is to guard living things. Even a single dahlia. Even if he loved it, what difference would it make? Hayati loves beds. Beds with clean sheets and freshly folded quilts. He loves tables with clean plastic covers. He loves sitting at such tables, being served peppery soup. The soup is piping hot. Its mist fragrant with oil. Hayati's mouth is watering. As soon as the day watchman arrives, he's going straight to the little soup place opposite the fire station. He'll lean over the bowl, to let the steam rise to his face. He'll season that steam with red pepper. Lots and lots of it. To his heart's content.

The night storm has left the waters of the Seyhan muddier than usual. In the fairgrounds over in Sığır Pazar, just across the bridge, the morning is well underway. Curses are passing between the Gypsy tents. Whatever these Gypsies are by night – acrobats, artistes – whatever skill they flaunt – by day, they care for their animals. Their snakes and their monkeys. The hedgehogs they prod with sticks to make the audience laugh. These animals mean everything to them. As much as life itself. These animals are their livelihood.

Şeker Karabacak is walking back from the Seyhan. She went there to have a wash. Ramiz is still there on the bank. If it were left to Şeker, she'd happily go without a wash. She loves to keep the sperm inside her. But what can she do? The dawn risers won't have it. If they see her racing around in the half light, her legs dripping, the other Gypsy wives call her names . . . But the day will come when she stops washing altogether. She's made a vow.

Right now, though, it's time to feed the hedgehogs. After that, her snake. And then the sun will rise, and she'll become "the girl who wrestles with wild beasts." She'll drape a snake around her breasts and belly dance. Looking after the monkeys – that Ramiz's job. His hair is still wet from the river. It sparkles in the early morning sun like silk. The other Gypsy wives eye him greedily. "So the river didn't cool you down, Ramiz?" They're ready to share this man. Sharing is something Gypsies learn in childhood.

Fadime Kocakarı is frying peppers. The braids she's not undone for many long years are hanging down over the pan. She takes out the peppers when they're done and scrapes in the tomatoes. Şeker, Ramiz, and Eyüp share out the bread they'll use to soak up the steaming sauce. Fadime sets the pan down on the table. They set upon it hungrily, clutching their bread, eating the peppers and tomatoes with their fingers.

The sun is rising now. Enough light now to read the signs in front of the show tents. "A man from Africa was attacked by a snake. He fought back like this. Just as the snake was about to strangle this man, he managed to kill it." Next to these words is a picture of a giant who could be Arab, or African, or both. He is holding a snake in his mouth, each tooth as big as a man's head. When the show begins, Şeker will do a belly dance in front of this sign. She'll reach between her breasts and pull out a snake. Eyüp has run off to the ferris wheel, with tomato sauce dripping from both sides of his mouth. Fadime Kocakarı cursing after him. The

Gypsy children gather together at the ferris wheel, so that that they can ride it until the operator arrives. They've worked out how to get it going somehow, like they work out everything else. Fact is, they all earn enough to buy themselves rides. But figuring out how to ride it for free – that's more fun. And anyway, once the day's work gets going, they won't have time. They'll be busy poking hedgehogs, doing flips in the acrobats' tent, swallowing fire, racing dogs, collecting money on trays.

The door of the Palace of Private Pleasures swings open. Şerife comes out swinging her wide hips. Her jet-black hair is braided. The bangs poking out from her tightly tied headscarf are all waves. Her purple trousers are tightly stretched around her ample thighs. Here and there a burst seam. Şerife is in a bad mood; her throat is sore. But soon – from the moment the first customer arrives – those low spirits will vanish into thin air. She'll be standing behind the microphone, cheering. Shouting, "Are you hard enough?" Goading the audience, joining in their cry for the belly dancers to give them a peek.

"Show it, girl! Show it!" She'll make an obscene gesture. The spectators will howl. "Want to stick yours in there? Then stick it in!" The men inside the tent just one big blur as her husband Rüsul makes his way with his tray through the clouds of sweat and cheap lust, collecting money from the men his wife has driven mad.

Şerife opens her mouth wide and pops her gum. No sign of

Rüsul. Not for the first time, either. From way over from here, she can smell Fadime Kocakarı's fried peppers. Delicious. Why not go over there and join them? Rüsul isn't here, because Rüsul is with Ulviye. So what, who cares. Before long the woman will be wriggling right next to her. Şerife will be asking the spectators if they've seen enough. Ulviye will bare her bruised thighs. Rüsul always begins by pinching women's thighs. Şerife sits herself down between Fadime and Şeker. Dunks her bread and forgets her troubles. No one asks after Rüsul. No one minds. Not about Eyüp. And not about Rüsul. We're used to living with our losses, we Gypsies. Dropping dead, landing in jail – those are the things we fear.

Oh, how good they are, Fadime's fried peppers. No one can match her fried aubergines either. They smack their lips and wolf the food down. No one says a thing. These fried peppers might be sweeter than sweet, but this morning she can barely taste them. Business is bad. Adana is under martial law. The police are all over them. Raiding their tents as if they had no permits to issue, no army deserters to chase, or hashish smugglers to collar. Some are using the threat of martial law to take protection money. If they weren't so worried about the gendarmes, they'd just pack up camp in the middle of the night and leave without paying what they owe to the council. But there's no escaping the gendarmes in times like these. They poke their greedy noses into everything. They have us coming and going. No time to breathe. This spells the end, in other words. The Gypsy life is dead. Fadime scours the pan with a page of newsprint and takes away the pan. Outside, the fairground is filling up with Öte-Geçe's wretched unemployed. Most are freeloaders, without a penny to their name. As for the scoundrels who poke holes in the tents, so that they can see inside – they'll get what's coming.

The Indian porcupines. The flea-bitten monkeys. The snake that Şeker pulls out from between her breasts. There are some who still pay for these pleasures, but most of them stand outside, gaping like the fools they are, craning their necks to catch a glimpse of a belly-dancing Gypsy girl for free. She keeps an eye out for the field laborers who spend the money the family has earned all together, just to watch the show. These are the types that Gypsy women most like to hunt. The biggest moneymakers? Şerife Yozan, the Ulkiyegils, and their Palace of Private Pleasures. Soldiers. Shopkeepers. Traveling salesmen and policemen. They all pay money to hear Şerife's vile curses and feast on Ulviye's bruised calves.

"Are you hard enough? Are you hard?" Şerife swings her broad hips. Her belly vibrates. Claps her hands as she sings. Teasing the men in the audience with her husky voice. When Rüsul makes his rounds with the money tray, no one returns it empty. But even this brings no pleasure. Rüsul is in trouble. He's a marked man. They'll get him soon, either for hashish or for gunrunning. If they lock him up, it's goodbye to all they've earned.

Eyüp has hidden the iron bar that turns the ferris wheel. Fadime clips him on the nape of his neck. He runs off to the tent before she can do worse. He picks up the metal-tipped rod to give the hedgehogs a prod or two. He'll be using it later to scare off the freeloaders. He loves nothing more than catching them at their peepholes, and chasing after them, waving his big stick. No one can do this better than he can. When he's chasing freeloaders, he thinks himself a policeman. "You think you can see me? Well, watch me grow up. Watch me get myself a fancy wife. I'm going to be a policeman. My pockets will overflow with money. I'll pull in all the Gypsies, lock up each and every one."

The day has dawned now. This morning, Rüsul will be caught. The Palace of Private Pleasures will see its door sealed shut. Şerife Yozan and Ulviye will pack up their sequinned stage clothes and put Adana behind them. Never once uttering Rüsul's name. Until Rüsul gets out, these two will be dunking their bread into the same frying pans. And perhaps, one day soon, there will be a new Palace of Private Pleasures, and a new Rüsul passing around a new tray to rake in the money.

Last night's downpour has washed the city clean. The clouds look ready to burst again. Soon the huge letters hanging over the huge entrance just over by the bridge will be glistening with rain. Bossa. Every street corner in this city has a Bossa sign. Every square, park, and empty wall. The stadium, too. They'll drink in the rain, these signs. Like the crops of the Çukurova Valley, they'll keep growing. A Fruko truck is rumbling across the bridge. The workers of Öte-Geçe have long since begun their day. It doesn't matter where the sun is: a worker's dawn never changes. It's the factory whistle, the clatter of rising shutters, the pounding of metal, the ticking of gathered cotton. The mountains of cotton and the cotton gin. Deaf to the vast Çukurova Valley's vast fields. Lost to shrill whistles. Tired footsteps. Clanking machines. The clamor of cotton remade. Just another harsh and unforgiving day of exploiting cotton's white purity. While children in shalwars and plastic shoes – their dirty faces wet with tears and snot, bushy-haired or shaven headed – pick their way across the open sewers.

The women in the mud-splashed, wooden shanties of 149th, 131st, and 141st Streets have been up for hours, tending to their chickens, their roosters, and their little ones, who wear no diapers, whose little penises are there for all to see. The lucky ones with jobs in the cotton mills pick their way through piles of mud, carrying the envy of the unemployed on their backs. A plane passes over them. A swarm of flies rises from the dusty pile of persimmons outside the grocery store to dive bomb into the open-air urinal just opposite. The grocer has put his wooden chair in front of the Filiz Akın poster. The store fills with customers looking to buy buttons, rubber bands, combs, and cologne.

Emsal is wearing his school uniform, which he never changes. He's sitting outside the grocery store crying. He needs to buy construction paper, the kind his teacher required, but his mother hasn't given him any money. Instead she knocked his head with her brass ring. Emsal's construction paper had just flown out of his hands. The chickens had walked over it. Now it was covered with their muddy prints. Emsal's sobs are growing louder.

"Scram! Get yourself to school!"

Emsal spends a few minutes envying those who don't have to go to school. Then he's on his way. When he gets to school, his teacher will scold him for having no construction paper, and knock his head, too.

Halil, the Ceyhans' boy, steps out of his house, his cap askew, and his jacket over his shoulder. His mother is just outside, beating the laundry with a stick. Halil jumps over her extended leg. Taking care not to dirty his newly shined shoes. But neglecting to give his mother so much as a look. No chance that he's up this early to go to work... Who knows where he's heading, and at the crack of dawn? Off to see that woman again? Halil has a friend over at the state brothel. He usually spends his mornings yelling at anyone who disturbs his sleep. He's been getting up early for a few days now. Let him snuff his candle wherever he wants to put it. So long as it doesn't land him in jail. If he lands in jail, all the breadwinning will fall to her.

Halil picks his way through the mud, reaching the fairgrounds without getting any on his trousers. He heads over to the nomads' tents. He's here to meet Rüsul and sell him some hashish.

The bridge party hosted by Muzaffer Bey, Retired Colonel, Factory Director, Mediterranean Industries only broke up at sunrise. The moment all his guests were gone, Muzaffer Bey opened the balcony door. The smoke inside began to dance with the fresh air rushing in. The apartment is on Atatürk Boulevard, just by Arı Cinema. Stepping out onto the balcony, Muzaffer Bey lit a cigarette. After a few puffs he grimaced. He just couldn't get used to these Kent cigarettes. If his years in the army hadn't made him so careful with money, he wouldn't have even touched these sissy things, which Turgut Bey had given him as a present. They offered nothing of the fragrance of a Harman. But never mind. The rainclouds are moving off. The sun is rising over the persimmon trees that interrupt Adana's flat expanse. The city beneath him resembles a great sea. The Çukurova Valley as endless as the great Mediterranean, whose shimmering waves offer shelter to all God's creatures. Muzaffer Bey is tired, but he's not going to bed. He's had trouble sleeping since stepping in as director. All this bother with the union. They have no idea what it means to have a work ethic in this city. They all want things to come easily, if not for free. The workers take no pride in their work. What does this factory produce, how does it serve the nation, what part does it play in its development? They couldn't care less. Am I or am I not getting compensation, insurance, a wage, a pension? It's always something else. But they never ask themselves: if this factory burned to ashes, what would happen then? Who would be there to feed these many mouths? Not for a minute has it occurred to these blockheads to ask such things. To them, the factory is a machine of perpetual motion. In fact, this factory is their insurance. Insurance that will vanish the moment it closes its doors. Let's see how you feed your sorry wives and snot-nosed children then. They worship money and nothing else. If only Atatürk could see . . . If only he could wake up to see what has become of his legacy. It's all the fault of these shameless villagers, pouring into the city. Encouraged by that cad Menderes. They should have hung him three times over and not just once. Was it like this in the old days? In those days, a villager would stay in his village, living by his means, and by his morals. Endlessly hospitable. Content with his lot . . . And now? They see a machine for the first time in their lives, and they're yelling about wages. What is this machine you see before you? Who invented it? Who brought it all the way here, from the far side of Europe? Which farsighted citizens should we be thanking? Who dreamed up our beautiful fabrics? How did they achieve the high quality that makes the whole country proud? Do you think it's easy, creating such designs? He passed his hand over his suit, made of Prince du Galle. Pinched his trousers. Raised his hand. So tell me, you scoundrels. Do you see a wrinkle? No. All you think about is your wage. Time for you to remember who fills your filthy stomachs, and keeps your shit-ass wives churning out babies. Don't waste a moment wondering how this cloth came into being. How could you begin to know? The boss spent years studying textile engineering in England. If he'd wanted, he could have spent that money on warm-hearted lovelies in Paris and Switzerland. Even then, the money wouldn't have run out. But what did he do instead? He decided one diploma wasn't enough. So off he went to England to work his head off, until he'd mastered textile engineering.

Any minute now, Muzaffer Bey's wife will come out with his coffee. She bows out early from these bridge parties. It was during his long years of service in the east that he got into gambling. What do these people know of life in the barracks? A worker lives like a king compared with a soldier. He'd play cards all night long with his friends in the barracks. Those long eastern nights, when you never knew if it was a dog howling, or a Kurd.

His wife, with the coffee tray. As always, across the years. Like a loveless but loyal dog. Her eyes, fogged with sleep, do not wish him good morning, but here she is, with his morning coffee. Which is all Muzaffer Bey cares about. All he asks of life is that it brings him no surprises. What he values most are the little routines that make each day the same. The wife who leaves the coffee tray on the balcony and withdraws without a word.

In Muzaffer Bey's opinion, words cannot be trusted: they can change things. They must not be allowed near the things that must never change, lest they sully their purity. How will this wife of his spend her day? Muzaffer Bey couldn't care less. He thinks about his wife while waiting for his morning coffee. But only to wonder if he can count on her to bring it out to him, or if today will be the day she fails in her duty. Once he's had his coffee served, he relinquishes control. Whatever Muzaffer Bey sees as important, he controls absolutely. Down to the last detail. However long it takes. Never for a moment taking his eye off the ball. Everything must be in accordance with procedures, which is to say that everything must be done exactly as it was done the time before. It's this, he believes, that made him a good soldier. At Sarıkışla, he held his men to the strictest standards. When on guard duty, they were not to deviate from the rules, no matter what. Nothing can or will excuse a soldier from turning up for his shift. Frost or no frost, wolf or no wolf, you must arrive at the appointed hour. Those who oversleep can expect no mercy. The rules can never bend. How many soldiers froze under his command at Sarıkışla? It's not important. What's important are the rules. Muzaffer Bey has never taken it upon himself to control the weather.

It's no accident he's now the Director of Mediterranean Industries Manufacturing. Put a soldier in charge of every business in this country and see what happens. Everyone will know their duty, place, rank, and limits. In the army, after all, superiors can criticize inferiors, but never the other way around. This is the key. Only thus can harmony between the ranks be achieved. Muzaffer Bey has in mind to bring military discipline to this factory. All employees, the engineers and foremen included, must comply with the chain of command. But if not even the workers know their place, well. The whole thing breaks down. What business do they have striking? When did you ever see soldiers go on strike? Or complain about conditions, and whatever else they don't like? The horrors we soldiers have had to face. Did we ever complain? No. We had a duty to the nation, and we honored it. The problem as I see it? We have yet to instill these workers with national pride. Our mission of unity continues to elude them. They are loyal only to their own kind. But in this nation of ours, there is only one kind. We are one nation, indivisible. So you're a worker. You should know your place in this topography. You should do the job that the nation has assigned you. But aren't these ignorant peasants the same ones who come to us for military service? Why don't they behave here as they did there? Because in the army, they had to go through basic training. These factory workers don't.

Muzaffer Bey puts his empty coffee cup back on the tray. He stands up to stretch his legs. He gazes down over the Adana plain. For just a moment, he allows himself to imagine it covered in white. With snow, pure as pure. He allows himself to speak as loud as if he were still taking soldiers through basic training.

"When on guard duty you will stay alert at all times! As if the Russians could arrive at any moment! The Russians could be here right now!"

Those soldiers did as they were told. Not a single one complained. Come snow or ice, they never let up their guard. They saw the danger. And that was because they'd been taught to see it. No one ever had to go into the reasons. We just sent them out to their guard posts, and they went. Job done. How else can a nation keep itself safe?

When he first arrived at the factory, it seemed to him to exist outside that nation. No shifts on holidays. No extra shifts either. Since when has a work ethic contained itself to standard working hours? Try showing some commitment first. Care for your job like the nation cares for you. It will never leave you hungry. We Turks never forget our nation's poor. All we ask is that they show some gratitude to those who bring them bread.

The Seyhan River is sparkling in the distance. The factory is near the river. He sees what he imagines: the workers flowing in. They must know he has his eyes on them. They must feel it. Soon Muzaffer Bey will be heading over to the factory. Sometimes he even gets there before the workers do. He'll stand at the door, examining them in turn as they file in. Tireless and undaunted. Seeing him, the workers falter. They're terrified of him. Just like all those soldiers, back in the day. Once, when he spotted a worker smoking by the machines, the man swallowed his cigarette. Or so he says. This is one of the stories Muzaffer Bey likes to tell at his bridge parties. Only last night, he told it to Zekai Bey. You civil police have no idea how to maintain public order. Pay no heed to the eye that sheds tears. That's Muzaffer Bey's favorite saying. If the job's not up to scratch, you don't waste time investigating twenty people to find the culprit. You punish all twenty. He tried this out a few times at the factory, but the union interfered. Once he cut the pay of an entire shift on account of one worker, and they went on strike. The owner, being a civilian, made concessions. And what happened next? Did these workers appreciate his good intentions? No. They refused to cool down. Give them a hand and they grab your leg. You must stand firm. From the word go, you must never yield. Fear is the only thing these simple, ignorant people understand. Zekai Bey has no backbone either. What the law didn't allow them to do. What claptrap. What law is there in the military? Did you ever see a soldier complain about the law? What counts is who's in charge. A leader must be strong, must never waver. Think of Atatürk. Did he ever stop to count how many he hanged? Citizens have only to look to his example to understand.

If Zekai Bey persists in his way of thinking, he'll never get his way with the workers. What law exists for workers? What right do they have to strike, or expect pensions? Put some fear in their hearts, that's the only way forward. Let them fear for their daily bread. Strike their hearts with terror, and they'll soon forget about these rights and laws. Their only desire will be to work harder, and then harder still. Know this: to crush a man is to control him. He must put his very life in your hands. A soldier must learn that his commanding officer can shoot him. One bullet, and the job's done. A martyr to duty. Duty, and the commitment to duty: these are the principles on which public order sits . . .

Muzaffer Bey has seen results from these views of his. He gets twenty thousand a month from the factory, in addition to his pension. On top of that, he received his first year's pay in advance. He looks after his interests, he does. One day soon he's going to buy himself an orange grove. Ten thousand square meters, all in all.

He steps back into the apartment. Zübeyir the foreman is busy emptying ashtrays and clearing up. When Muzaffer Bey leaves the house, he says no goodbyes. He never says goodbye when he's leaving a place: that would be like asking permission. They shouldn't even notice I've left. They should think that I am watching their every move, that any moment I might pounce.

The elevator isn't working. The floor buttons are broken. No one's bothered to fix them. These people can't even look after their own property. The company car is waiting outside. The chauffeur jumps out. He stands at attention until Muzaffer Bey is seated. The car glides down Atatürk Boulevard. The asphalt's still wet. Last night brought them a flood, it seems. Ankara Boulevard has yet to rouse itself. They turn into İnönü Avenue. Soon it will be across the bridge to Öte-Geçe and the factory. The shift began some time ago. Soon Muzaffer Bey will go in to inspect them. To strike fear in their hearts.

And now he's arrived in Öte-Geçe where farm laborers and workmen live alongside nomads, Gypsies, and Arab lackeys. Where no one must forget, not even for a moment, that they are here because they are conscripts under the command of superior offices who enjoy the comforts of Atatürk Boulevard.

Ali's lying half-conscious on a wooden bench in the hallway of the police station. His right hand is cuffed to the bench. The bench is right next to the toilet. The hallway, too, stinks of piss. But Ali can't smell a thing, can't hear a thing either. He's in a cradle rocking back and forth between sleep and oblivion. He doesn't like all this swinging, though. He longs to bury his tired, aching head in a great white cloud as soft as cotton. If only he could stop his aching head from swinging. The pain wins every time it moves. It wins and it grows. If only he could just chop off his head, to stop this unbearable pain. If only he could find that white cloud. That pillow that eludes him even in his dreams. No pillow could be big enough, soft or soothing enough. If only he could rest his head on a cloud pillow, he could fall into a sleep as sweet as the rain of plenty. He's asleep, and still longing for sleep. And then, just as the dream comes true in all its grandeur, just as he sinks his head into that soft cloud, it turns into a pillow, he falls through its soft false promise and into the void. Sleep comes to claim him, sending him off into an abyss that has no end. As its full weight presses in on his head, denying him any respite, his aches turn into moans.

Ali's head is hanging off the side of the bench. He's not actually asleep. His body has stilled, to heal itself. He was beaten, he must now find the strength to rise. But he can't rest with his head hanging off the bench like that. With his neck in such agony. It keeps waking him up, this aching neck of his. And soon his whole body is racked with a terrible pain.

He wants to open his left eye, but he can't. He remembers Sezai punching him. Someone yelling son of a dog. Sezai's face, looming large and venomous. Grabbing Ali by the neck and shaking him. "So tell me. Tell me now. Tell me why you brought together all those Communists." Sezai's eyes. So big and so mean. His right eye keeps blinking. Still in shock about the way this night has gone, Ali thinks it's blinking to keep him company. When Sezai grabbed his neck, he'd taken it as his secret way of saying, "I have no choice but to do this, my friend." He'd tried to reciprocate, by smiling at Sezai with his eyes. That was when he got that punch in his left eye. This was not the sort of punch you threw because you had to do your duty or put on a show. It was the hardest punch Sezai had in him. Full of force. Bursting with hatred. Then everything went dark. All he could hear was his own screaming, from afar. Now it's just exhaustion. It's just his neck hurting. He lifts up his head. Lets it sink onto the wooden bench.

It feels softer even than the cloud in his dreams. No pain in his left eye. No reason, either, to open it. Ali's no stranger to bodily pain. He knows how to turn pain into numbness. The torments that caused those screams last night have softened into exhaustion. Just his neck aching now. And that was because his head rolled off the side of the bench when he was unconscious. He tries to sit up. When he realizes that his right hand is cuffed to the bench, he's jolted. To be arrested. To be guilty. To be charged. These prospects terrify him so much more than pain ever could. Pain always passes. To lose his job, to be ejected from the factory, to lose all hope of a pension, to be banned forever from the river through which life's waters flow – what is a hard punch next to such things? Or an eye that won't open?

Ali feels himself on the brink of Hell. Of hunger. Poorhouses. Begging on the street. Shivering. In the hell he learned to fear so very long ago. As fear overtakes him, his neck stops aching. If they came to him now and said he was free to go he could walk out showing no sign of the torments he just suffered. He can't move his legs. He needs to pee. Basic needs can be so comforting. They distract us from our fears. He looks around him. Searching for someone who might show him some concern. He starts coughing, can't stop.

"What's wrong, my fellow countryman?"

Ali can't believe his ears. Isn't this Abdullah? The Abdullah whom Ali had addressed in the same way last night, only to have the man insult his mother's honor? But now he is all politeness. A puzzle. As puzzling as it would be if Muzaffer Bey made allowances for workmen who missed shifts without an excuse.

"Never mind, my fellow countryman. If I could ask for some water?"

"With pleasure. We hail from the same lands do we not? It's our duty to look after each other."

Though these words sent Ali reeling back into the horrors of the night, reminding him how Abdullah had honored his obligations to a man who hailed from the same lands. But still his heart softened, to think of the lands they both loved.

"Try and move your arms and legs a little, my fellow countryman. Take your time. When you're ready, I'll escort you to the toilet."

"Thank you."

"Two men who come from the same lands. It's as good as a blood tie, in my mind."

"You're from Maraş like me, I take it."

"Now you're offending me, brother. Do you think I'd be calling you my fellow countryman all this time for no reason?"

This is not the cursing Abdullah of the interrogation. But never mind. Ali is ready to believe him.

"What part of Maraş are you from?"

"The interior."

This answer is a bit puzzling. The people of Maraş have a

passion for geography. The interior is a general and abstract term. Ali doesn't dwell on it. Ali, so recently delivered from the brink of hell, is ready to embrace Abdullah as a man of Maraş.

He stands up. The moment his feet touch the floor, his mouth lets out a scream. The pain takes him back to the interrogation room, and the falaka breaking the soles of his feet. It is real, this pain, so much more so than Abdullah's fine words. As he stumbles toward the toilet, those words are soiled by doubt. How tense he is suddenly, this Abdullah.

"Stop, my fellow countryman. Let me help you."

Why is he being so solicitous? Especially when there's no reason? Ali will be getting out soon, that much is clear. It no longer matters, how well or badly he's been treated. All that matters to Abdullah now is that Ali's from Maraş. Abdullah is feeling frail and lost. What rotten luck, that the house they raided last night belonged to a fellow countryman. There are no flowers in his life. No one to love, either. All that deigns to spread across its empty spaces is ugly. The company of fellow countrymen his only consolation. His only hope for honor or for love. Usually he can manage it. When a fellow countryman ends up in here, he can usually count on special consideration. When the war-wounded march on Independence Day, he cries from pride. So many brave soldiers wounded in Maraş. When they changed its name to Kahramanmaraş, making it the official city of heroes, he felt even prouder. It had a ring to it: Abdullah from Kahramanmaraş. It gave him the chance to wear his city's mantle of pride. These heroes who gave so much to our own nation. May Allah turn all they touch to gold.

He longs for Ali to take his arm. But Ali has not warmed to his advances. He's not about to push Abdullah away, but he has no wish to take his arm. "Let me go it alone, brother. I need to walk off the falaka. You also mounted my back last night, by the way, and dunked me in saltwater."

Abdullah makes like he's offended. Now he's the one babbling. This Abdullah is acting as if he wasn't one of the men who'd beat him. But Ali knows this. He remembers it all now. They'd all played different parts, and Abdullah had played the enemy. Leaving no room for fellow feeling. This he remembers well.

And now he's all smiles. So concerned about Ali's injuries. When causing injury is the only way he knows to get what he wants.

"Come on now, my lion. My fellow countryman. Show yourself a hero."

Ali stops. What's this scoundrel doing? Having a laugh?

"Fuck off, you!"

He isn't surprised when these words burst from his mouth. His soles have stopped aching. He is no longer in a police station, fearing arrest and the freezing cold of hell. He's forgotten that Abdullah is a policeman. He's simply cursing a scoundrel who claims to be from the Maraş *interior.* Even when he remembers the rest of it, he doesn't care. He even feels relief. He hobbles off to the toilet, leaving his so-called countryman to scratch his head. He can manage the floor fine.

Abdullah stays on the bench. Like a fool. Punch drunk from his sleepless night. Troubled by what the dawn might bring. Recalling how much of his life he's spent helpless and alone. And tired, so very tired. For a moment he considers lying down on the bench Ali has just vacated. Only for terror to overtake him. As if he's been carted in for just this kind of crime. What would happen if Zekai Bey walked by and caught him dozing on this bench? Having unlocked Ali's handcuffs and sent him off to the toilet unescorted? What's wrong with him? What has caused him to feel so bereft? His intentions were good, this he knew. I tried to help the old fellow. Appeal to our common bond. How could that be wrong? Human kindness. Nothing in this world matters more.

Last night, during the beating, Ali's mouth kept opening and shutting like a fish. Exactly like a fish. And Abdullah had started thinking about fish. Wondering about them. Abdullah is just crazy about aquariums. He acquired this passion just after moving to Adana. There was an Arab errand boy at the station. A bachelor named Hüsrev, who bred fish. When he fell ill, he asked Abdullah to look after his aquarium while he was in the hospital. He didn't come out alive, and so the aquarium had stayed with Abdullah. And those fish had become Abdullah's sole obsession. If he couldn't get home, he'd go mad with worry. The other people in his house couldn't be trusted. He's always talking about these fish of his, boring everyone to tears. It bothers him now, to think that the thing Ali did with his mouth while he was beating him had reminded him of fish. He'd been meaning to change their water today. What if they've died? Dear God, what if they've died? Now he is angry at Ali again. If I hit him, it was because I am a patriot. To think that this countryman of his had welcomed Communists to his house. It betrays all we stand for. It spits on our heroes, who martyred themselves for the national cause.

To hell with the fainthearted. In our struggle for independence, the streets of Maraş ran with the blood of our heroes. The likes of that flood never before seen. We've paid so dearly for the national cause. Sacrificed so many animals. Are we going to stand by and let a fellow countryman stuff his house with Communists? What man can stand higher than we who call Maraş our home? We were killing infidels long before Mustafa Kemal stepped in. They've never dared set a foot in Maraş since. These Communists are a thousand times worse than infidels. Especially when they're Russians. Who are infidels to boot.

We are the descendants of the Aslanbeys. An easy thing to say. We send blood running through the streets on Independence Day. Abdullah is cheering up now. He's taken himself back to Maraş. And there before his eyes is the National Square. On

Independence Day, an army jeep stands there, displaying a bust of Atatürk.

Before he picked up his quilt and moved into the police force, he worked for the Maraş city council. One Independence Day, he was on duty in that square. Standing on the asphalt. In the noonday heat. The tar was melting. His nostrils stinging. He'd felt as if he'd fallen into a cauldron of asphalt. They'd just put loose gravel over it. The army jeep riding around with the bust of Atatürk had sent a speck of that burning gravel flying into his eye. Oh, how he'd cursed his job. Whenever he thinks back to that day, the image of the bust of Atatürk covered with black specks of gravel and tar rushes back to him. And he can feel his eye burning again, melting into its socket.

Ali has returned to being his enemy again. Not a fellow countryman but a nobody. To think that we tried to help this scoundrel who filled his home with Communist dogs, just because he happened to come from Maraş. We have our living to think about. Let them throw me off the force. No way I'm letting this scoundrel kick more gravel in my eye. What does this shameless creature know about work? Abdullah has forgotten that Ali is in fact a worker. Ali has become a man who's never had to lift a finger. A man who's never had gravel kicked into his eye in the heat of the Maraş midday sun. He's sorry now that he uncuffed him. He's forgotten that Ali will be getting out soon, that by then they would have uncuffed him anyway. He's thinking that he's

risked Zekai Bey's ire, and for a man as worthless as Ali. Zekai
Bey never hesitates to fire men he finds lacking. They talk about
job security. Well, forget it. They'll do anything Zekai Bey asks.
Plant hashish in his house, even. Would he stop at anything?
Don't doubt it. The police all know. They all have horror stories
to share. No one in the police has faith in the law. When the law
does not work in the state's favor, it casts the law aside. No law
can protect you then. This is what the police hold to be true.
So forget about a law that can keep some bigwig from snuffing
out a penniless wretch. It doesn't exist. Abdullah owes his job to
a relative, who works as a driver for one of the Maraş national
deputies and got his boss to put in a good word for him. How
could he ever forget how easy it would be for his own boss to
boot him out?

Ali's coming back from the toilet now. Keeping one hand on
the wall. Abdullah doesn't move a muscle. Forget Maraş. Forget
fellow feeling. His countryman can see to himself. Ali is not at
all troubled by this change of attitude. These police have been
running hot and cold on him all night. One minute kicking and
punching. The next minute offering kindly advice. Slowly, very
slowly, he lowers himself onto the bench. He holds out his hands
so that Abdullah can cuff him again.

As he turns the lock on Ali's handcuffs, glowering just as
menacingly as he'd done in the interrogation room, Abdullah
remembers his job. What's come over me? Am I so tired I can't

even think? Zekai Bey sent me down here to release this man. My brains must be well and truly scrambled. Just a few minutes ago he was worried about getting into trouble for undoing Ali's handcuffs. Now he'll be in trouble for putting them back on. Abdullah's anxiety grows. He can't think straight, that's for sure. They want me to curse a man's mother all night, and then, in the morning, to treat the same man as innocent. This is one part of his job here that he's never understood. And he's always having to do it. But here he is now, with this man who's just told him to fuck off. How can his hands be the ones to set Ali free? He needs to give him a fresh beating first . . . but what might Zekai Bey do to him, if catches him beating a man he'd ordered him to release? He forgot all about that when was unlocking Ali's handcuffs, and waxing poetic about Maraş and its heroes. Now, if it were up to him, he'd be putting ten handcuffs on this Ali, and dragging him down to a dungeon to shut his other eye. Work us night and day, jam these dogs into the room where we eat our suppers, and then what? The pashas on high decide not to lock up any more Communists. Zekai Bey's not too bothered either. That's why soldiers don't trust the police anymore. The police are always telling the colonel that they don't have any men to help them. *You have no idea what sort of people we have to work with.* How many times has Abdullah heard Zekai Bey complain like that to the colonel. Abdullah's getting angrier now. He's ready to give this Ali the beating of his life.

Ali sits there in silence. He's ready for anything now. He feels strong.

"Hold out your arms!"

He must want to check the lock on these handcuffs, Ali thinks. He holds out his arms.

Abdullah draws back, willing great mountains, wide seas, and rolling plains into the gap between them, to chase away all chance of fellow feeling. He undoes Ali's handcuffs.

"You can fuck off now. Get going. If I ever see you in here again, be sure I'll close your other eye too."

Now it is Ali who doesn't know what to think. He thinks maybe Abdullah has lost his mind. He doesn't move. He can't believe what Abdullah has just said.

"Are you deaf? I said go, you fool. You're released."

"Who said I was released?"

"I did. Look at this clown. He can't even hear me."

"When your boss says I can go, I'll go."

Now Ali's really pushing it.

"Who brought you in here? My boss? Who raided your Communist nest? Was it my boss, or was it me? When I took you in last night, did you say you'd only come with me if my boss gave his permission?"

Ali doesn't answer. Doesn't move a muscle either. He just sits there with his handcuffs.

Abdullah is struggling to keep himself under control now. If he weren't so worried about facing Zekai Bey's fury, he'd be laying into this Ali now. But just the thought of Zekai Bey turns his anger into desolation. *Haven't you sent that fool away yet?* That's how he would scold him.

"Stand up, idiot!"

Saying nothing, Ali stands up.

"Where are we going?"

"That's for me to know. You get busy sending prayers to Maraş. We're off to see the director."

Restored to enmity in the morning light, the two men make their way toward Zekai Bey's office.

Zekai Bey is opening and closing his hands, trying to speed up his pulse. He doesn't like staying up all night, not unless he's gambling. And this time, he's gone without sleep for nothing. He's angry at everyone. At the martial law command, for making them do these raids, only to turn around and demand that the suspects be released. At himself, for letting things go this far when it was clear they had raided this house for nothing. At Abdullah most of all. *If that clumsy fool had thought to bring in just one or two pieces of evidence, we could have arrested them. All he knows, this one, is how to ruin a night of bridge.*

There are too many ignorant men like Abdullah in the police force. You could work all day every day, and you'd still get nowhere. I've lost count of the number of times I've told the commander myself. But those guys sure know how to drag us down. If they know so much, why don't they do the raids themselves? They have no idea what they're doing – that much is clear. Zekai Bey hasn't the faintest idea why they wanted this house raided in the first place. His best guess is that they'd wanted to intimidate this Oya, on account of her being here in exile. His next best guess is that they'd wanted to scare Mustafa, on account of their just having let him out of prison. But in Zekai's mind, there wasn't sufficient justification for either. Who does a raid, without having first gathered intelligence? What are the police for? So you want to put the squeeze on this woman. Send an agent in to talk to her, gain her trust, and get ready to play. You need to know what the game is before you go around hunting for evidence and grounds for arrest. Police work requires patience. Cunning. Trickery. Gamesmanship. Calculation. In Zekai Bey's view, soldiers lack all of the above. Go bumbling into a house like that, and all you've done is open the woman's eyes. From here on in, she'll be careful to cover her trail. And the teacher? He just got out of prison, the house belonged to his uncle, so how's that going to play out? You have to wait a little, let him settle in at home. See where he goes and who his new friends are. Now, though, he'll be watching his every step.

The more he thinks about all this, the angrier he becomes. No arrest without evidence, they tell him. You can't get evidence with a raid like this. Who can know what mischief they were up to? You don't find evidence, you create it. But they could still have found some evidence if they'd bothered. What else are spy methods for? That's Zekai Bey's term for torture. Spy methods get results. You catch a spy and you get that spy to admit to spying. A confession! In this country you can find a culprit for every crime. Thanks to confessions. And isn't that what public order is all about?

This time there'd been no need for confessions. Why not? They'd taken them by surprise. They'd missed their chance. Who could say what fishy business they were up to? The more he thinks about it, the more it troubles him. He's been in this job for forty years but he's still struggling to understand it. He feels like a housewife who after cooking the same dishes for forty years is suddenly forced to cook new dishes, dishes she's never before tasted, with only a slapdash recipe to guide her. He'll be going home soon. Before he goes to bed, he'll spend some time playing with his daughter.

A knock on the door. Abdullah walks in, and Ali follows. Just when he's managed to get them out of his mind.

"What's this fool doing here? Didn't I tell you to send him home?"

"He didn't believe me, sir."

"Fuck off! Who gave you the right to doubt a police officer? Screw your head back on! Whatever passes across a police officer's lips, it's the law! You clear out of here. Out of my sight, now."

As they head for the door, Zekai Bey calls for Abdullah to stay. "You are to ask for a transfer, with immediate effect. I can't work with you."

Abdullah crumbles. He stands there dumbfounded. With Ali beside him, looking just as confused. What has become of the scowling man who raided his house last night? He's a wreck now, on the verge of tears. It was as if he'd just been told that the raid had resulted in just one arrest: his own.

He escorts Ali out of the station, just to see it with his own eyes. Seeing him wandering up and down the corridor in a daze, Zekai Bey called him back into his office.

"What are you doing?"

"I'm waiting, sir!"

"Waiting for what, you imbecile? Did you think it might have been a good idea to wait last night, before raiding that house? Where's the woman?"

Abdullah is shaking. This cursed raid that has brought him such misfortune.

"I was about to send the woman off, sir."

"Stop there! I'm done with you and your two-bit brain making a mess of things. Who told you to let the woman go? Let her wait. The teacher too. Who was the other one?"

"Zekeriya . . ."

"Fine. Let him go too. Why are you still standing there? Get going!"

"Sir. There's someone. Someone else. What shall I do with him?"

"What? There's someone else? You could drive a man mad! Who's this someone else, then? When did *he* turn up?"

"The lawyer."

"What do you mean, the lawyer? None of them have been arrested yet."

"Not that kind of lawyer, sir. I mean the lawyer we brought in from the raid. The teacher's cousin . . ."

"What – did you bring in the whole tribe? All right then. Why didn't you bring this lawyer up for questioning last night?"

"You didn't ask for him, sir."

"Never mind, then. Let him wait too."

"Are they going to be arrested?"

They have to arrest someone. If dawn is not to bring Abdullah even more trouble. Making him the most pitiful wretch in the world.

"Arrested for what? As if you haven't blotted your copybook enough. Is there a jeep free outside?"

"I'll go and see, sir."

"What do you mean, you'll go and see. Find a jeep. Pile all three of them inside. Put a policeman in there with them. Send them off to the Martial Law Command."

Abdullah looks so confused it almost makes Zekai Bey laugh.

"Time to stir some fear in them . . . Have the jeep stop at the entrance. You go inside. When you come back out, don't say a word. Not even if they ask . . ."

"And then I bring them back here, sir?"

"What do you think, you dunce? Is this place a hotel? You can let them go somewhere near the bridge."

"If they ask me where we're going when I get into the jeep, what shall I say?"

"Say you're going to Martial Law Command. That will be enough."

Ali had a hard time making it to the station entrance. The soles of his feet were killing him again. He had no money with him for a taxi. For a while he just stood there, not knowing what to do. Then he saw Veyis and Teberdar getting into the prison van parked just outside the entrance. He'd exchanged a few words with Veyis before going off for his beating. Just a sentence or two. "They'll let you go," Veyis had said. "Don't you worry." When they came to drag him away like a common criminal, Veyis had seemed remorseful, for having given Ali false hope. So they'd been arrested, these two. "They'll let you go, don't you worry," he had said. "And you?" Ali had asked.

"They'll arrest us, for sure. We've stirred up a wasp's nest."

That's all Veyis had said. Not a word more about that wasp's nest. So Ali has no idea. No idea either why Veyis and Teberdar were so sure they'd be arrested, or why he'd been the only one from the raid to have had a beating. But he'll think about it. How serene they look as they step into that prison van. When Veyis looks over at Ali to give him a warm smile, Ali feels his strength coming back. The soles of his feet hurt a little less. But he still can't face walking all the way home. He hobbles past the park. How hungry he is. What he would give for a bowl of soup. His head is pounding. Pounding with thoughts. Aching, unbearable thoughts, seeping in through the sides of his swollen eye and straight into his brain. He's walking through the market now. Slippers and shoes spread across the pavement. To get past them without losing his balance, he'd need to be a tightrope walker. But his soles aren't bothering him anymore. No. Not a bit. All the pain is in his head. His head, which so longs to lie down on a gigantic pillow as soft as a white cloud and drift off to sleep. A single sentence drifts in, to push away all other sentences. He needs to go to the factory. But he can't do that without a doctor's note. No tardiness allowed without it. Muzaffer Bey insists. He needs to get to the factory. With a doctor's note. He needs to go to the hospital. Doctor's note. Factory. Muzaffer Bey. The words circle around his brain, knocking into each other. It's not enough to walk the tightrope among these shoes and slippers. Sit down. How good these two words are. He hobbles on. To the beckoning coffeehouse.

The Abdullah who unbolts the holding cell is wearing the same face as last night. Grim and menacing. The face all police officers must wear in the presence of the guilty. This face, Abdullah hopes, will save him his job.

The moment he sees Abdullah, Zekeriya scrambles to his feet and stands at attention. Abdullah pays him no attention. Zekeriya is not the one who will save him his job. He goes over to Mustafa.

"Up on your feet, you!"

Mustafa lifts up his head very slowly, to look at Abdullah with blank eyes. As if to underline the fact that Abdullah's job is at risk. To fail to provoke a reaction – to Abdullah this morning, nothing could seem more ominous. He's going mad. Never has he felt so humiliated. But now his shame changes shape, sending forth the storm that has been brewing inside him for too long. He gives Mustafa a hard kick. Sending Mustafa onto the floor. Restoring Abdullah's confidence. But only for a moment. Then Mustafa sits back up. As cool and indifferent as before.

"Stand to attention, you worthless rat!"

Mustafa looks up at Abdullah. Looking back, Abdullah sees something like pity in his eyes. This scoundrel knows that Zekai Bey is pushing me out. Pushing me out of my job. He might even be the one who is making it happen. They have influence, these people. Who can say who pulled what strings to get him into teaching? Who gets anything in this country unless someone pulls a few strings? Abdullah's mind is spinning like a top now. The Colonel was never going to arrest these people – that much is now crystal clear. Something's fishy. Something tells him that this is why Zekai Bey is so out of sorts. Something's going on here. Abdullah can tell.

So now he doesn't know how to act toward this man he was ready to grind under his feet only moments earlier.

"I knew you were in the wrong place. You can claim your rights at the Martial Law Command."

"We are being taken to Martial Law Command, brother?"

Zekeriya isn't asking this question so much as sobbing it.

Zekeriya. Another one he's late releasing. He feels Zekai Bey breathing down his neck, noting down Abdullah's every clumsy, stupid mistake. Next thing he'll be wagging his tail.

"No, son, you can go. You're freed. Get along home now."

He wants Mustafa to ask him. Aren't we free to go too? But the indifferent bastard shows no concern, no interest. He just looks up at Abdullah with a mixture of hatred and pity. Once again, Abdullah howls like a kicked dog.

"To your feet, both of you! I'm taking you to Martial Law Command!"

Hüseyin puts out his cigarette. Mustafa stands up. They're ready. They have no questions for Abdullah.

Abdullah is seething now. His heart, his hands, his head, all whirling. So not just Mustafa. Hüseyin, too. They both have men of influence looking out for them. He needs to get them off his case at once. Why am I the wretch who has to shake them down? Zekai Bey gave me this job on purpose. To get me into big, big trouble. Why else would he be asking me to cart people to and from the Martial Law Command, when they haven't even been arrested?

"Say, brother. Am I really free to go?"

What – is this one still here? Are they all ganging up on me now? In his confusion, or is it fury and fear, he punches Zekeriya in the face.

"Didn't I tell you to fuck off?"

"Please, brother. I can make it up to you. Anything . . ."

"I told you to get the hell out."

At last, Zekeriya understands that he is being released.

"Brother, let me kiss you."

He takes Abdullah's hand and gives it a sloppy kiss. Abdullah feels a bit better. He needs many more like Zekeriya, if he is ever to regain his confidence.

"Go on now. Don't let me see you in here again."

"You know all about me, brother. I . . ."

"How wouldn't I know all about you? Think how long I've been in the police, my son."

His mind is on Mustafa now.

Mustafa and Hüseyin are standing by the door. They're waiting to be taken to Martial Law Command.

Finally convinced that no one means to arrest him, Zekeriya heads out of the station, offering a respectful greeting to every police officer he sees along the way. Out on the street, he stays sheepish. But once he has put the police station far behind him, he straightens up. Holds his head up high. He's full of himself now. And angry . . . With a number of people. But most of all, his wife. He'll give her something to think about tonight. On his way to Atatürk Boulevard, he considers how he'll punish her. She's in her sister's house right now. Crying her eyes out, for sure. But he's not going back there. She can sit there worrying all day. No way she's ever going to dare talk back to him after this, or remind him that they are eating her brother-in-law's food. We know now what sort of a man he is. From tomorrow, we're off to Iskenderun. If she refuses to break off from her sister's family, she's asking for it. One thing is for sure: Zekeriya has no room for traitors in his life. He passes the kebab restaurant, turning into the National Struggle Association just next door. It's been ages since he's been here. He asks for Mahmut Bey. He hasn't yet arrived but is expected soon. He sits himself down on one of the wooden chairs in the corridor to wait for Brother Mahmut. He'll tell him how he pounced on the Communists in his wife's family. He'll kiss his hand and thank him for the job in Iskenderun. He'll be doing God's work there, pouncing on every Communist he finds!

Mustafa and Hüseyin are still waiting at the door. Abdullah gives them a shove.

"So you think you can just stand there?"

Mustafa opens his mouth, as if to say something. But then he changes his mind. He thinks back on last night, when this Abdullah seemed to know his job at least. Now, though, he's just a sad little man.

Abdullah's just about ready to give up on Mustafa. The jeep is waiting in front of the station. Abdullah considers how he's going to fit four people in the back seat. Hüseyin, Mustafa, the blonde bitch, and the police guard. He'll sit next to the driver. Those cuckolds in the back will just have to make room for the woman. He cuffs Hüseyin to Mustafa. Joined together, they have a hard time getting into the car. Mustafa looks around him, searching for Oya. He must be wondering what they've done with her. Only now does Abdullah himself remember her. He goes running back into the station, to tick off the police who've been guarding her.

With Abdullah out of the car, Hüseyin loses the cool that had left his brother feeling almost impressed. He can't stop jiggling his legs now.

"Do you think they'll arrest her?"

"Well, why shouldn't they?"

"They don't have anything on her!"

"Do you really think they need to have something on her?"

"They didn't even question me."

"They must not have seen the need."

"You've been impossible to talk to, from the moment you arrived."

"What exactly do you want me to talk about? Are you expecting me to say that they can't arrest us when we're innocent? Or that the guilty all end up inside?"

"That's not what I meant. But if you wag a finger at a blind man . . ."

"Don't worry. The fascists will restore your sight soon enough. Only then will people like you face reality. Right now, it suits you to stay blind. You haven't had to suffer yet. And until you have, you're ready to hold everyone else responsible for their suffering."

"You know what? I'm glad they locked you up. You think you know everything, don't you?"

"Well, I do know this. We'll understand each other a lot better, once you too have spent time inside."

Hüseyin falls silent. He's too tense to be angry with his brother. He has to think. But when he starts thinking, he can't get past the big case that he's been trying and perhaps failing to pull together, so as to pay his three months of back rent. It won't be long before Metin goes looking for a new partner. After this business, though, who would want to have me as his partner? He'll have to take a leave. But what if they charge him under Article 141? The thought of an eight-year sentence runs like burning oil down his gullet. He belches. His ulcer is festering.

When he sees Oya at Abdullah's side, Mustafa relaxes a little. This surprises him. Why is he glad that she too was heading to Martial Law Command to be arrested, when he should be sorry that she'd not yet been released? She walks with her two cuffed hands before her. In the morning sun, she's looking very pale. She is taller than Mustafa remembers. She has her fair hair tied back. How did she have it last night? It must have been different. As if you could change your hairstyle in a police station. Her trousers are navy blue and wrinkled. He remembered lusting after her in the night, and this memory shamed him. Even so, it gives him some pleasure to be sharing something with her just now. The strangest things can make you happy sometimes. He's not thinking of his wife now, or his daughter. He might as well have no one in the world. He's just glad that he and Oya have gone through this whole fiasco, this utterly meaningless fiasco, together. As if this is what it means to be free. As if they weren't on their way to prison, but off on a romantic spree. Mustafa knows it's all bullshit. Even so, he feels as light as a bird. A bird flying into the forest after long years in a dark cage. Freed of life's grim burdens! I must have been missing this, I guess. Missing what? Lightness and joy. Love and sheer nonsense. Who knows. The things that everyday life is made of. Yes, that's it.

Oya greets Mustafa and Huseyin with a quick nod. She can't bring herself to look them in the eye. After a moment's pause, Abdullah seats her in front, next to the driver. He squeezes in next to the police guard in the back. The jeep sets off at once.

There in the front seat, Oya is lost in thought. She gazes blankly out the window. Then her eyes fix on the palm trees lining the streets. She loves palm trees. It might be a long time before she sees palm trees again, or any trees at all. She thinks this without twisting up inside. She tries to give them her full attention. For the first time since she arrived, Adana looks beautiful to her. You can learn to love nature. Life has given her this chance. What my life has given me, whatever happiness it has brought me, whatever wealth or wisdom, it's been through small sorrows. The jeep is crossing over the bridge now. Gazing at the crowd on the field opposite, with their quilts and their trays, their babies and their bundles, she sees one large mass. Night and day, the workers who've earned their keep picking cotton always gather around this bridge. They're waiting here for whatever truck or car can carry them home to their villages. This is Oya's first sight of them. Of their place in the landscape.

She turns around to look at Hüseyin. She has a few questions for him. But he looks away. Why is he treating her like this? Is he pretending he doesn't know me? Fine, but who is he pretending for? Abdullah, the driver, or this guard sitting next to him? Is that what he's going to say when they get to Martial Law Command? I don't know this woman. Ask Abdullah, or the driver, or the guard. Is that what he's planning to say? Oya feels like laughing. Hard not to, when things get this ridiculous. As they so often do. She thinks of the people who tried to ingratiate themselves in court by claiming to have fought the Communists in Korea. And that's just one of the absurd moments she can remember. Now she can add Hüseyin to the list.

The Seyhan River sparkles in the morning light. Maybe she's being unfair to Hüseyin. He's yet to be tested. Like the rest of us. Even so, she needs to give this little shared moment its due. A glance, a shared smile – they mean so much at moments like this. But it's not going to happen right now with Hüseyin. She's sorry she ever met him. The darkness that had lifted with the morning light now seeps back inside her. How wrong she'd been, to trust in Hüseyin's friendship. He's full of fine words, but when he's in a tight spot, he acts like he doesn't know me. This man should be feeling some responsibility for what's happened. Wasn't it Hüseyin who arranged the evening, knowing full well that I was under observation and might be followed? No, I shouldn't be making things easier for myself by blaming Hüseyin. Blaming him for getting me in trouble would just be an evasion.

A plane passes overhead. Interrupting her thoughts, returning her to sorrow. My exile was to have ended in a week's time. I was to have been heading back to Ankara. Flying back, probably. Her eyes well up. Is she crying? Or is she just tired? Never mind.

Perhaps Hüseyin averted his eyes because he was having the same sad thoughts and trying to hide them. She has to pull herself together. Stop thinking about Hüseyin and all that. Her nerves are shot. She keeps thinking of more things to laugh about, more reasons to cut loose.

Wednesday visitors. Five or ten-minute visits. Shouting to be heard through the bars that call to mind a cage in a zoo. Summoning up enough love to erase the uniformed guards standing on both sides, and their weapons, too. The iron doors, so much heavier after visiting days. The hearts and the thoughts that the visitors take away with them. Restoring them to freedom. Leaving only bodies behind bars.

Is she going to have to go through all that again now? Why wouldn't she? She has only to think about all the others still languishing inside. But still, something inside her rebels at the thought. How could she have been so foolish as to . . . Stop it, girl. This has nothing to do with brains or foolishness. This is oppression. The oppressors have brains, they know just what they're doing. So don't forget that. They know exactly what they're doing, and what they're out to prevent. They need their scapegoats. Why else did the kings and emperors of old put so much faith in cruelty? The spectacle of cruelty most of all. They used it to change the past to suit their story. And to prevent what might become. Did they throw their slaves to the lions just for fun?

Oppressors need a constant stream of victims to survive. Here I am again, turning life into literature. Giving life a bit of glamor, with a few fine words. How stupid I am. I could just open this door and jump out. But where would I go? What's wrong with us? We know how to trot along to the station and turn ourselves in. No one even has to chase us or catch us. If only Gülay were in my place right now. She'd be out of this jeep in a second. She'd be running away, looking for a place to hide, work out the rest from there. Even if it meant getting caught or shot in the end. Next to her I'm just a fool. Still struggling to work out the rules of the game. Like a pampered child surprised by a speck of mud. Playing ball in the mud and expecting to come out untouched. No, my girl. That's not how it works. If you don't like mud, you should protect your pretty clothes by staying inside.

Now they're passing the factory. There's a thickset man shouting at the men gathered outside. "Get into line!" This is Muzaffer Bey. Oya doesn't know him. To her, he's just an officious fool. She can tell he must be one of the directors. But making them get in line still doesn't make sense. It's not as if it's going to make the factory any more efficient. Oya senses a military mind at work here. She thinks back to her military prison's commander. Not a roll call went by without his speaking about lines.

"Tell me, old woman, how do you line up to go to the mess?"

As if all you had to do to keep political prisoners in line was to line them up. As if by assigning them places at the long mess table in the middle of their barrack, they would make the Communists a little less Communist, and the anarchists a little less anarchic.

"Tell me, ladies, how do we line up the beds?"

He'd wait for their mumbled answers:

"We sit at the mess table in the same order as for roll call."

"Our beds are in order of height."

"Ladies! In what order do you go to the bathhouse?"

"In the order of beds. Six by six . . ."

Though they didn't really go in any sort of order to the bathhouse where the water was never hot enough. But they did form some sort of line between the two soldiers who escorted them with submachine guns held chest high.

Oya had always wondered what those soldiers were thinking when they pointed their submachine guns at the straggly line of flip-flop-clad women prisoners clutching sponge bags, plastic bags, and towels.

It was during one of those trips to the bathhouse that Gülay had almost escaped. The commander in charge of roll call didn't like how one of the soldiers was holding his submachine gun. So he was knocking him about. Seeing the commander's attention elsewhere, the second soldier had lowered his submachine gun to give his arm a rest. And that was the moment Gülay made a run for it, fast as an arrow.

Neither the commander nor the malingering soldier had

noticed. But it wasn't long before they brought Gülay back. When they spotted her strolling calmly towards the gate, they assumed at first that she must be someone's relative. But just as she was passing through that gate, a colonel came through in his jeep. The colonel recognized her instantly. He reached out from the slow-moving jeep and grabbed her by the arm.

"If I'd known it was the colonel in that jeep, I'd have bolted."

"They'd have shot at you."

"So what. They might have missed. The way they treat their weapons . . ."

To believe in adventure was to believe in *her own* adventure. That was Gülay in a nutshell. Who else would dare to attempt an escape from a yard patrolled by armed guards? If she hadn't crossed paths with the colonel, might she have succeeded?

After she was frogmarched back to the barrack, there were many who spoke against her. "This woman is crazy!"

"But she almost got away with it."

"She could never have escaped. If you want to escape, you do so when escape is possible. Not just because a random opportunity arises."

"This is adventurism."

"Escapees get shot and killed."

"But she might just have pulled it off," Oya had said. "It might have been freedom's hour, and she was heeding its call."

"You're as bad as she is," Feza had replied.

"You're a dreamer. Put dynamite in one pair of hands, and a pen in another. The results are the same. Two clocks, working by the same perfect rules. It's the setting sun that gets the time wrong. Even if you decide to believe a faulty clock, you still can't turn sunset into sunrise."

"It was a mistake, I agree . . ."

"One of many. Why else would we be in here?"

"So you're saying we all believe what our faulty clocks tell us."

"What I mean," said Feza, "is that dawn is still a long way away."

They've left brutish Muzaffer Bey far behind them now. The jeep stopped next to the guard booth. Abdullah jumps out and hurries into Martial Law Command.

Mustafa can't take his eyes off the back of Oya's neck. He's looking at the band that's holding back her hair, and the little wisps of blond hair that have escaped it. He wants to kiss that neck right now. That's how he wants to spend his last moments of freedom. Find something to say to her. But what? "Last night I fell in love with you." Really? Too ridiculous for her even to laugh off. And a big fat lie, to boot. I didn't fall in love with her last night. I lusted for her. That's how it was. I used her image to give a shape to all the yearnings I've never dared to name. He has no idea what to do with such thoughts. He has no experience of it.

Will he ever see Oya again? Maybe in court, if we're arrested. Just the thought cheers him up. We can greet each other when we meet in court. Exchange smiles. Arrested together, for the same absurd reasons. The words we don't say are so much better than the words we say. He sits back. As if he were happy.

"Come on now. Get out!"

When did Abdullah get back? He looks distraught, destroyed. And his face – it looks so much smaller. He's about to tell them they're free to go. With this sentence, marking himself as a man of no significance. A nothing. Right now he's everyone's enemy. The whole world has banded together to mock him. Zekai Bey. This menace of a teacher. This lawyer. The woman who has dressed herself up like a man. They've all bonded together to destroy him, grind him into the dust. They'll make him suffer. A thousand and one punishments before they kick him right out of the force. They'll keep rolling past him, sending specks of asphalt flying at him in the Maraş noonday sun.

"I said get out!"

Though they are already out of the car. The driver grinning at his confusion. So he's on their side too.

Mustafa, Hüseyin, and Oya wait in silence. The two men aren't even looking at Abdullah, they have no inkling of his doubts. They think they're waiting to surrender to Martial Law Command. Only Oya's mind is on what she's left behind.

How am I going to get my things from the hotel? There must be a way. Someone is sure to help. People are sure to hear I've been arrested. Someone will take it upon himself to pack up my things and bring them over. But what about my hotel bill? Will they keep running it up if they're not informed right now? She can't bear to think of what she'll lose if she's arrested, so instead she frets over little details like her hotel bill. She must be afraid to think about what lies ahead. This is her way of escaping.

Mustafa can't take his eyes off Oya. When he should be thinking about his wife and daughter. No chance of another teaching job. So what is he going to do? He has to think about that. Think about his responsibilities. And not the wisps of hair on the neck of a woman he doesn't even know. He needs to write his wife a letter. He needs to start composing his words right now. But where should he send this letter? He's not even sure his wife is still in Urfa. If he asked Hüseyin to make inquiries. If he could find out. He's forgotten that Hüseyin might be going inside with them. He wants to think of this fiasco as something he and Oya can keep for themselves. Will the Teachers Association keep paying my salary to my wife? Who's going to look after me while I'm inside? Is this it? My life snapped in two, like a cheap necklace of evil eyes? My struggle, our struggle? His head is throbbing. The pain so bad his eyes water.

He will once again let his eyes rest on Oya's neck. While he sinks into a deep, dark misery.

Whereas Hüseyin is preoccupied neither by his feelings or the bills he might have run up or might have to pay in the future. He's still trying to figure out what's going on here. His eyes dart from Abdullah to Mustafa, from Mustafa to Oya. Hoping to find some sort of answer in their expressions. Mustafa and Oya are deadly pale. Is this from lack of sleep, or fear? He hopes it isn't fear. If it isn't fear, then it means they're not going to be arrested, and Hüseyin could relax. He decides they're not frightened. But that makes him angry. They're showing off. Making as if fearlessness is an acquired skill. Such idiocy! This brother of his. He's always been irresponsible. He didn't mention his wife and daughter even once last night. Here he is now, ogling Oya instead. He'll be flirting with her next. Playing the revolutionary. The revolution! That's all he has left. What is he going to do with his life after this? Look for work in a factory? That won't be easy, either. The state might be a harsh employer, but the factories of Adana are even worse. They're not going to hire a marked man like him. So what's left for him? He'll have no way of supporting his wife and child. He'll be a burden on his family. And all the while, he'll be cursing and criticizing everyone around him who dares to find success in life. All the poison he spread last night – that was just the beginning. When Abdullah walks out of Martial Law Command empty-handed, Hüseyin feels reassured. He's starting to think nothing will come of this. If I can get myself out of this mess, then nothing I put my mind to is beyond me. Mustafa knows that, too. Which is why he is so angry. When Socialists should act like Socialists. How is he going to save anyone, if he can't save himself? And what just happened here? He stopped off in Adana, got him and Ali's family into a ton of trouble.

He has to nab this Unity Party case. This would be a big win for the practice. They're lining up already. All the Alevis of the Çukurova Valley are coming his way. This could end with his becoming a national deputy. Why not? Just think what I could do then. Who will be working for the struggle then? Him or Mustafa?

"You're released!"

Relieved to have finally uttered the dreaded words, Abdullah unlocks their handcuffs. Without another word, he gets back into the jeep. In a single moment, it's all over.

For a while, the three of them just stand there at the side of the tree-lined street. Then they begin walking, side by side, but acting as if they don't know each other.

Oya's legs are wobbling. Freedom has turned her into a puppet with loose strings. Is she relieved? If she is, then she's ashamed to be showing it. I'm flying back to Ankara. My exile finishes in a week. And then? I'll go to the seaside. Any sea will do. She imagines herself sailing past Alanya and into the Aegean, savoring each curve of its glorious coastline. Those blue skies. Those wide spaces. That sea. Those rocky shores. Those forests. But where in all this is her husband? Her home? Her children? Or all her other responsibilities? There are no blue skies awaiting her.

No forests. No freedom. Just that endless list of things she must now do. Start a new life. Finalize my divorce. That could count as her new start. But how is she going to support her children? There's no new start for me. I'm going back to a ruined home to try and put it back in order. That's all I have to look forward to.

It's too soon still to be thinking about all this. Let alone enduring it. She's still learning how to walk in the sun-speckled shade of these trees. Still letting the world back in. Hüseyin is walking along the sidewalk. She isn't angry at him anymore. He might be all talk. And not to be trusted. But couldn't I say the same of most of my friends? And he's never had it so easy. Not like her friends, with their elite schools, their languages, their lovely girlfriends, their fine arts. All he has are the yearnings he's gathered up inside him. A boy from the provinces, who had to struggle to get this far. Who wants it to make it as a lawyer. That's his only hope, and he's embraced it. But what do I have to embrace? A new order? A cause that has lost its center?

Mustafa has his eyes on the road. She doesn't find him as interesting as she did last night. What could she expect from him? She hardly knows the man. He's like her: thrashing about, looking for something to cling to. Trying not to drown. Liberty is so much more than that, and so much nobler. While he and I – we're both still fighting for our lives. Yes, I can see that now. We're fighting for our lives. Each in our own way. It's not such a relief then, to have been set free.

Ali cannot remember how he got to the coffeehouse. Someone is shaking his chair.

"This isn't a hotel, my friend."

He tries to pull himself together. This waiter might not be so friendly, but Ali still welcomes the sight of him. Any one will do, so long as it isn't Abdullah.

"Make me a strong coffee."

Now he sees some pity in the waiter's face. He is looking at Ali's bruised and swollen eye.

"They really worked you over, didn't they, brother?"

"Never mind," says Ali. "It's over now." The waiter accepts this. Men will fight. Men will get beaten. Quarrels will erupt. Guns will come out, and someone will get shot. This is the world he knows. He finds it natural.

As he sips his coffee, Ali tries to make a plan for the day. If he goes straight home, he'll end up collapsing into bed. He'll cease to be the last thing between his family and disaster. If he lets himself relax, even his body might give up on him. So he has to get himself to the factory. Muzaffer Bey will insist on a doctor's note. How is he going to get a doctor's note? What is he going to say, when he gets to the hospital? That he got his beating at the police station? He knows those hospital people inside out. They're all in on it together. They'll want to know how he ended up at the police station. They'll look into it. Just a matter of time before Muzaffer Bey finds out he was taken in and beaten on suspicion of being a Communist. And if Muzaffer Bey thinks you're a marked man, he'll fire you on the spot.

If he goes straight to the factory, though. How is he going to work? They won't have a hard time guessing what's happened. But it's pointless to worry about all this. The news will be all over the neighborhood by now. They took Ali away. They raided the house. A clandestine meeting. It would be worse not to go in. If I don't get myself in there, they'll use my absence as an excuse to fire me. Yes. The best thing is to go to work. Shake it all off by showing my face. Let them see that they've released me. That I've committed no crime. Even so. He knows what the odds are for a man who's been beaten to a pulp. Who has one eye bruised shut. Whose soles have been burst open by the falaka. In their eyes, he's a guilty man. This he knows.

"So I'm off, now. Stay well."

Oya says nothing. Mustafa, for his part, is not surprised to see his brother walking away. It's not what you'd expect of a brother, or of anyone, let alone a member of the Maraş tribe. Even so, he doesn't dwell on it. He's glad to be rid of him. He's gone his separate way, Mustafa thinks, because he knows he's not wanted. He watches his brother race toward a shared taxi parked a way ahead.

Oya's feeling nervous. She's not happy being left alone with Mustafa. She remembers how Zekai Bey looked her over last night. How he bared his tar-stained teeth and spat out the word.

Prostitute. And now here she is, alone with Mustafa, in the dawning light. As if Zekai Bey's curses had come true. As if she had to do something now, to prove him wrong.

"Are you going to keep walking?"

"Maybe. I'm not sure."

Mustafa can tell what Oya is thinking. She's right to think it, too. He feels shame for all he's done to her in his thoughts. If Oya had any inkling of all that, she'd have every right to feel uneasy. Not at all good, to part on these terms.

"I'm heading to the bus station."

". . ."

"Yes . . . I'm off to Urfa. My wife and daughter . . ."

Thinking that he's mentioning his wife and daughter to douse water on her heart, Oya feels even more annoyed than before.

"So you have a wife."

He turns to look at Oya. Is she mocking him? The tension in her face has slackened.

He sees that he has hurt her, by mentioning his wife.

"Does your wife know you've been released?"

"I don't know. I haven't told her."

"She'll be glad to see you, then."

He only mentioned his wife to reassure Oya. But now he's back where he was. Will his wife really be happy to see him? She might hate me by now. What if she'd picked up her daughter and gone back to Istanbul? Where did this idea come from, that my wife no longer loves me? Or am I the one who no longer loves her? Actually, he's sure his wife and child are still waiting for him in Urfa. Wherever they are, Urfa or Istanbul, they'll be waiting for him.

"I'm not sure they're even in Urfa."

Why is he opening up to Oya?

"They'll be there."

It feels good, to be comforting Mustafa.

"What's it to you, if they're there or not?"

"You're right. What's it to me?"

She's just as mad at herself now as she is at Mustafa. The sooner they part company, the better. Mustafa stops short, as if he's read her thoughts.

"I apologize. I was talking nonsense. I'm just tired. Very tired. What I mean is . . . right now, things are hard."

"You're right. Right now, everything is hard."

The only thing they can agree on.

It will be hard right now for Mustafa to go back to Urfa. Hard to face the fear that he might find his wife waiting there for him. Hard to face the fear that he won't be able to find her. Hard to go back to teaching. Hard to be barred from teaching. Hardest of all to try and live better, and do better. Do more good. To prove that he didn't go through all this suffering for nothing. To rise above empty regrets. To refuse all foolishness. That is how it must be. But how hard it is, how much strength it takes, to make a fresh start. To embark on something that difficult – to love it for being difficult – you must first embrace it. He understands now why he wasn't afraid of getting arrested again. Prison was so much easier than the challenges he now faces. Prison puts off the day when you have to make a man of yourself. It frees you of all responsibility.

His eyes have clouded over again. Oya thinks they might be brown. Whatever color they really are, all she can see in them right now are his wounds. They shake hands and part ways. Thinking it wise to end things there. When in fact they are going the same way. Mustafa quickens his pace. Keeping his eyes on the road ahead. He's starving. Just ahead of him, outside Sığır Market, he can see a row of köfte peddlers. He walks toward them, garlanded in the aroma of grilled meat.

"Inside bread. Lots of it. A double portion. Pile on the pepper. Onions and radishes, too."

The köfte peddler picks up two big hunks of bread and deftly cuts each in half. He fills them with finely sliced onions, radishes, and parsley. After placing the köftes on top, he gives them both a good shaking of pepper. Mustafa can barely contain himself. Suddenly he's ravenous. Even more so when he takes he bread into his hands. His mind has vanished. All feeling too. Nothing left in him but ravenous hunger. As if Oya never existed. As he walks across the fairground past the shaven-headed boys kicking up the dust, the road ahead seems crystal clear to Mustafa.

He'll cross this bridge and take the first bus to Urfa. If he doesn't find her at home, he can find someone who knows where she's gone. The landlord will know if she's gone back to Istanbul, if not him, then the neighbors. And maybe, just maybe – why is it even maybe – Gülay will be at home. She has read her horoscope in the newspaper, and now she is waiting. She's just out of a bath. The baby is sleeping peacefully in her crib. When Mustafa gets home, she'll make him that pilaf with peppers and tomatoes. A big salad. Cheese and raki. They won't speak much. As if he'd never been away. Best not to mention the dawn when they took him away. When those police officers pointed their submachine guns at her head.

We'll talk about the dawns we have ahead of us. I'll tell her what I'll do to get us back on track. I'll find a job in a private school . . .

He starts walking faster. His thoughts are racing, jumping all over. He slows down again. He thinks of his friends, on the day of his release. Their words, their looks, the anthems they'd sung together. Their farewells. "Don't forget us." That's what one of them said. Which one? One way or another, in gestures if not in words, they'd all said the same thing. Don't forget us. Always putting the emphasis on the word *us*.

Don't forget how the barrack's stone walls would ring with the echoes of marching boots – thousands of them, tens of thousands – at every headcount, every changing of the guard. Don't forget how we felt coming back after court. How, when our applications for release were denied, we buried our hopes deep inside. How, after torture, we found ways to continue torturing ourselves. How we did our best to pick up the pieces of our despised selves and mend them as best we could. How we made our broken bodies into healthy ones, suffering the birth pangs in silence. How we'd stay up half the night talking. How we found joy in a glass of tea, a cup of coffee. How our hearts pounded every time they passed out the mail. How, if there was nothing for us, we'd hate the whole world. How hard we tried not to bow our heads, not to forget, not to accommodate, and not to weaken. How we shared our sorrows. Don't forget the joy of going back to the beginning, to think everything afresh, to embrace it all afresh, knowing what we truly believed. Or the clean, necessary, long-awaited fury. Are you ever going to forget these things? A question, and a hope. A belief, and a doubt. In everything they did or said, there had always been the thing, and its opposite.

He looks across the fairground, with its tents painted as brightly as prostitute's faces. And there they all are his, his cellmates, all in a row. Just as he last saw them. On the day he was set free.

You haven't passed the test yet, have you, Mustafa?

He's not been able to finish his köfte bread. Too tired. But his friends would never be this hard on him. They're patient. They'll wait. More tests await him. So many of them, on the road ahead.

When after a sleepless night Ziynet heard from the neighbor-hood children that Zekeriya had not been arrested, and had been seen walking around town, she felt relieved. She took a look at herself in the mica mirror she'd bought at the corner shop not long ago. She passed her fingers over her eyebrows. Such a long time since they'd seen a pencil. Zekeriya got angry when she put on make-up. She rearranged her hair, four times in all. She didn't lift a finger to help her sister with the house. Gülşah, meanwhile, on hearing her Ziynet's news hoped that Ali would be on his way home. But when he didn't turn up, she began to fear the worst. *When they take in the likes of us, they wear us down.* That was some-thing her father or uncle used to say, or something like it. And now it comes back to her. To think they'd arrested Ali was to think he'd get a hiding. She's so worried that she can't even find it in her to be annoyed at Ziynet's selfish joy. And she herself has never enjoyed the habit or the luxury of wallowing in sor-row. Instead she puts herself to work. Takes the mats outside and gives the stone floor a good scrub with Arab soap. Takes the laundry that has been piling up for who knows how many days and puts it in the pot to boil. Throws in Ali's long underwear, too, and his thick flannel undershirt. Thinking he might need them. In other words, thinking like the sort of woman who always does what's needed, without complaint. She doesn't let up until the laundry is as soft as gum. Rinsing it three times, and then boiling it, and then letting it sit. She doesn't even feel her arms aching when she's wringing it out. Three times she takes down the gas canister, without a peep. Grates three bars of green soap, fills three canisters, forgetting her aching back.

After prettying herself up as much she can and with still no sign of Zekeriya, Ziynet becomes suspicious and goes out in search of the neighborhood urchins. They tell her that he's been spotted in front of the National Struggle Association on Atatürk Avenue. That makes her angry. After all they'd been through the night before, he's run off to see his brothers instead of coming home to her. Well, let him go there! Let him see what sort of blessing they have in mind for him. Where's his gratitude. After all Brother Ali has done for him. You'd think he'd at least come back to give his sister-in-law some news. It is only now that Ziynet notices how upset her sister is. She offers to help her, but by then Gülşah is done with the cleaning and the laundry.

Ziynet goes to sit down on the divan. After sulking for some time, she comes up with a plan. She'll go next door to see Meral. And this week's photoroman. If Zekeriya comes back while she's out, let him fume by himself! She'll be next door reading *Fate Weaves its Web*. She can't wait to find out how it ends.

Rüstem, the Akdeniz Industries gateman, was reading the newspaper when Ali walked into the factory. Today's column by Mehmet the Wrestling Wolfman, to be precise. At first he didn't recognize Ali. Thinking him a stranger, he'd taken affront.

"Where do you think you're going, my fellow countryman?"

Ali stopped to look Rüstem in the eye. Now Rüstem recognized him. Everyone in the factory had heard that Ali's house had been raided, on account of him being an anarchist. Seeing Ali's sorry state, he could only think that Ali had fought off the police and escaped. He couldn't stretch his mind enough to ask himself why a man on the run from the police would then turn up for work at a factory. But even if he had, he would have then been left with the equally illogical proposition that Ali, having been caught with a nest of anarchists by night, could be free again by morning. He said nothing to Ali now. What point was there, in messing with an anarchist? As soon as Ali had passed through the door, he picked up the phone to call the director's secretary.

"Hello? Is this the director?"

"Who's calling?"

"I have something to tell the director."

The woman on the other end of the line now spoke more harshly.

"I asked who's calling."

"It's me. The gateman."

"What gateman?"

"Rüstem the gateman. At the entrance."

"All right, then. Just a minute."

"No, it's not like that. I need to tell the Director something."

"The Director is busy."

"No, it's not like that. I mean, it's not about me. It's about Ali."

"Ali? What Ali? If this Ali has a problem, he should come in himself."

"He can't. Because he's running away."

"What do you mean he's running away? If he's running away this early in the morning, he's running away from his job."

"No, it's not like that. He's running away from the police."

"Are you crazy or what? Do you think we're a police station?"

"Mr. Director will know what I'm talking about. Make sure you tell him."

He puts down the phone. Rüstem curses himself a thousand times over for having let Ali walk right into the factory. What use is a gateman if the anarchists are already inside? What would Muzaffer do to him? His head was spinning. He rushed into the factory. He was racing around with no idea where to go when he was stopped in his tracks by a loud noise.

"What are you doing in here?"

This is just the sort of thing that drives Muzaffer Bey crazy. He might as well be a soldier caught abandoning his guard post. He steels himself for the slaps and punches that are sure to come next. He is in for a beating now, for sure. God's truth. He has it coming. He has been here before, after all. He begins to tremble. As for Ali. He's forgotten all about him. With Muzaffer's permission, he's heading straight back to the guard box.

"And why are you standing there like that?"

Rüstem is standing at attention.

"Is this your idea of a uniform? Where's your jacket?"

Rüstem had been in such a rush to catch Ali that he'd left his jacket hanging on the back of his chair in the guard box. It's lost to him now. No jacket, no Ali, no anarchy, no job, nothing. Only Muzaffer Bey, and the fear his commanding officers instilled in him during his military service.

"Did you swallow your tongue? Is this how you guard a big factory? What if there was an enemy attack? The factory could be on fire and its walls caving in and you wouldn't even know it."

With this mention of fires and walls caving in, Ali came sailing back into Rüstem's mind. Ali and anarchy. What would Muzaffer Bey do to him, if he found out he'd let the enemy walk right inside?

"Do you know how many people there are out there who are longing to do your job, you idiot dog? Get out of my sight! Go find yourself a job somewhere else!"

Rüstem is ready to do anything. Anything that will save him from Muzaffer Bey's wrath. At just that moment, he sees the foreman approaching, with Ali at his side.

"What happened to this one?"

"He spent the night at the police station."

"What was he doing there?"

"Someone denounced me. They picked me up and took me in."

"You be quiet. I didn't ask you."

The foreman quickly explains what happened.

"They'd been holding a clandestine meeting in his house. Someone from the neighborhood informed me this morning."

Muzaffer Bey fixes his eyes on Ali. With a glare that knows how to rip a man apart – his clothes, his flesh, his bones, his internal organs, and the rest of him too. He's back in his element now. Protecting life's order. What he has before him is not a workman in trouble but an agitator who is out to disrupt that order. Ali is fed up. He'd done nothing to deserve what they'd done to him last night, but he'd picked himself up and moved on. Muzaffer Bey's glare doesn't frighten him anymore. It unsettles him, yes, but nothing more. If this goes on any longer, he won't be able to contain his rage. And that does frighten him. Don't burn your quilt to chase off a flea. He learned that when he was a boy. But his patience is being stretched.

"So tell me, you fool. Describe this meeting."

And suddenly it's not Muzaffer Bey before Ali, but Abdullah. He forgets about his job, and his pension. All he can see is Abdullah the prick.

"I've been cleared. They released me."

"So he's been cleared. If he were truly an honorable citizen, would they turn his face into the Wednesday market?"

Ali's head is spinning. Whatever he does, he's done. If he's still standing right now, it's his fury at Muzaffer Bey's unjust words that's giving him his strength. If he collapses, Muzaffer Bey will see it as proof of his guilt. Seeing as he thinks a beating at a police station is proof enough. But his face is blank. Half asleep, almost. Muzaffer Bey's suspicions grow.

"Who did you have with you in that house of yours?"

As if Ali's house were an extension of the factory. As if Muzaffer Bey were not just the factory director, but the director of Ali's home, too. As if Ali were not just another factory worker, but his personal possession. This man seems to think he can violate Ali's right to his own home.

"Some relatives came from Maraş."

"So you're from Maraş, are you?"

With this question, Muzaffer Bey opens new roads to new crimes: Why are you from Maraş? If you're from Maraş, then why are you in this factory? Why do you have relatives in Maraş? Why do your relatives come to visit you in your home? And so on.

But all Ali does is nod and say, "Yes, I'm from Maraş."

"So he's from Maraş. Did you come down to Adana to stir everyone up?"

"I've been working in Adana for twenty years."

Is this Ali's way of saying that he's been here a lot longer than Muzaffer Bey?

And that he's been working in this factory far longer, too?

"So you've been hiding away in this factory for twenty years. But you can't hide from me, let me tell you. No one can hide in my factory."

No hope now of keeping his job. All Ali wants now is for this to be over. If this crazy guy wants to beat him, then fine. He wants to lie down, at home, on his divan. Gülşah will boil him up a lemon and peppermint tea. The rest can take care of itself. His head is throbbing again. The pain unbearable. He shuts his one working eye.

"Don't you dare hide your eyes. Look at my face. No one hides from me."

Muzaffer Bey doesn't seem as angry now, somehow. He turns to his foreman.

"Send this one home. Tell Accounts to dock three days' pay. One because he won't be working today. The other two to teach him a lesson. If he doesn't get himself into work tomorrow morning, he knows what to expect."

With that Muzaffer Bey takes leave of Ali, Rüstem, and the foreman. Off he rushes down the corridor, to see to a matter of some importance. The cafeteria is to be raided. Someone's made an accusation about the food they've been feeding the engineers and technicians. Someone has been stealing meat. He's sent someone in to check, someone he trusts to do the job. It won't be enough just to check what's in the pans. But never mind. The important thing is to threaten the cook. It's for him to prove his innocence. The burden is on him. One false move, and in Muzaffer Bey's eyes he becomes a guilty man.

Ali looked at Rüstem, who was staring at him open-mouthed. No sense in taking offense. Time to leave the factory. He hobbled over the riverbank. Sat himself down on a bench. Soothed by the rush of water, he rested his tired right eye. Let his thoughts drift away with the current. On the next bench were two boys who should have been in school. They had their transistor radio turned up as high as it could go. A jingle. After which a joyous woman cried out:

"Mediterranean Industries!"

The boys aren't listening. They're shouting over the music and each other, as adolescents will. "So you haven't been to Iskenderun yet, you sucker? The women they have there ... They grind you like millers. They could squeeze the life out of you ..."

Industries. Sucker. When Ali rises from the bench, these words are bouncing against the walls of his head. He's not going to let them dock his pay. He won't be wronged like this. So what if it's only three days. He's going to insist on his rights. Yes, he will.

Mustafa had no trouble finding a seat on the Urfa bus. It had just pulled out when he remembered Ali. He should have gone back to the house and put Aunt Gülşah's mind at rest. Maybe Ali's back by now, too. He should have gone to say goodbye. When Aunt Gülşah saw what they'd done to Ali, would she wail and curse? No, of course not. Aunt Gülşah. How much love had she put into that bumbar she'd made for him, last night and so many other nights before that? His heart aches. As the bus turns into the road, he thought how it would be a long time before he came back to Adana. First he had to mend his shattered life. Adana has shamed Mustafa, crushed him. Adana is his debt to Ali. Its interest rate still rising.

While crossing the bridge, Oya caught sight of the fairground. Oh, to jump onto that ferris wheel and feel free as a child. Oh, to go back to the days when she believed that a world of limitless freedom awaited her, if only she could escape the strictures of home. Oh, to feel that giddy rush again. To be back on the ferris wheel. Racing across those gardens and parks and fields. To think herself free. To have yet to learn how hard freedom was, and how easy it was to lose. How so much in life had to be taken from the lion's mouth. There was no going back there. Her innocence long lost. She has two choices. Either she goes back to dawdling. Or she returns to the struggle. To the war. If you're up to it.

The köfte peddlers in front of Sığır Pazar cut the dreams of hungry children down to size. The coins in their pockets can buy them a köfte bread or it can buy them a taste of freedom on a ferris wheel, but it cannot stretch to both. The adults tell them they must choose. "One more simit, and there's no ferris wheel, do you hear?"

She sees Mustafa in front of a köfte stand. She pretends not to see him. Enough, she thinks. Time to stop trying to wrap her head around this man. Better to make the most of the morning air. Which is fresh and clean, thanks to last night's rain. She breathes it in. She loves mornings. Loves all new starts. Though she knows that no good can come from a new start that hasn't been thought through. If there's not enough trust, or enough forethought. If it wasn't your choice to start with. So many reasons to be wary of making yet another new start now. It's visible from the way she walks. Does she look like a woman striding toward a new dawn? Life has undone her. She is limping toward a setting sun. My days here are numbered. And then, after I've signed in at the police station for the last time, it's straight to Ankara. And then? Yes, what then? What sort of new beginning can she expect coming out of prison and exile? Bearing in mind that she has no wish to return to the Oya she once was. If that choice is even open to her. It's not clear. The past few years have been a litmus test. Opened her eyes to so much foolishness. So much degeneracy and rot. She's cleansed herself of all that now. Or at least, resolved to do so. The things that gave the old Oya's life meaning, the things she most valued – they mean nothing to her now. Is it as easy as she thinks, to rid herself entirely of her old habits? They say habits are the single person's friend. If you're not single, you can shed them easily. The important thing is not to be alone. Not to be alone. You need more than a husband and children for that. More than family and friends who come and go. Or maybe this new life will come with new habits. After all she's been through, she's pretty much forgotten her old habits. Or rather she cut away from certain things. She has been through harsh times, but they've opened up a space for her own desires, her own choices. But where are its foundations? How exactly does she plan to re-engage with life? In the bright light of an Adana morning, she counts her doubts.

In prison it was easy to cut old ties. To convince herself she'd made new ones. She'd shared her days with others who were suffering the same injustice. Together they'd found ways to hold body and soul together. Together they'd endured hardship. Together they'd resisted. They'd put up a common front. They'd learned what a beautiful thing it could be, to act with honor. To honor the struggle. To struggle as one. How much confidence all this had given her. How could she ever have endured these months of exile, had she not brought with her all she'd shared in prison, and learned. Things that would break anyone with a little bit of pride. Things like the daily trip to Hacıbayram Police Station to sign in. Like the so-called chestnut peddlers stationed next to the hotel entrance. Like the plainclothes policemen stationed in the half-finished building across the street. And the enforced solitude. She'd never tried to give a meaning to all this. She'd not tried to make any changes. Instead she'd let time gnaw away at her sentence. Kept time from gnawing away at her. To do so all alone could make a person just a little steadier, a little stronger. To find a space inside the press and make it yours. Waking up every day at the same time, every morning doing exercises, and reading a few papers. Setting times for reading and times for work and keeping to them. Talking a walk through the city at some point every day. Adana had been one big prison for Oya, a prison where she could choose when to go out into the exercise yard. This was the daily routine she had created for herself to make her term of exile easier. All addicts know how comforting such daily habits can be.

Now her time in Adana is coming to an end. And with it, this life that had been forced on her. To tell the truth, she had fought off tyranny by being hard on herself in little ways. In the days of so-called freedom soon to come, she would need to be hard on herself in new ways. It was prison and exile that taught her how to resist, work with others, and protect humanity. But now her circumstances were changing. She had to find a way to bring her fine ideas about freedom and humanity into lived experience. How easy it would be to create a spineless, apathetic, and confused Oya who was still convinced that she was carrying on the struggle. Because from this point onward, she would find herself up against things that were much more difficult to grasp. It would be much harder to distinguish between a right or wrong turn. Can she really be sure she's forgotten the old Oya, and left her old habits behind? Or did she just think so because those old habits were taken away from her? As she makes her first steps toward freedom, her joy is tempered by fear. A fear of the Oya to come.

The Oya who is waiting for her at home in Ankara. Who on mornings when there is no water, is angry only at the water. Who trots from task to task as placidly as a pack horse. Her days revolving around relatives, friendships, newsprint, and television. Battling more with the dust than with her books. The pots she can never manage to scrub clean. The endless tidying. The aubergines she brings home from the market only to find that they're full of seeds and past their prime. The dishes that must be cooked to perfection, or else. The mayonnaise that refuses to bind. Packing up the winter clothes and taking the summer clothes out of the trunk, or vice versa. The moths circling around her like plain clothes policemen. Peace in name only. Fretting over details and calling it anxiety. All this is so close now. All this talk about fresh starts and new commitments, but how? Such things don't just happen by themselves on a Wednesday. From this moment on, every step she makes must reflect a consciousness. Every meeting and greeting. Her daily habits must reflect a higher purpose. She must live by her ideas. She wants to stay connected. Work with others. Belong. Fine. But where exactly does Oya belong? She's a writer, an intellectual who tries to do the right thing instead of chasing 'the good life.' She's paid a price for that. But what else? She's worked hard to keep her worst fears about herself from coming true, but how could that ever be enough? As the Adana sun rises higher in the sky, so too do her thoughts. The more her mind lights up, the slower her steps. So much to think about now that freedom looms.

New opportunities beckon. But also, so many tests. These will become clear over time. It's still too early to tell. Right now everything's up in the air. Why is that, though? What if I'm tested and fail utterly? What if I miss out on a chance to be tested? That's not a random question for someone like me. Chance itself will decide if I'm offered a chance. What if over time I gravitate toward a life in which I can be sure never to be tested? Something is going on here. An open and deliberate mistake. Something that is bringing her these doubts about the life ahead. Yet again, she's putting herself at the center of things. This being her experience of freedom. That's where her mistake lies. That's what she fears.

She didn't land in prison because of anything she did. She ended up behind bars due to circumstances beyond her control. But now that the cage has opened, she needs structures. To resist, she needs to be pushed. In concrete ways. She knows all this, but she has no idea how to reconnect. I thought I'd figured all this out. But no. I'm still confused. I simply have no idea.

She was in the middle of the fairground now. Right in front of the Palace of Private Pleasures. For a time she stood there, watching the Gypsy girls belly dance at the entrance. Just to escape her thoughts. One of her worst habits: looking at something just to escape her thoughts. She had to stop playing the observer. She put the fairground behind her. Only to stop on the bridge to look down at the water. It occurred to her that she had never seen blue water in a river. On its own water wasn't blue. It had no color whatsoever. A little bit of water was a little bit of nothing. There was nothing to see in a river but water's flow. But in prison, whenever she'd thought about water, it had been blue. She'd imagined a sea, the bluest sea that nature could provide. A sea that brought her joy and washed her clean. Water is only blue when it has joined the sea, the sea that no horizon can ever contain. This river, too, will find its way to the sea. There to begin anew. How she misses the sea at this moment. The great blue expanse that makes a nonsense of little worries and narrow thoughts. The sea that sets nature free.

When my exile ends, I'm not going straight back to Ankara. First I'll go to Iskenderun. No, then, to the Aegean shore. Its red soil and turquoise sea and gentle western sun. I'll start off in Iskenderun. There, in that little patch of nature, I shall have no choice but to start each day anew.

She has to laugh. What am I trying to do, turn my life into a Godard film? Whenever a woman in a Nouvelle Vague film gets angry at a home, she hops on a plane and flies off to another continent. A train annoys her. A trinket. And she's off to Africa. While everyone else is stuck in their nine to five jobs, these people are racing across the sands, spinning the threads of their dull daily lives into lofty abstractions.

Never do these women speak of how they earn their money, how they can afford all these last-minute plane tickets, or how, after deciding they've had enough of a shitty whatever, they can start anew, just like that. Was it a job that gave them the where-withal to lead such a fine and colorful existence? Or was it an inheritance? We are not to know, and neither are we told how they ended up with so much free time on their hands. Or the ugly price they paid to look so thin and gorgeous on screen.

They find their chic little patch of nature, there to make their chic fresh starts. Oya doesn't want to be like them. Though in fact she could never be. She lacks the resources.

She turns her gaze on a nearby peddler. On the syrupy dough-balls piled high behind the glass of his two-wheeled cart.

A man's breath on the back her neck. A strangled voice:

"Eat a sweet, to be a sweet fuck . . ."

Oya jumps, wheeling around so fast that she bumps into the man standing behind her.

"Sorry!" she says. Another old habit.

Only afterward does she realize that this was the man who'd breathed those obscene words down her neck. Blushing, she rushes off. Why is she so surprised? Does she think it will be any different, on her solitary travels? Does she really think she could roam free? Here she is, a woman forever fearful of unwanted attention and surprise assaults. In Iskenderun she'll count as an outsider. A woman without a man. What sort of welcome can she expect? She could look for the same sort of job she had in Ankara. Teaching. Or translating. She could try something new, she thinks. But then in her mind's eye she sees a man fiddling with his moustache before showing her the door. She'll end up in the same sort of circle she had in Ankara. Just a bit more provincial and pretentious.

Do I really think I can change life's conditions singlehandedly, for myself let alone others? That's not how revolutions happen. Fine, but say I go straight back to Ankara. What can I expect there? Will I sit there waiting for others to change me? She isn't thinking straight. Her head is spinning. If only she'd bought something sweet from that peddler. With a bit of sugar rushing through her blood, she might be able to compose a thought. But she can't turn back now. She's afraid of seeing that man again. So she continues her walk to freedom, carrying her fears, frail and small, on her back.

"Hey, tourist! Hey you!"

She's still on the bridge. And someone is shouting at her. Shouting at her, but also at something else. He's right in front of her, but looking through her. Again she blushes. She looks into the crowd and works out who it is. The bastard who called her a tourist. A tourist! He can't be more than ten or eleven, this boy. He's wearing black plastic shoes. His loose black shalwars are held up by a piece of string. His eyes both fearful and taunting. He's surprised that this tourist has understood his words. Shocked when she walks over to him. Should he run away, or seize this chance to take a closer look?

"What's your name?"

What a stupid question. What good will it do, to know his name? That's what we always ask first, when we're looking down at someone. I've never seen anyone ask this question of an equal. Other people introduce us. Or rather, we already know each other well enough already.

"My name's Cevdet."

"Are you from around here?"

Cevdet lifts his eyebrows, to indicate that he is not.

"I'm from down there."

He points to below the bridge. Oya turns to look at the crowd she noticed on her way over to Martial Law Command. The men, women and children with their packages, pots and pans.

"What are you waiting for?"

"For a truck."

"Where will that truck take you?"

"To Siverek."

"How long have you been waiting here?"

"A week or so. I'm on my way back from picking cotton in Karataş."

So the fieldworkers have been paid their wages, and now they're waiting for a truck to carry them back to their villages. Nothing unusual about that. She might as well be standing here with a notebook, camera, and microphone, pointing out a little piece of reality! Lowering the microphone to let a real person speak. Pushing it into his throat and asking, "What are you waiting for here? Are you hungry? What did you eat at lunchtime? What did you eat last night? Are you a worker or are you unemployed? Do you earn enough to live? Why not?" For some reason, people can ask such questions without anyone hitting them. People like Oya. Think what else she could do now, if she had a microphone, if she'd fancied it was her job to shape public opinion. "The families gathered down over there beside the river are cotton pickers. They earn such and such per diem working the Çukurova Valley's fertile fields. They've now been paid their wages. On average they earn such and such in a season. This will see them through the months until the next season." And now, she lowers her microphone to the child.

"What did you eat this morning?"

"We drank tea."

"What did you have for lunch?"

"We drank tea."

"What did you have for supper?"

"We drank tea."

"Tea and nothing else?"

"I ate some bread."

Question by question, Oya gathers information that will help other tourists understand this foreign land. How lovely. How easy. As easy as learning German in ten lessons or English in twenty. She's on to a bestseller, for sure.

Oya has reached the other side of the bridge now. Police whistles. People running. The peddlers are being dispersed. The police are on the job. She sees one peddler pushing a cart laden with mirrors, condoms, copper bracelets, safety pins, elastic, scissors, nail files, evil eyes, padlocks, and keychains. He is threading his way through the crowd with an agility Oya finds impressive. But then he bumps into her, and a keychain falls to the ground. There's an eye on the keychain. An eye on the keychain! A winking eye. An optical illusion, in fact. An image that appears to wink when you see it from another angle. Like the freedom awaiting her. Oya's sentence is served now. Her exile will soon end. The police have released her. But she still isn't free. Nor can she ever be. She must stay inside. With the Cevdet who is locked up in Ankara Central Prison with his mother, Firdevs. And with the Cevdet who is waiting for the bus to Siverek. Unless they can all live together in freedom, she will remain with them, behind bars. If she doesn't, she'll have only tricked herself into believing that this eye is really winking, and that she's truly free. Until she's locked up again by another Cevdet. By every Cevdet under the sun.

archipelago books
is a not-for-profit literary press devoted to
promoting cross-cultural exchange through innovative
classic and contemporary international literature
www.archipelagobooks.org